Lady Catherine MacAlister's Hard Struggles

A Short Story about Catherine's Struggles

GRAHAM LOMAS

BALBOA.
PRESS
A DIVISION OF HAY HOUSE

Balboa Press books may be ordered through booksellers or by contacting:

Balboa Press
A Division of Hay House
1663 Liberty Drive
Bloomington, IN 47403
www.balboapress.com.au
1 (877) 407-4847

Print information available on the last page.

ISBN: 978-1-5043-1249-3 (sc)
ISBN: 978-1-5043-1250-9 (e)

Balboa Press rev. date: 06/26/2018

Contents

A very Special Dedication to My Wife Patricia,

With All My Love, Graham.

A Short Story About Catherine's Struggles

This is a romance story that is set in the 1900's in Scotland about love, tragedy, and struggles.

It is about a young lass by the name of Catherine MacAlister, who lives with her father, the Earl of MacAlister, in a castle in Scotland called MacAlister castle.

Catherine was an only child who lived in MacAlister castle in Scotland. Catherine was very beautiful, with a beauty of a rare kind.

Hoping for an heir, the earl had remarried when Catherine was seven but the second Lady MacAlister died a few years after her union with him.

Catherine's half-brother, Matthew, who had been only a small child of two years old when he first came to MacAlister castle, knew nothing, of course, of any other home. Matthew has epilepsy and Catherine had called for the doctor in the night, a Johnathon Pendrill, to check on his brother; who five years ago had an accident on the cliffs and fell. Matthew's doctor is also his cousin.

Johnathon said to Catherine, "I will look in on him tomorrow, but I assure you there is no cause for anxiety. He is no worse than usual."

Johnathon bid good night to Catherine while buttoning up his heavy driving coat. At the end of his sentence, he opened the heavy oak door letting in a blast of cold air and a fine sheet of penetrating rain.

"Oh Johnathon, what weather! I ought not to have sent for you." Nonsense! You know I am weather - proof. Old Jack will find his way home, if I cannot. Good-bye again".

The door closed upon the tall and strong figure and Lady Catherine

MacAlister was left standing alone upon the wide staircase, amid the gathering shadows of the great hall.

Catherine, who held herself sternly responsible for all, nursed Matthew with a devotion that no mother could have surpassed. She now vowed deep down in her heart that she will devote her own life to him. That for him she would live, and that whatever she could do to lighten his load of pain and make his future happier should be done, at whatever cost to herself.

Chapter 1

The MacAlisters of MacAlister Castle

"Good-bye, Catherine. I will look in again tomorrow: but I assure you there is no cause for anxiety. He is not worse than usual, and will be better soon. "The doctor was buttoning up his heavy driving coat as he spoke, and at the conclusion of the sentence he opened the heavy oak door, letting in a blast of cold air and a sheet of fine penetrating rain.

"Oh Johnathon, what weather! I ought not to have sent for you." "Nonsense! You know I am weather-proof. Old Jack will find his way home, if I cannot. Good-bye again."

The door closed upon the tall and strong figure, and Lady Catherine MacAlister was left standing alone upon the wide staircase, amid the gathering shadows of the great hall.

MacAlister Castle was, in truth, a sufficiently grim and desolate place both within and without. Tangled park, dense pine woods and a rocky harsh-bound coast surrounded it, cutting it off, as it were, from communication with the outside world. Within its walls lay a succession of vast, stately chambers. Few of them now inhabited-regions where carved black oak, faded tapestry, rusty armour, and antique relics of by gone day's seemed to reign in mournful grandeur, telling their own tale of past magnificence and present poverty and decay.

Yes, the MacAlister's were a fallen race; for the past three generations the reigning earl had been poor, and the present Lord MacAlister had failed to do anything towards restoring the decaying fortunes of his house. He to was very poor, hence the air of neglect that reigned around and within the castle.

Catherine, however, his only child, was far too well used to the gloom and grimness of the old castle to be in the least oppressed by it. She loved her lonely desolate home with a curious, passionate intensity, and could not picture anything more perfect than utter silence and isolation that hemmed in her life. The idea of desiring a change had never so much as occurred to her, Catherine was very beautiful, with a beauty of a rare kind that haunted the memory of those who saw her, as a strain of music sometimes haunts the ear. Her face was always pale and grave, and at first sight cold even to hardness, observation, though it never failed to make itself felt. It was a lovely face-like that of a pictured saint for purity of outline of a Greek statue for perfection of feature—almost as calm and colourless as marble itself.

Yet, behind the statuesque severity lay the strange, sad wistful sweetness which could not quite be hidden away, and grave to the beholder the idea that some great trouble had over shadowed the girl's life. Let us go with her, and see what that trouble was. When the door closed upon Johnathon Pendrill, she stood for a moment or two silent and motionless, then turned and mounted the shallow stairs once more, and passing down a long corridor, opened the door of a fire-lit room, and entered softly. The room had two tenants: one a great mastiff dog who acknowledged Catherine's entrance by gently flopping his tail against the floor, the other, a lad of seventeen, who lay upon an invalid couch, his face very white and his brows drawn with pain.

As Catherine looked at him her face quivered, and a look of unspeakable tenderness swept over it, transfiguring it for the moment, and showing wonderful possibilities in every line and curve. She bent over him, laying one cool, strong hand upon his head.

"Better Matthew?" "Yes, getting better. That stuff Johnathon gave me is taking the pain away. Stir up the fire, and sit where I can see you.

I like best." Matthew Pendrill, cousin to Johnathon Pendrill, the young doctor who had just left the castle, was the only child by a first marriage of Lord MacAlister's second wife. Hoping for an heir, the earl had married again when Catherine was seven years old, but his hopes had not been realised, and the second Lady MacAlister had died only a few years after their union. Matthew, who had been only a child of two year's when he first came to MacAlister Castle, knew nothing of course, of any other home., and he and Catherine had grown up like brother and sister, and were tenderly attached, perhaps all the more so from radical differences of character and temperament. Their childhood had been uncloudedly happy; they had enjoyed a glorious liberty in their wild Cornish home, that could hardly have been accorded to them anywhere else. Catherine had always been the leading spirit; physically as well as mentally, she had always been the stronger; but he adored her, and emulated her with the zeal and enthusiasm of youth. He followed her wherever she led like a veritable shadow, until that terrible day, five years ago, which had laid him upon a bed of sickness, and had turned Catherine in a few hours time from a child to a woman.

Upon that day there had been a sad end to the mad-cap exploits in cliff—climbing in which the girl had always delighted, and Matthew had been carried back to the castle, as all believed, to die he did not die, however, but recovered to a suffering, helpless, invalid life; and Catherine, who held herself sternly responsible for all, and who nursed him with a devotion that no mother could have surpassed, now vowed deep down in her heart that her own life should henceforth be devoted to him, that for him she would live, and that whatever she could do to lighten his load of pain and make his future happier should be done, at whatever cost to herself, as the one atonement possible for the rashness which had cost him so dear.

Five years ago that vow had been recorded, and Catherine from a bright, high-spirited girl, had grown into a pale, silent, thoughtful woman; but she had never wearied of herself-imposed charge-never faltered in her resolution. Matthew was her special, sacred charge. Anything that would conduce to his welfare and happiness was to be accomplished at whatever cost. So far, to tend and care for him had been her aim and object of life, and her deep love had made the office sweet. It had never occurred to her that any contingency could possibly arise by which separation from him should prove the truest test of her devotion,

Whilst Matthew and Catherine were dreaming their own dream upstairs, by the light of his dancing fire, no thought of coming changes clouding the horizon of their sky, downstairs, in the earl's study, a consultation was being held between him and his sister which would have startled Catherine not a little had she heard it.

Lord MacAlister was a tall, stately, grey-headed man of sixty-five, with a finely——chiseled face and the true MacAlister of countenance that his daughter had inherited. His face wore, however, a look of pallor and ill-health that, to a practised eye, denoted weakness of the heart, and his figure had lost its old strength and elasticity, and had grown thin and little bowed. His expression had much of gentleness mingling with its pride and austerity, as if with the advance of years, his nature had softened and sweetened, as indeed had been the case. Lady Louise, on the other hand, had grown more sharp and dictatorial with advancing age. She was a "modish" old Lady, who although quite innocent of such adamants, always suggested the idea of powder and patches, high-heeled shoes and hoops. She generally carried a fan in her hand, dressed richly and quaintly, and looked something like a human parrot, with her hooked nose keen black eyes, and quick, sharp voice and movements. She had an independent and sufficient income of her own, and divided her time between her London house and her brother's Cornish castle. She had always expressed it as her intention to provide for Catherine, as her father could do little for his daughter, everything going with the entail in the male-line; but there was a sort of instinctive hostility between aunt and niece, of which were both well aware, and Lady Louise was always deeply offended and annoyed by Catherine's quiet independence, and her devotion to Matthew. It was of Catherine they were talking this boisterous autumn evening.

"She has a sadly independent spirit," remarked Lady Louise, sighing and fanning herself slowly, although the big paneled room was by no means warm. "I often think of her future, and wonder what will become of her." "Why of late?" was the rather sharp question. "I have not been feeling so well since my illness in the spring. Johnathon Pendrill and his brother have both spoken seriously to me about the necessity for care. I know what that means——they think my state critical. If I am taken, what will become of Catherine?" "I shall. Of course, provide for her." generous; but money is not everything. Catherine is peculiar: she wants controlling, yet——

"Yet no one can control her: I know that well; or only Matthew and his whims. My blood runs cold every time I see her on that wild black thing she rides, with those great dogs bounding round her. There will be another shocking accident one of these days. She ought to be controlled——taken away from her extraordinary life. Yet she will not hear of coming to London with me even on a short visit; she will not even let me speak of it. "Lady Louise's face showed that she was much affronted. That is just it," said Lord Alister, slowly; "her life and Matthew's both seem bound up in MacAlister castle." Lady Louise made a significant gesture, which the earl understood.

"Just so; and yet——unless under most exceptional circumstances—— unless what I hardly dare to hope should happen——she must, they must both leave it, at some not very distant date." The hesitation in Lord MacAlister's manner did not escape his sister. "What do you mean?" She asked abruptly.

"I mean that I have been in correspondence lately with my heir, and that I expect him shortly at MacAlister castle." "Your heir?"

"Yes, Edward MacAlister, one of the Dunbar branch. The extinction of the MacAlisters of Brodie last year, you know, the next in succession. I made in inquiries about him, and then entered into personal communication."

Lady Louise looked keenly interested. "What have you made out?" "That he is very well spoken of everywhere, as a young man of high character and excellent parts. He is wealthy——very enriched by a long minority. He is twenty seven and he is not married."

Lady Louise's eyes began to sparkle "And he is coming here?" "Yes, next week. of course I need not tell you what is in thoughts. I object to match-making, as a rule. I shall put no pressure upon Catherine of any kind, but if those two should by chance learn to love, one another, I Would give my blessing to depart at any time. "Lady Louise looked very thoughtful. "Catherine is undoubtedly beautiful," she said, "and she is interesting, which perhaps is better." her brother, however, made no reply, and as he did not appear inclined to discuss the matter farther——they were seldom in entire accord in talking of Catherine she presently rose and left the room, saying softly to herself as she did so, "I should love to see that proud girl with a husband's strong hand around her."

Catherine, do you never want a little variety? What would you say to a visitor at MacAlister castle?" "I would try to make them comfortable, Are you expecting any one, father?" "Yes, a kinsman of ours: Mr. MacAlister, whose acquaintance I wish to make."

"Who is he? I never heard of him before."

"No, I have not known much about him myself till lately, when circumstances made him my heir. Catherine, have you ever thought what will happen at MacAlister castle in the event of my death?"

A very troubled look crept into Catherine's dark unfathomable eyes. Her face looked pained and strained. "I think you ought to know Catherine," said the earl gently. "Perhaps you thought that the estates would pass to you in due course of time."

Catherine pressed her hands closely together, but her voice was steady, her words were quietly spoken. "I do not know if I have ever thought about it; but I suppose I have fancied it."

"Exactly, you would naturally inherit all I have to leave; but MacAlister castle is entailed in the male line, and goes with the title. At my death Mr. Edward MacAlister will be the next earl, and all will be his. "Catherine sat very still, feeling as if she had received some sudden stunning blow; but she could not take in all in a moment the meaning of such intelligence. A woman in some matters, she was a child in others.

"But father," she said quietly, and without apparent emotion, "Matthew is surely much nearer to you than this Mr. MacAlister, whom you have never seen?" The earl smiled half––sadly, and shook his head. "My dear, do not understand these things; I feel towards Matthew as if he were my son, but he is not of my kindred. He is my wife's son, not mine he not a MacAlister at all.

Catherine's troubled gaze rested on her father's face, "He cannot live anywhere else but at MacAlister castle," she said slowly. "It would kill him to take him away; "and in her heart she add––a little jealous hostility rising up in her heart against the stranger who was wrongfully coming––" He ought to have it. He is a son and a brother here. By every law of right MacAlister castle should be his.

Foolish, irrational Catherine! Where Matthew was concerned her eyes were blinded, her reason was warped by her love. And the ways of the great outside world were so difficult to understand. Presently she spoke in very low, measured tones, though not without a little falter in her voice now and then.

"You mean that if——if you were to die——Matthew and I should be turned out of MacAlister castle," "You would neither of you have any right to remain," answered Lord MacAlister, choosing his words with care. "You will fine a home with your aunt; and as for Matthew, I suppose he would go to his cousins——unless, indeed, if he seemed unable to live away from the place, some arrangement with my successor could be made. Everything would depend on him of course it would be a difficult thing to manage.

She drew a long breath, and passed a hand across her eyes. "Mr. MacAlister is coming here, you say?" "Yes, next week. I think it is right that we should become acquainted with our kinsman, especially as so much may depend upon him in the future." "I think so too," answered Catherine; and then she quietly left him, without uttering another word.

Chapter 2

Catherine's Ride

The next morning dawned fair and clear, as is often the case after a storm. Catherine rose early, her first thought was for Matthew. She crept on tip-toe to his room, to find him as she had left him, sleeping calmly––as he was likely now to do for hours, after the attack of the previous day; and finding herself no longer required by him, the girl was not long in making up her mind how these early hours of glimmering daylight were to be spent.

Seven o' clock found her in the saddle, mounted on her glossy black thorough bred, who gentle under her hand, would tolerate no other rider, and showed his spirit and courage in every graceful eager movement, and in the restless quivering of his shapely limbs. His coat shone like satin in the pale early sunlight; he pranced and performed as he felt his rider upon his back. Catherine and her horse together made a picture that for beauty and grace could hardly meet its match in the length and breadth of the land.

The girl was perfectly at home in the saddle. She took no attention of her horse striking the ground with his hoof impatiently, or the delighted baying of the great hounds who formed her escort, and whose noise caused James' delicate nerves many restive start. She gathered up her reins with practised hand, soothed him by a gentle caress, and rode quietly and absently out of the great grass––grown court-yard and through a stretch of tangled park beyond. Once outside the gates, she turned to the right, and quickly gained a narrow grass-grown track, which led for miles along the edge of the great frowning cliffs that almost overhung at a giddy height the tossing ocean far below. It was a perilous-looking path enough——one false step would be enough to hurl both horse and rider to certain destruction, but Catherine rode fearlessly onward; she and her horse were familiar with every step of the way, both knew the wild cliff path, and both loved it; and James stretched his delicate supple limbs in one of those silent gallops over the elastic turf in which his heart delighted.

Catherine seldom passed more than a day without traveling across that well known track. She loved to feel the fresh salt wind as it blew off the sea and met her face. Sometimes it was warm and tender as a caress, sometimes fierce and violent, a wet, blinding blast, laden with spray from the tempest-tossed waves below, but today it was a keen, fresh wind, salt, and strong, and life giving——a wind that brought the warm colour to her cheek, the light to her eye, and gave a peculiar and indescribable radiance to her usually cold and statuesque beauty.

Today she felt strangely restless and uneasy. A sort of haunting fear was upon her, a presentiment of coming trouble that was perhaps all the harder to bear from its very vagueness. She had never before realised that future would bring any change to the course of her life, except that of gradually increasing age. Not for an instant had it ever occurred to her that a possibility such as the one hinted at last night by her father could by any chance arise. That she and Matthew might ever have to leave MacAlister seemed the wildest of all wild dreams, and yet that is what in all probability must happen in the event of her father's death. Catherine shuddered at the bare idea. Her beautiful dark eyes glowed strangely. It must not, it should not be. It would be too cruel, too hard, too unjust!

In deep abstraction, Catherine rode along the cliff for some three miles, then turning her horse's head inland, she crossed an open space of wind-swept down leaped a low stone wall, and found herself on a road, which followed for some considerable distance. It led at length to the quaint little town of St. Maws a pretty little place, nestling down in a wooded hollow, and intersected by a narrow inlet from the sea, which was spanned by a many——arched bridge. All the trees in the neighbourhood seemed to have collected round St. Maws, and its inhabitants were justly proud of their stately oaks and graceful beeches Catherine rode quietly through the empty street, returning now and again in a salutation from some tradesman or rustic. It was still early—only eight o' clock—and the sleepy little place was slowly awaking from its night's repose. At the far end of the town stood a good-sized house, well hidden from view behind a high brick wall. James turned in at the gate of his own accord, and following a short, winding carriage drive, halted before the front door. The house was of warm red brick, mellowed by age; there was an indescribable air of comfort and hospitality hanging over it. It was mantled by glossy ivy, and its gables, steep pitched roof, twisted chimneys were charmingly picturesque. The door stood wide open as if to invite entrance. Catherine's hounds had already announced her approach, and a tall, wiry looking man of some thirty year's was standing upon the threshold. He was not much like his brother, the blue-eyed, brown bearded Johnathon having a thin, sharp, closely shaved face, very keen penetrating eyes, and cynical mouth. Bruce Pendrill was himself a doctor, like his brother; but he did not practise on his own account, being a man of scientific predilections, with a taste for authorship. His college fellowship rendered him independent of lucrative employment, and for assisting his brother with critical cases, his time was spent in study and research. "Well, Catherine, you are abroad early today." was his greeting. Matthew's cousins had been like cousins to Catherine almost ever since she could remember, "you have to breakfast, of course?" "I came to tell Johnathon not to trouble to call at MacAlister today, if he is busy. Matthew is much better. I want to see Aunt Jennifer; but I should like some breakfast very much."

"I will take your horse," said Bruce, as the girl slipped from the saddle. "you will find Aunt Jennifer in the breakfast-room."

The "Aunt Jennifer" thus alluded to was the widow of the Pendrill's uncle, and she lived with them for many years, keeping their house, and bringing into it the element of womanly refinement and comfort which can never be found in a purely bachelor establishment. The young men were both warmly attached to her, as was her other nephew, Matthew, at the castle. As for Catherine's "Aunt Jennifer" had been to her almost like a mother, supplying that great want in the girl's life of which she was only vaguely conscious—the want of tender, womanly comprehension and sympathy in the trials and perplexities of childhood and youth.

It had been her habit for many years to bring all her troubles to Mrs. Pendrill. She did not discuss them with Matthew. Her mission was to smooth and cheer him, not to infect him with any fears or sorrows. He was her boy, her charge, her dearly-loved brother, but Aunt Jennifer was confidante and friend.

She was a very sweet-looking old Lady, with snow-white hair, and a gentle, placid earnest face. She greeted Catherine with a peculiarly tender smile, and asked after Matthew with the air of one who loved him.

"He is better," said Catherine, "much better, or I could not have come. He is asleep; he will most likely sleep till noon. I want talk to you Aunt Jennifer. I felt I must come to you. When breakfast is over, please let us go somewhere together. There is so much I want to say."

When they found themselves at length secure from interruption in Mrs. Pendrill's pretty little parlour, Catherine stood very quiet for a minute or two, and then turning abruptly to her aunt, she asked—"Is my father very much out of health?" Mrs. Pendrill was a little startled. "What makes you ask that, my love?" "I can hardly say—I think it is the way he looked the way he spoke. Please tell me the truth, dear Aunt Jennifer, I have nobody but you to turn to," and there was a pathetic quiver in the voice as well as in the pale, sweet face.

Mrs. Pendrill did not try to deceive her. She knew from both her nephews that Lord MacAlister's health was in a very precarious state, she loved Catherine too well not to wish to see her somewhat prepared for a change that must inevitably fall upon her sooner or later. She had always shrank from thinking of this trouble, she shrank from bringing it home to Catherine now; but a plain question had been asked, and her answer must not be too ambiguous.

Catherine listened very quietly, as was want, not betraying and emotion except in the strained look of pain in her great dark eyes. Then very quietly too, she told Mrs. Pendrill what her father had said the previous evening about his heir, and about the prospective visit.

"Aunt Jennifer," said Catherine suddenly, after a long pause, betraying for the first time the emotion she felt, "Aunt Jennifer, I do not wish to be wicked or ungenerous, but I hate that man! He has no right to be at Mac Alister, yet he will someday come and turn out Matthew and I. I cannot help hating him for it; but oh, if only he would be good to Matthew, if only he would let him stay, I could bear anything else, I think! Do you think he would be generous and would let him keep his own little corner of the castle? It does not seem much to ask, yet father it might be difficult. Matthew is so patient, so good, he might learn to love him––he might even adopt him, so to speak. Am I very foolish to hope such things, Aunt Jennifer?––they do not seem impossible to me. Mrs. Pendrill pondered a little while. "Has this Mr. MacAlister any family?" "I do not know. Father did not speak of a wife. I fancy he is an old bachelor. "He is old, then?"

"I fancy he is elderly, or at any rate middle-aged, or father would hardly care to have him on a visit. He must be younger than father, of course, but I do not know anything more about him. Oh, it will be very hard; but if he will only be good to Matthew, I will try to bear the rest.

"I am sure you will, my Catherine," said Mrs. Pendrill. "I am sure you will never be ungenerous or act unworthily. A dark cloud seems hanging over your life, but there is light behind, though we cannot always see it. And remember, my darling that gold shines all the brighter for having been tried in the furnace."

"I know the fellow," said Bruce Pendrill, an hour later, when Catherine had gone, and he heard from his aunt part of what had passed between them Catherine is about his age; he can't be more than twenty seven and a right good fellow he is too, and would make my Lady a capital husband, if he is not married already. Edward MacAlister was at oxford; I knew him there pretty well, though he was only an undergraduate when I had taken my degree. The name sounded homelike, and I made friends with him. He wasn't anywhere near the title then, but I suppose there have deaths in the family since. Well, well, the earl is quite right to have him down, and if he could manage to fall in love with Catherine and marry her, it would simplify matters wonderfully; but that wild bird will need a good deal of training before she will come at a husband's call, and in the sight of the quarry. "No thought of this, kind, however entered into Catherine's head. She was far too unversed in the ways of the world to entertain the smallest suspicion of the hopes entertained on her account. She thought a good deal of the coming guest as the days went by thought of him with bitterness, with aversion, with mistrust; but in the light of a possible husband––never for a single instant.

It was the day before the stranger was expected and Catherine, as the sun was sinking in the sky, was riding alone in the pine wood the surrounded the castle. She was grave and pre-occupied, as she had been for the week past, haunted by the presage of coming sorrow and change.

Her face was pale and sad, yet there was a wonderful depth of sweetness in its expression of wistful melancholy. The setting sun, slanting through the healthy-looking trunks of the tall pines, shone full upon her, lighting her golden hair, and making an aureole of glory round her head, showing off with peculiar clear distinctness the graceful outline of her supple figure and the beauty of the horse she rode.

She was in a very thoughtful mood, so absent and pre-occupied as to be quite lost to outside impressions, when James suddenly swerved and reared, with a violence that would have unseated a less practised rider. Catherine was not in the least alarmed, but the movement aroused her from her reverie, and she was quickly made aware of what had frightened the horse. A tall broad-shouldered young man stepped forward, and laid a hand upon James bridle, lifting his hat at the same time, and disclosing a broad brow, with a sweeping wave of dark hair lying across it.

"Beg a thousand pardons; I believe I frightened your horse he is evidently unused to the sight of trespassers. I trust you have not been alarmed."

Catherine smiled at the notion; her face had been somewhat set and cold till the apology was made. The stranger had no right to be there, certainly, but his frank admission of the fact went far to relieve the crime. She allowed her self to smile, and the smile was in itself a revelation.

"It does not matter," she said quietly. "I know the wood is bewildering; but if you keep bearing to the west you will find the road before long. No I was not frightened, thank you. Good-afternoon."

She bent her head slightly, and the stranger uncovered again. He was smiling now, and she could not declare that he was very good-looking, and every inch the gentleman.

She had no idea who he was nor what he could be doing there; but it was no business of hers. He was probably some tourist, who had lost his way exploring the beauties of the coast. She was just a little puzzled by the look his face had worn as he turned away: there was a sort of subdued amusement in the dark blue eyes, and his long brown moustache and quivered as if with the effort to subdue a smile.

Yet there had been nothing in the least impertinent in his manner; on the contrary, he had been particularly courtly and polished in his bearing. Catherine dismissed the subject from her mind, and rode home as the sun dipped beneath the far horizon.

Chapter 3

Lord MacAlister's Heir

Lord MacAlister sat in his study in the slowly declining daylight, waiting the arrival of his expected guest. Now that the moment had come, he shrank from the meeting a good deal more than he had once believed he should do. It was so long since he had seen a strange face, and his relations with this unknown heir would perhaps be difficult: undoubtedly the situation was somewhat strained. Would the young man think a trap was being set for him in the person of the beautiful Catherine? Was he acting a wise or fatherly part in scheming to give her to this stranger, if it should be possible to do so?

He had liked the tone of Edward MacAlister's courteously-worded acceptance of his invitation. He had liked all that he heard of this man himself. He had a presentiment that his wish would in time be realised, that this visit would not be fruitless; but his child's happiness: would that be secured in securing to he the possession of a well-love home? Edward MacAlister would hardly be likely to spend any great part of his life at this lonely sea-bound castle. He might pass a few months there, perhaps; but where would the bulk of his time be lived?

Lord MacAlister tried to picture his beautiful, wayward, and freedom-loving daughter mixing in the giddy whirl of London life, learning its ways and following its fashions, yet he utterly failed to do so. She seemed indissolubly connected with the wild sea-coast, with the gloomy pine woods, with the rugged independence of her sea-girt home. Catherine a fashionable young countess, leading a happy life of social distraction! The thing seemed impossible.

But he had no time to indulge his imaginings farther. The door opened, and his guest was ushered in. The old Earl rose and bade him welcome with his customary simple, stately courtesy. It was growing somewhat dark in that oak-panelled room, and for a minute or two he hardly distinguished the features of the stranger, but the voice and the word's in which the young man answered his greeting pleased his hard to please taste, and a haunting dread of which he had scarcely been fully aware, faded from his mind forever in the first moment of introduction.

Lord MacAlister heaved an unconscious sigh of relief when he resumed his seat, and was able to give a closer scrutiny to his guest. One glance at his face, figure, and dress, together with the pleasant sound of his voice, convinced Lord MacAlister that this young man was a gentleman in the rather restricted sense in which he employed that elastic term. He was a handsome, broad-shouldered, powerful man, with a fine figure, dark hair and moustache, dark blue, eyes frank and well-opened, a quiet, commanding air and carriage, and that cast of countenance which plainly showed that blood of the MacAlister's ran in his veins.

Lord MacAlister eyed him with quiet satisfaction, and from the conversation that ensued he had no reason to rescind his favourable impression. Edward MacAlister was evidently a man of culture and refinement, with a mental capacity distinctly above the average. He was moreover, emphatically a man of the world in its truest and widest sense——a man who has lived in the world, and studied it closely, learning thereby from its silent teaching the good and the evil there of.

The two men talked for a time of the family to which they belonged, and the deaths that had lately taken place, bringing this young man so near to the title.

"The MacAlister's seem to be a dying race," said the old Earl, half sadly. "Our family is slowly dying out. I suppose it has done its work in the world, and is not needed any longer in these stirring times. You and my daughter are now the sole representatives of the MacAlister's in your generation, as my sister and I are in ours."

Edward MacAlister looked into his kinsman's face with a great deal of reverence and admiration. He liked to meet a man who was a genuine specimen of the "old school." He felt a natural reverence for the head of this house, and was gratified, whilst the younger man was pleased to feel himself in accord with his host. The interview ended with mutual satisfaction on both sides, and Edward was taken up the great oak staircase, down or two dim, ghostly corridors, and landed finally in a couple of large panelled rooms, most antiquely and quaintly furnished, in both of which, however, great fires of pine logs were blazing cheerily.

"We dine at eight," Lord MacAlister had said, in parting with his guest. "I shall hope then to have the pleasure of introducing you to my sister and my daughter.

Left alone in his comfortable but rather grim-looking quarters, Edward broke into a low laugh. "And so this somber old place, full of ghosts and phantoms of departed days––this enchanted castle between sea and forest––is the home of the lovely girl I saw yesterday! Incongruous, and yet so entirely appropriate! She wants a setting of her own, different from anything else. It must have been Lady Catherine I encountered, the Lady of the pine wood. What a sad, proud, lovely face it was, with its frame of golden hair, and soft eyes like a deer's; and her voice was as sweet as her face, low, rich, and full of music. What has been the secret of her life? Sorrow, I am certain, has overshadowed it. Who will be the happy man to bring the sunshine back to that lovely troubled face? Edward MacAlister, do not run on so fast. You are no longer a boy. You must not judge by first impressions; you will know more of her soon." Edward's encounter with Catherine the previous day had been purely accidental.

The young man reached St. Maws one day earlier than had intended, one day earlier than he had been invited to arrive at the castle. Some business in Plymouth which he had expected would detain him some days had been dispatched with greater speed than he had anticipated, and he had gone on to St. Maws to renew acquaintance with his old friend Pendrill, who lived, as he remembered, in that place.

When he descended to the drawing-room it was to find the earl and Lady Louise there before him, and he made as favourable an impression upon the vivacious old Lady as he had done before upon her brother. Yet he found his attention straying sometimes from the animated talk of his companion, and his eyes would wander to the door by which Catherine must enter.

She came at last, stately, beautiful, statuesque, her dress antique cream-coloured brocade that had, without doubt, belonged to some remote ancestress her golden hair coiled like a crown upon her graceful head. She had that same indescribable air of isolation and remoteness that had struck him so much when he saw her riding in the woods. She did not lift her eyes when her father presented the stranger to her, but only bent her head very slightly, and sat down by herself, somewhat apart.

But when dinner was announced, and Edward gave her his arm to lead her in, she raised her eyes, and their glances met. He saw that she recognised him, and yet she gave not the slightest sign of having done so, and her face settled into lines of even more severe gravity than before. He felt that she was annoyed at his having met and addressed her previously, and that she would brook no allusion to the encounter.

His talk with the Pendrill's had prepared him some what for Catherine's coldness towards himself. It was natural enough, he thought, and perhaps a little interesting, especially as he meant to set himself to win her goodwill at last.

He did not make much way during dinner. Catherine was very silent, and Lady Louise engrossed almost all his attention; but he was content to bide his time, conscious of the charm of her presence, and of the haunting, pathetic character of her beauty, and deeply touched by the story of her devotion to the crippled, suffering Matthew, which was told him by the earl when they were alone together, with more of detail than he had heard it before.

When he returned to the drawing-room, he went straight up to Catherine, and said "I am going to ask a favour of you, Lady Catherine. I want to know if you will be good enough to introduce me to your brother?" Her face softened slightly as she raised her eyes to his. It was a happy instinct that had led Edward to call Matthew by the name she most loved to hear, "your brother." "You would like to see him tonight?"

"If it is not too late to intrude upon an invalid, I should very much." "I think he would be pleased," said Catherine. "It is so seldom he has any one to talk to."

The visit to Matthew was a great success. The lad took to Edward at once, delighted to find him so young, so pleasant, and so companionable. Of course he identified him at once as the hero of Catherine's adventure yesterday, and was amused to hear his account of the meeting. Catherine did not stay long in the room; but her absence enabled Matthew to sing praises as he loved to do, and Edward listened with a satisfaction that surprised himself. He was very kind to the boy, sincerely sorry for his helpless state, and more than ready to stand his friend if ever there should be occasion. Before he left the invalid that night, he felt that in him, at least, he had secured a staunch and trusty friend.

But during the days that followed he could not hide from himself the fact that Catherine avoided him. Indeed, he sometimes hardly saw her from morning till night, and when they did meet at the luncheon or dinner-table, she sat still and silent, scarcely vouchsafing him a word or a look. The first time Edward found himself alone with Catherine was in this wise: he had been riding about the immediate precincts of the castle with the earl one morning, and his host was just expressing a wish to extend their ride farther, in order to see some of the best views of the neighbourhood-hesitating somewhat on his own account, as he had been forbidden to exert himself by much exercise––when Catherine suddenly appeared, mounted on James, and attended by her convoy of dogs, ready for her daily gallop.

Lord MacAlister's face softened at her approach; he loved his fair daughter with a deep and tender love. "Catherine, my dear, you have come in good time. I want Mr. MacAlister to see the view of the castle from the black cliff, and the wonderful archway in the rocks farther along the coast. These fine days must not be wasted; and I feel too tired to undertake the ride myself. Will you act as my substitute, and do the honours of MacAlister?"

Catherine glanced with a sort of mute wistfulness into her father's pale face, and assented quietly. The next moment she and Edward were riding side by side over the close soft turf of the sweeping downs. The girl's face was set and grave, she seemed lost in thought, and was only roused by the eccentricities of James' behaviour. The spirited little barb resented company even more than his mistress did, and showed his distaste by every means in his power. He was so troublesome that Edward was half afraid for Catherine's safety, but she smiled at the idea of danger.

"I know James too well," she answered; "it is nothing. He only hates company. He is not used to it." "Had you not better have another horse today?" "Let myself be conquered? No, thank you. I always say that if that once were to happen, it would never be safe ever for me to ride James again." The battle with the horse brought the colour to her face and the light to her eyes. She looked more approachable now as she cantered along beside him (victorious at last, with her dogs bounding about her) than she had ever done before. He drew her out a little about her four-footed favourites, and being a lover of animals himself, and knowing their ways, they found a good deal to say without trenching in any way upon dangerous or personal topics.

They visited the places indicated by Lord MacAlister, and Edward admired the beauties of the wild coast with a genuine appreciation that satisfied Catherine. Had her companion been anybody but himself––an alien usurper come to spy out the land that would some time be his own––had his praises been less sounded in her ears by Lady Louise, whose praise was in Catherine's eyes worse than any open condemnation she could almost have found it in her heart to like him; but as it was jealous distrust drove all kindlier feelings away, and even his handsome person and pleasant address added to her sense of hostility and disfavour.

Why was he to win all hearts––he who would so ruthlessly act the part of tyrant and foe, as soon as his chance came? Did not even his friend, Lady Louise, continually repeat that his succession to the MacAlister estate must inevitably mean an immediate break-up of all existing forms and usages? Was it not an understood thing that he would exercise his power without considering anything but his strict legal right? Lady Louise knew the world––that world to which Edward evidently belonged. If this was her opinion, was it not presumably the right one? She sneered openly at the suggestion her niece had once thrown out of the possibility of his granting to Matthew liberty to remain at MacAlister.

"You foolish child!" she said sharply. What is Matthew to him? Men do not make sentimental attachments to each other. Matthew has no right here, and Mr. MacAlister will show him so very plainly when time comes."

Was it any wonder that Catherine's heart rose in revolt against this handsome, powerful stranger, who seemed in a manner to hold her whole future in his strong hands? Was it strange she should avoid him? Was it difficult to understand that she distrusted him, and that only his present kindness to Matthew, and the lad's affection for him enabled her to tolerate with any kind of submission his presence in the house? He tried now to make her talk of herself, of Matthew, of her home and her life there, but she became at once impenetrably silent. Her face assumed its old look of statuesque hauteur. The ride back to the castle was a very a very silent one, Edward had enjoyed the hour spent in the company of Lady Catherine, but he could not flatter himself that much ground had been gained.

Chapter 4

David MacRae

Whether Catherine would ever have thawed towards him of her own free will Edward MacAlister could not tell; during a sharp attack of illness that prostrated Matthew at this juncture, he was so much in the sick boy's room, and so kind and patient and helpful there, that the girl's coldness began insensibly to melt; and before the attack had passed, he felt that if she did not share her brother's liking for him, at least the old antipathetic hostility had somewhat abated.

They rode out together sometimes now, exploring the country round the castle, or galloping over the wind-swept moors. Catherine was generally silent, always reserved and unapproachable, and yet he felt that a certain vantage-ground had been gained, and he did not intend to allow it to slip away. Unconsciously almost to himself, the wish had grown to win the heart of this wild, beautiful, lonely young creature. Yet the charm of her solitary timelessness was so great that he hardly wished the spell to be too suddenly broken. He could not picture Catherine other than she was––and yet he was growing to love her with every fibre of his being.

But fortune was not kind to Edward, as an incident that quickly followed showed him. He and Catherine had ridden one day across a wild sweep of trackless moorland, when they came in sight of picturesque Elizabethan house, in a decidedly dilapidated condition, whose red brick walls and mullioned windows took Edward's fancy. He asks who lives there.

"No one now," answered Catherine, with a touch as of regret in her voice; "no one has lived there for years and years. Once it was such a bright, happy home we used to play there, Matthew and I, when we were children; but the master died, the children were taken away, and the house was shut up. That was ten years a ago. I have never been there since."

"Who is the owner? Does he never reside here now?" "He has never been back. I believe he is not rich, and could not keep up the place. He must be about twenty-five by this time. He is Sir David MacRae he was such a nice boy when I used to play with him."

Edward started; he controlled himself in a moment, by Catherine's eyes were very quick, and she had seen the instinctive recoil at the sound of the name. "Do you know David MacRae?" she asked. "We have met." he answered, somewhat grimly. "I do not claim the honour of this acquaintance. "Catherine glanced at him. She saw something in the stern lines of Edward's face that told a tale of its own. She was not afraid to state the conclusion she reached. "That means that you have quarreled," she said.

"I am not at liberty to explain what it means," was the answer, spoken with a certain stern gravity, not lost upon Catherine. She had never seen her companion look like this before. The strength and resolution of his face compelled an involuntary respect, yet she revolted against hearing the friend and playmate of her childhood tacitly condemned by this stranger.

"I do not like innuendoes, Mr. MacAlister," she said. "If you have anything to say against a man I think it is better spoken out." "I have nothing at all to say upon the subject of Sir David MacRae." he answered quietly. Ungenerous! Unmanly!" was Catherine's mental comment.

"I cannot bear hearing a character hinted away. I loved David once, and he loved me. I do not believe he has done anything for which he should be condemned. "Edward thought little of these few chance words respecting Sir David MacRae at the time when they were spoken; but he was destined to think a good deal about that individual before many days had passed.

Making his way to Matthew's room towards dusk one day, as he often did, he was surprised to find quite a little group around the glowing fire. Catherine and the dogs were objects sufficiently familiar to him by this time, but who was that graceful, fair-haired youth, who sat beside the girl, his face turned towards her and away from Edward, whilst he made some happy laughing rejoinder to her in a very sweet, musical voice?

Edward recognised that laugh and that voice with another start of dismay. His face set itself in very stern lines, and he would have withdrawn in silence had he been able to do so unobserved; Matthew saw him as he moved to go, and cried gladly "Oh, here is Edward——that is right. Our old friend and new one must be introduced. Sir David MacRae-Mr. Edward Alister."

Edward's eyes were fixed full upon the face of the younger man, as made the slightest possible inclination of the head. His hand unconsciously clenched itself in a gesture that was a little significant. Catherine's eyes were upon David. Was it possible that he quailed and flinched beneath the steady gaze bent upon him?

She did not think so, she was sure it could not be; no, he was only drawing himself up to return that cold salutation with one expressive of sovereign contempt. Not a word was exchanged between the two men. Edward sat down beside Matthew, and began to talk to him. David drew nearer to Catherine, and entered into a low-tone conversation with her. His voice sounded tender and caressing, and ever anon such words as these reached young MacAlister's ears-

"Do you remember, Catherine?"——"Ah, those sweet days of childhood!"——"You have not forgotten?"——"How often have I thought of it all."

Evidently they were discussing the happy past the bright days that had been shared by them before the cloud fell upon Catherine's life. Edward could not keep his eyes away from her face. It was lit up with a new expression, half sad, and yet strangely, infinitely sweet. David's face was very beautiful too, with its delicate, almost effeminate colouring and serious, melancholy blue eyes. He had been a lovely child, and his beauty had not faded with time. It had stood him in good stead in many crises of his life, and was doing so still. There is an irrational association in most minds between beauty and goodness.

But Edward's face grew more and more dark as he watched the pair opposite. Old memories were stirring within him, and at last he rose and left the room, feeling that he could no longer stand the presence of that man within it, could no longer endure to see him bending over Catherine, and talking to her in that soft, caressing way. David looked after him, a vindictive light in his blue eyes. As the door closed he uttered a low laugh. "What is it?" asked Matthew.

"Oh, nothing. I was only wondering how long he would be able to brazen it out!" "Why, sitting there with my eye upon him. Couldn't you see how restless he got?" "Restless!" repeated Matthew quickly. "Why should he be restless?" David laughed again.

"Never mind, my boy. I bear him no malice. The least said the soonest mended." Catherine was silent and a little troubled. She liked to understand things plainly. It seemed to her an unnatural thing for two men to be at almost open feud, yet unwilling to say a word as to the cause of their mutual antagonism. She thought that if they met beneath her father's roof they should be willing to do so as friends.

Her gravity did not escape David's notice, "Has he been maligning me already?" he asked suddenly, with a subdued flash in his eyes. "No" answered Catherine, with a quick involuntary coldness. "He has not said a word. I do not think," she added presently, with a gentle dignity of manner, "that I should listen very readily from the lips of a stranger to stories detrimental to an old companion and playmate, told behind his back." David gave her a look of humble gratitude. He would have taken her hand and kissed it had she been anybody else, but somehow, demonstrations of such a kind always seemed impossible where Catherine was concerned. Even to him she was decidedly unapproachable.

"It is good indeed of you to say so," he answered; "but Catherine—may I call you Catherine still, I may not? As I have always thought of you all these long years—you might hear stories to my detriment that would not be untrue. There have been faults and follies and sins in my past life that I would gladly blot out if I could. I have been wild and reckless often. I lost my parents very young, as you know, and it is hard for a boy without a home and home influences to grow up as he should do." David paused, and then added, with a good deal of feeling "Catherine, can a man do more than repent the past? Can nothing ever wipe away the stain, and give him back his innocence again? Must he always bear about the shadow of sorrow and shame?"

Catherine's face was grave and thoughtful. She shook her head as she replied "It is no use coming to me with hard questions, David; I know so little, so very little of the world you live in. Yet it seems to me that it would be hard indeed if repentance did not bring forgiveness in its wake." quoted

Matthew, lazily. "What is it you have done? Can't you tell us all the story, and let us judge for ourselves––old friends and playmates as we are?"

"I should like to," answered David, gently. Some day I will; but do not let us spoil this first meeting with bitter memories. Let it be enough for me to have come home, and have found my friends unchanged towards me. May I venture still to call you my friends?"

"To be sure," cried Matthew readily; but David's eyes were fixed on Catherine's face; and she saw it, and looked back at him with her steady inscrutable gaze. "I do not think I change easily," she said, with her gentle dignity of manner. "You were my friend and playmate in our happy childhood. I should like to think of you always as a friend." "Of course, put in Matthew, happily; of course we are all friends, and you must make friends with Edward too. He is such a good fellow." "I have no objection at all," answered David, with a short laugh. "The difficulty I imagine, will be on his side. Some men never forget or forgive any one who succeeds in finding them out."

"Oh, we will manage Edward, never fear. You are ready, then, to make it up if he is?" Most certainly, "was the ready answer." He is the nobler of the two," said Catherine to herself––at least her reason and judgment said so; her instinct, oddly enough, spoke in exactly opposite strain; but surely it was right to listen first to the voice of reason.

"I say Edward," said Matthew, half-an hour later, when the young baronet had taken his departure and the other guest had returned to the invalid's room, "David is quite willing to make it up with you." Edward's smile was a little peculiar.

"Sir David MacRae is very kind." "Well, you know, it's always best to make friends, isn't it? Deadly feuds are a nuisance in these days, don't you think so?" Edward smiled again; but his manner was certainly a little baffling. "Come now Edward," persisted Matthew, with boyish insistence, "You won't hang back now that he is ready for the reconciliation. He is the injured party, is he not?"

There was rather a strange light in Edward's dark blue eye. His manner was exceedingly quiet, yet he looked as if he could be a little dangerous. "possibly," was the rather inconclusive answer. "You know he come to stay little time in the neighbourhood, he will often be here. It will be so awkward if you are at daggers draw all the time."

"My dear boy, you need not put yourself about. I will take care that there shall be no annoyance to anybody." you will make friends then?" "I will meet Sir David MacRae, whenever he is your father's guest, with the courtesy due from one man to another, when circumstances bring them together beneath the roof of the same hospitable host. But to take his hand in reconciliation or friendship is a thing that I cannot and will not do. Do you understand now?" Matthew looked at him intently, as for once Catherine was doing also.

"Edward," he said, a little inconsequently, "do you know I think I could almost be afraid of you sometimes. I never saw you look before as you looked just then." Then stern lines on Edward's face relaxed a little, but he still looked grave and pre-occupied, sitting with his elbow on his knee, leaning forward, and pulling his moustache with an abstracted air.

"You are rather unforgiving too, I think," pursued the boy. "David admitted he had done wrong, but is very sorry for the past; and I think it is hard when old offences, repented of, are not consigned to oblivion," Edward was silent. "Don't you agree?" still only impenetrable silence. "Come, Edward, don't be so mysterious and so revengeful. Let us have the whole story, and judge for ourselves.

"Excuse me, Matthew; but the life of Sir David MacRae is not one that I choose to discuss. His affairs are no concern of mine, nor, if you will pardon my saying so, any concern of yours, either. You are at liberty to renew past friendship with him if it pleases you to do so; but it is useless to ask me to do the same." And with that Edward rose, and left the room without another word.

"There is something odd about it all," said Matthew, who was inclined to indulge a good deal of curiosity about other people's affairs: "but I think David behaves the better of the two."

Catherine quietly assented; but perhaps she might have changed her opinion had she heard the muttered threats breathed by David as he rode across the darkening moor––"So Edward MacAlister, our paths have crossed once more! I have vowed vengeance upon you to your very face, and perhaps my day has come at last. I see through you. I see the game you are playing. I will discourage you if I can; but in any case I will have my revenge."

Chapter 5

Sunday at MacAlister

It was Sunday, and Catherine, with Edward beside her, was making her way by the path along the cliff towards the little old church perched high upon the crags, between MacAlister and st. maws, but nearer to the town than the castle. Edward had found out the ways of the house by this time. He knew that Catherine played the organ in the little church that she started early and walked across the downs, instead of going in the carriage with her father and aunt. He knew that she generally lunched with the Pendrill's betweens services, and that one of her cousins walked back with her to the castle, and spent an hour with Matthew afterwards.

He had found out all this during his first two Sundays, and upon the third he ventured to ask permission to be her escort. Edward was quite aware that he had lost ground with Catherine of late; that the barrier, partially broken down during the week of anxiety about Matthew, had risen up again as impenetrable as ever. How far Sir David MacRae's appearance upon the scene was to blame for this he could not tell, nor could Catherine herself have sense of restraint experienced in his presence. Yet was conscious that his love for her increased every day, and that no coldness on her part checked or stunted its growth. He sometimes wondered at himself for the depth and intensity of his passion, for he was a man who had passed almost unscathed here to fore from the shafts of the blind god, nor was he by nature impulsive or susceptible. But then Catherine was like no woman he had ever met before, and from the very first she had exercised a curious fascination over him. Also their relative positions were peculiar; the daughter and the heir of the old earl, whose life was evidently so very frail. Edward had a shrewd idea that his kinsman had little to leave apart from the entail, and in the event of his death what would become of the fair girl his daughter? Would be fate to be placed in the keeping of that worldly spinster, the Lady Louise? Edward's whole soul revolted from such an idea.

So, altogether, his interest in Catherine was hardly more than natural, and his sense of protecting championship not entirely uncalled for. One thing he had resolutely determined upon—that she should never suffer directly or indirectly on his account. He had made no definite plans as regarded the future, but on that point his mind was made up. Today, for the first time, he ventured to allude to a subject hitherto never touched upon between them. "You have a very beautiful home, Lady Catherine," he said. "It is no wonder that you love it." Her glance met his for a moment, and then her eyes dropped again.

"Is it true that you have never left MacAlister all your life? "Except for a few days with Matthew, never." "You have never seen London?" "No, never," very emphatically. "Nor wish to do so?" "No."

He reflected a little. Somehow it was more difficult than he had believed to convey to her the information he had desired to hint at. He entered upon another topic. "Have you ever been advised, Lady Catherine, to try what the German baths could do for Matthew? Very wonderful cures are sometimes accomplished there. "She her head suddenly, with something of a flash in her eyes.

"Bruce Pendrill has been talking to you!" Indeed, no." "That is what he wants—what he is always driving at. He does not care how my poor boy suffers, if only he has the pleasure of experimenting upon him for the benefit of science. You do not know how he suffers in being moved; a journey like that would be murder. He can live nowhere but at MacAlister-MacAlister or the neighourhood, at least. Promise me never to suggest such a thing, never to take sides against me in it. Mr. MacAlister, I appeal to your honour and your humanity. Promise me never to league with Bruce Pendrill to send Matthew away to die!"

He had never seen her so vehement or excited. He was astonished at the storm he had aroused. "Indeed, Lady Catherine, you may trust me," he said. "I have not the least wish to distress you, or to urge anything in opposition to your wishes. The idea merely occurred to me, because I happen to have heard of many wonderful cures. But I will never allude to the subject again if it distresses you. It is certainly not for me to dictate to you as to the welfare of your brother."

The flush of excitement had faded from Catherine's face. She turned it towards him with something of apology and appeal. "Forgive me if I spoke too hastily," she said, with a little quiver in her voice he thought infinitely pathetic, "but I have so few to love, and the thought of losing them is very sad. And then Bruce has so often frightened me about Matthew and taking him away; I know that I understand him better than anybody else, though I am not a doctor, nor a man of science."

He looked at her with grave sympathy. "I think that is highly possible, Lady Catherine. You may trust me to say or do nothing that could give anxiety or pain." "Thank you," answered Catherine with unusual gentleness. "I do trust you." His heart thrilled with gladness at those simple words. They had almost reached the church now, and Catherine paused at the edge of the cliff, turning her gaze seawards, a strange, sad wistfulness upon her face.

Her companion watched her in silence. "There will be a storm before long," she said at last. The air was curiously clear and still, and the sea the same; yet there was a sullen booming sound far below that sounded threatening and rather awful. "You are weather-wise, Lady Catherine?" he asked with a smile. "I ought to be," she answered, turning away at length with a long-drawn breath. "I know our sea so well, so very well." And then she walked on and entered the church by her own little door, leaving Edward standing alone without.

He, too lunched with the Pendrill's that day. He had been over several times to see them since his arrival at MacAlister, and had made his way in that house as successfully as he had done at the castle. Bruce walked with him to church for the afternoon service. He spoke of Catherine with great frankness. "I have always likened her to a sort of undine," he remarked, "though not in the generally accepted sense. There are latent capacities within her that might make her a very remarkable woman; but half her nature is sleeping still. According to the tradition, love must awake the slumbering soul. I often think it is that which wanted to transform and humanise my Lady Catherine."

Edward was silent. The smallest suspicion of criticism of Catherine jarred upon him. Bruce saw this, and smiled to himself. They reached the little cliff church long before the rustic congregation had begun to assemble. The sound of the organ was audible from within. Bruce laid his fingers on his lips and made a sign to his companion to follow him. They softly mounted a little quaint stairway towards the loft, and reached a spot where, hidden themselves by the shadows, they could watch the player as she sat before the instrument.

Catherine had pushed back her heavily-plumed hat, and the golden sunshine glowed about her fair head in a quivering misty brightness. Her face wore a dreamy, softened look, pathetically sad and sweet. Her lustrous dark eyes were full of feeling. It seemed as if she were breathing out her soul in the sweet, low strains of music that sounded in the air. Edward gazed for one long minute, and then silently withdrew; it seemed a kind of sacrilege to take her unawares like that, when she was unconscious of their presence. "Saint Mary!" he murmured softly, as he descended the stairs once again. "Catherine, my Catherine! Will you ever be mine in reality? Will you ever learn to love me?" Catherine's face still wore its softened dreamy look as she joined Edward at the close of the service. Music exercised a strange power over her, raising her for a time above the level of the region in which she moved at other times. She looked pale and a little tired, as if the strain of the week of anxiety about Matthew had not yet quite passed off. As they reached the top of the down and turned the angle of the cliff, the wind, which had been gradually rising all day and now blew half a gale, struck them with all its force, and Catherine staggered a little beneath its sudden fury.

"Take my arm, Lady Catherine," said Edward. "This is too much for you." "Thank you," she answered, gently; and a sudden thrill ran through Edward's frame as he felt the clinging pressure of her hand upon his arm, and was conscious that she was grateful for the strong support against the fury of the elements. "It will be a dreadful night at sea," said the girl presently, when a lull in the wind made speech more easy. Look at the waves now. Are they not magnificent?" The sea was looking very wild and grand; Edward halted a moment beneath the shelter of a projecting crag, and gazed at the tempest-tossed ocean beneath. "You like a storm at sea, Lady Catherine?" She looked at him with a sort of horror in her eyes. "Like a storm!" "You were admiring the grandeur of the sea just now."

Ah, you do not understand!" she said, and gazed out before her, far-away look in her eyes. Presently she spoke again, looking at him for a moment with a world of sadness in her eyes, and then away over the tossing sea. "It is all very grand, very beautiful, very wonderful; but oh, so cruel, so pitiless in its strength and beauty! Think of the sailors, the fishermen out on the sea on a night like this, and the wives and mothers and little children, waiting at home for those who, perhaps, will never come back again. You do not understand. You belong to another world. You are not one of us. I have been down amongst them on wild, stormy nights. I have paced the beach with weeping women, watching, waiting for the boats that never came back, or came only to be dashed in pieces against the cruel rocks before our very eyes. "She paused a moment, and he felt her shudder in every limb; but her voice was still low and quiet, just vibrating with the depth of her feelings, but very calm and even. "I have seen boats go down within sight of home, within sound of our voices, almost within reach of our outstretched hands—almost, but not quite; and I have seen brave men, men I have known from childhood, swept away to their death, whilst we—their wives, their mothers, and I—have stood at the water's edge, powerless to succor them. Ah you do not, you cannot understand! I have seen all that, and more—and you ask me if I like a storm at sea!" She stood very still for a few seconds, and then took his arm again. "Let us go home," she said, drooping a little as the wind met them once more. "I am so tired." He sheltered her all he could against the fury of the gale, and presently as they neared the castle they were able to seek the shelter of the pine wood. Catherine's face was very pale, and he looked at her with a gentle concern that somehow in no wise offended her.

"You are very tired," he said, compassionately. "The walk has been too much for you." "Not the walk exactly," answered Catherine, with a little falter in her voice; "it was the music and the storm together, I think. I am glad we sung the hymn for those at sea tonight." He looked down at her earnestly. "And yet the sea is your best friend, Lady Catherine. You have told me so yourself." She looked at him with strange, wistful intensity.

"Yes, it is, it is," she answered; "my best and earliest friend; and yet-and-yet--" she paused, falling into a deep reverie; he roused her by a question "yet what, Lady Catherine?" Again that quick, strange glance. "Do you believe in presentiments?" "I am not sure that I do." "Ah! Then you cannot be a true MacAlister. We, MacAlister's, have a strange forecasting power. Coming events cast their shadow over us, and we feel it--we feel it!" He had never seen her in this mood before. He was intensely interested. "And you have a presentiment, Lady Catherine?" She bent her head, but did not speak. "And having said so much, will you not say more, and tell me what it is?" She stopped still, looked earnestly at him for a moment, and then passed her hand wearily across her face.

"Sometimes I think," she said, "that it will be the great sea, childhood's friend, that will bring to me the greatest sorrow of my life; for is it not the emblem of separation? Please take me in now. I think a storm is very sad and terrible." He looked into her pale, sweet face, and perhaps there was something in his glance that touched her, for as they stood in the hall at last she looked up with a shadowy smile, and said "Thank you very much. You have been very kind to me." That smile and those few simple words were like a ray of sunlight in his path.

Chapter 6

In Danger

Perhaps there was some truth in what Catherine had said about her ability to presage coming trouble. At least she was haunted just now by a strange shadow of approaching change, that future events justified only too well.

She often caught her father's glance resting upon her with a searching wistfulness, with something almost of pleading and appeal in his face. She had a suspicion that Matthew sometimes looked at her almost in the same way, as if he too would ask some favour of her, could he but bring his mind to do so. She felt that she was watched by all the household, that something was expected of her, and was awaited with a subdued expectancy; but the nature of this service she had not fathomed, and greatly shrank from attempting to do so. She told herself many times that she would do anything for those she loved, that no sacrifice would be too great which should add to or secure their happiness; but she did not fully understand what was expected of her; only instinct told her that it was some way connected with Edward MacAlister.

Sir David MacRae came from time to time to the castle. He was cordially recieved by the Earl and Lady Louise, who had respected and liked his parents, and remembered him well as a fair-haired boy, the childish playfellow and friend of Catherine and Matthew. Old feelings of intimacy sprang up anew after the lapse of time. It seemed as if he had hardly been more than a year or two away. It was difficult to realise that the young man was practically an entire stranger, of whose history they were absolutely ignorant.

Catherine felt the change most by a certain instinctive and involuntary shrinking from David that she could not in the least explain or justify. She wished to like him; she told herself that she did like him, and yet she was aware that she never felt at ease in his presence, and that he inspired her with a certain indescribable sense of repulsion, which, oddly enough, was shared by her four-footed friends, the dogs.

Catherine had a theory of her own that dogs brought up in human society became excellent judges of character, but if so, she ought certainly to modify some of her own opinions, for the dogs all adored Edward, and welcomed him effusively whenever he appeared; but they shrank back sullenly when David attempted to make advances, and no effort on his part conquered their instinctive aversion. David himself observed this, and it annoyed him. He greatly resented Edward's protracted stay at the castle, as he detested above all things he necessity of encountering him.

"How long is that fellow going to palm himself upon your father's hospitality?" he asked Catherine one day, with some appearance of anger. He had encountered Edward and the Lord in the park as he came up, and he was aware that the cold formality of the greeting which passed between them had not been lost upon the keen observation of the latter, "I call it detestable taste hanging on here as he does. When is he leaving?" "I do not know. Father enjoys his company, and so does Matthew. I have not heard anything about his going yet."

"Perhaps you enjoy his company too?" suggested David, with a touch of insolence in his manner. A faint flush rose in Catherine's pale face. Her look expressed a good deal of cool scorn. "Perhaps I do," she answered. David saw at once that he had made a blunder. Face and voice alike changed, and he said in his gentle, deprecating way "Forgive me, Catherine. I had no right to speak as I did. It was rude and unjustifiable. Only if you knew as much as I do about that fellow, you would not wonder that I hate to see him hanging round you as he is doing now, waiting it were, to step into place that is his by legal, but by no moral right. It would be hard to see any one acting such a part. It is ten times harder when you know your man." Catherine looked straight at David. "What do you know against

Mr. MacAlister? My father is acquainted with all his past history, and can learn nothing to his discredit. What story have you got hold of? I would rather hear facts than hints."

David laughed uneasily. "I know that he is a cad, and a sneak, and a spy; but I have no wish to upset your father's confidence in him. We were at oxford together, and of course it was not pleasant to me to hear his boasting of his future Lordship at MacAlister. That was the first thing that made me dislike him. Later on I had fresh cause."

Had Catherine been more conversant with the family history, she would have known that his boasting could never have taken place, as Edward had been far enough from the peerage at that time. As was, she looked grave and a little severe as she asked "Did he do that?" and listened with instinctive repugnance to the details fabricated by the inventive genius of David.

He next cleverly alluded again to his own past follies, and appealed to Catherine's generosity not to change towards him because he had sinned. "It is so hard to feel cast off by old friends," he said, with a very expressive look at the girl. "I know what it is to see myself cold-shouldered by those to whom I have learned to look up with reverence and affection. I have suffered very much from misrepresentation and hardness––suffered beyond what I deserve. I did fall once––I was sorely tempted, and I did commit one act of ingratitude and deceit that I have most bitterly repented of. I was very young and sorely tempted, and I did something which might have places me the felon's dock, and would have done so had somebody not far away had his will. But I was forgiven by the man I had injured, and I have tried my utmost since to make atonement for the past. The hardest part of all has been to see myself scorned and contemned by those whose good-will I have most wished to win. Sometimes I have known sorrow that has been akin to despair. I have been met with coldness and disdain when most I needed help and sympathy. Catherine you will not help to push me back into the abyss? You will not help make me think that repentance is in vain?" She looked at him very seriously, her eyes full of thoughtful surprise.

"I, David. What have I to do with it or with you?" This much, "he answered, taking her hand and looking straight into eyes:" this much Catherine that nothing so helps a man who has fallen once as the friendship of a noble woman like yourself; nothing hurts him more than her ill-will or distrust. Give me your friendship, and I will make myself worthy of it; turn your back coldly upon me, and I shall feel doomed to despair." "We have been friends all our lives, David," said Catherine, with gentle seriousness. "You know that if I could help you in the way you mean I should like to do so." "You will not change you will not turn your back upon me, whatever he may say of me?" She looked at him steadily, and answered, "No." "You promise, Catherine?" "There is no need for that, David. When I say a thing I mean it. We are friends, and I do not change without sufficient reason."

He saw that he had said enough; he raised her hand to his lips and kissed it once with a humility and reverence that could not offend her. Catherine wandered down by the lonely cliff path to the shore, revolving many thoughts in her mind, feeling strangely absorbed and abstracted.

The wind blew fresh and strong off the sea. The tide rolled in fast, salt, and strong. Catherine felt that she wanted to be alone today-alone with the great wild ocean that she loved so well, even whilst she feared it too in its fiercer moods. She therefore made her way with the agility and sure-footed steadiness of long practice over a number of great boulders, and along a protruding ledge of rock that stretched a considerable distance out to sea——a sunken reef that had brought to destruction many a hapless fisherman's craft, and more than one stately vessel.

At high tide it was covered, but it would not be high water for some hours yet, and Catherine, in her restless state of mental tension, had forgotten that the high spring tides were lashing the sea to fury just now upon this iron-bound coast, rendered more swift and strong and high by the steady way in which the wind set towards the land.

Standing on the great flat rock at the end of the sunken reef, a rock that was never covered even at the highest tides, Catherine was soon lost in so profound reverie that time flew by unheeded; and only when the giant waves began to throw their spray about her feet as they dashed up against the rock, did she suddenly rouse up to the consciousness that for once in her life she had forgotten herself, and forgotten the uncertain temper of her tryant play-fellow, and had allowed her retreat to be cut off.

She looked round her quietly and steadily, not frightened, but fully conscious of her danger. The reef was already covered; it would be impossible to retrace her footsteps with the waves dashing wildly over the sunken rocks. Catherine was a bold and practised swimmer, but to swim ashore in a heavy sea such as was now running was obviously out of the question. To stand upon that lonely rock until the tide fell again was a feat of strength and endurance almost equally impossible. Her best chance lay in being seen from the shore and rescued. Some one might pass that way, or even come in search of her, only the daylight was already failing, and would soon be gone.

Catherine looked round her, awed, yet calm, understanding, without realising, the deadly peril in which she stood. There was always a boat-her little boat lying at anchor in the bay, ready for her use at any moment. Her eyes turned towards it instinctively, and as they did so she became aware of something bobbing up and down in the water—the head of a swimmer, as she saw the next moment, swimming out towards her boat.

Some one must have seen her, then, and as all the fishing-vessels were out, and there was no way of reaching the anchored boat, except by swimming, had elected to run personal risk rather than waste precious time in seeking aid farther afield.

A glow of gratitude towards her courageous rescuer filled Catherine's heart, and this did not diminish as she saw the difficulty he had first in reaching the boat, then in casting it loose, and last, but not least, in guiding and pushing it towards an uncovered rock and getting in. But this difficult and perilous office was accomplished in safety at last, and the boat. Was quickly rowed over the heaving, angry waves to the spot where Catherine stood alone, amid the tossing waste of water. Nearer and nearer came the tiny craft, and Catherine experienced an odd sensation of mingled surprise and dismay as she recognised in her preserver none other than Edward MacAlister.

But it was not a time in which speeches could be made or thanks spoken. To bring the boat up to the rock in the midst of the rolling breakers was a task of no little difficulty and danger, and had not Edward been experienced from boyhood in matters pertaining to the sea, he could not possibly have accomplished the feat unaided and alone. There was no bungling on Catherine's part, either. With steady nerve and quiet courage she awaited the moment for the downward spring. It was made at exactly the right second; the boat swayed, but righted itself immediately. Edward had the head round in a moment away from the dangerous rock. In ten minutes they had reached the shore and had landed upon the beach.

Not a word had been spoken all that time. Catherine had given Edward one expressive glance as she took her seat in the boat, and that is all that had so far passed between them. When, however, he gave her his hand to help her to disembark, and they stood together on the shingle, she said, very seriously and gently——"It was very kind of you to come out to me, Mr. MacAlister. I think I should have been drowned but for you," and she turned her eyes seaward with a gaze that was utterly inscrutable.

He looked at her a moment intently, and then stooped and picked up his overcoat, which lay beside his pilot jacket and boots, upon the stones "Will you oblige me by putting this on in place of your wet jacket? You are drenched with spray." She woke up from her reverie then and looked up quickly, doing as he asked without a word; but when she had donned the warm protecting garment, she said——"You are drenched to the skin yourself." "yes, so a garment more or less is of no consequence. Now walk on, please; do not wait for me; I will be after you in two minutes." Again she did his bidding in the same dreamy way, and walked on towards the ascent by the steep cliff path. He was not long in following her, and they walked in almost unbroken silence to the castle. When they reached the door, Catherine paused and raised her eyes once more to his face. "You have saved my life today," she said. "I am I think I am-very grateful to you." Matthew's excitement and delight when he heard of the adventure were very great.

"So he saved you, Catherine-at the risk of his life? Ah, that just proves it!" "Why, that he is in love with you, of course, just as he ought to be, and will marry you some day, make us all happy, and keep us all at MacAlister. What could be more delightful and appropriate?"

A wave of colour swept over Catherine's face. "You are a foolish boy, Matthew." "I am not a foolish boy!" he answered, exultingly; "I know what I am saying. Edward does love you; I see it more plainly every day. He loves you with all his heart, and some day soon he will ask you to be his wife. Of course you will say yes——you must like him, I am sure, as much as every one else does; and then everything will come right, and we shall all be perfectly happy. Things always do come right in the end, if we only will but believe it."

Catherine sat very still, a strange, dream-like feeling stealing over her. Matthew's playful words shed a sudden flood of light upon much that had been dark before, and for a moment she was blinded and dazzled.

Edward MacAlister loved her! Yes she could well believe it, little as she knew of love, thinking of the glance bent upon her not long ago, which had thrilled her then, she knew not why.

Catherine trembled, yet she was dimly conscious of a strange undercurrent of startled joy beneath the troubled waters of doubt, despondency, and perplexity. She could not understand herself, nor read her heart aright, yet it seemed as if through the lifting of the clouds, she obtained a rapid passing glimpse of a land goldened sunshine beyond, whither her face and footsteps alike were turned-as a traveller amid the mountain mist sees before him now and again the bright sunny smiling valley beneath which he will shortly reach. The land of promise was spreading itself out already before Catherine's eyes, and a dim perception in her heart was telling her that this was so. Yet the sandy desert path still lay before her for awhile, for like many others, her eyes were partially blinded, and she turned from the direct way, and wandered still for awhile in the arid waste. She lacked the faith to grasp the promise; but it was shining before her all the while, and in her heart of hearts she felt it, though she could not yet grasp the truth.

Chapter 7

"Will you have this Woman?"

Lord MacAlister was not unobservant of the feelings with which Edward regarded Catherine. Quiet and self-contained as the young man was, his admiration and the pleasure he took in her society was still sufficiently obvious, and his own opinions were triumphantly endorsed by those of Lady Catherine.

"He is head over in love with her!" exclaimed that sharp-eyed dame to her brother, about a couple of days after Catherine's rescue by Edward, of which, however, she luckily knew nothing. Indeed, the story of that adventure had only been told by the girl to Matthew and her father, and both had had the tact and discrimmination not to broach the subject to Lady Louise.

"He is head over heels in love with her, but she gives him not the smallest encouragement, the proud sly! And he is modest, and keeps his feelings to himself. It seems to me that the time has come when you ought to speak out yourself, MacAlister; we cannot expect to keep a happy young man like Edward for ever in these solitudes. Speak to him yourself, and see if you cannot manage to bring about some proper understanding."

Lord MacAlister had, in fact, some such idea in his own mind. He and his young kinsman were by this time upon easy and intimate terms. They felt a mutual liking and respect, and had frequently very nearly approached the subject so near to the hearts of both. That very night as they sat together in Earls' study, after the rest of the household had retired, Lord MacAlister spoke to his guest with frankness and unreserve of the thoughts that had for long been stirring in his mind.

He spoke to his kinsman and heir of his anxieties as to the future of his dearly-loved and only child, who would at his death be only very inadequately provided for. He did not attempt to conceal the hope he had cherished in asking Edward to be his guest that some arrangement might be made which should conduce to her future happiness; and just as the young man's heart began to beat high with the confusion of conflicting feelings within him, the old Earl looked him steadily in the face, and concluded with a certain stately dignity that was exceedingly impressive.

"Edward MacAlister, I had heard much in your favour before I saw you, so much, indeed that I ventured to entertain hopes that may sound scheming and cold-blooded when put into words, yet which do not, I trust, proceed from motives altogether unworthy. My daughter is very dear to me. To see her happily settled in life, under the protecting care of one who will truly love and cherish her has been the deepest wish of my life. In our secluded existence here there has been small chance of realising this wish. I will not deny that in asking you to be our guest it was with hopes I need not farther specify. Some of these hopes have been amply realised. I will not seem to flatter, yet let me say that in you I have found every quality I most hoped to see in the man who is to be my successor here. You are a true MacAlister, and I am deeply thankful it is so; and besides this, I have lately entertained hopes that another wish of mine is slowly fulfilling itself. I have sometimes thought-let me say it plainly—that you have learned to love my daughter."

"Lord MacAlister," said Edward, with a calmness of manner that sighed deep feeling held resolutely under control, "I do love your daughter. I have done so ever since our first consent to try and win her hand, I shall count myself a happy man indeed, although I fear her heart is not one to be easily moved or won."

Lord MacAlister's face expressed a keen satisfaction and gladness. He held out his hand to his young kinsman, and said quiet—"You have made a happy man of me, Edward MacAlister. In you hands I can place the future of my child with perfect confidence. You love her, and you will care for her, and make her life happy." Edward squeezed the offered hand. "Indeed you may trust me to do all in my power. I love her with my whole heart. I would lay down my life to serve her."

"As you have demonstrated already," said the old earl, with a grave smile. "I have not thanked you for saving my child's life. I hope in the future she will repay the debt by making life happy, as you, I am convinced, will make hers. "Edward's bronzed cheek flushed a little at these words." Lord MacAlister," he said, "to gain your good-will and assent in this matter is a source of great satisfaction to me; but I cannot blind my eyes to the fear the Lady Catherine herself, with whom the decision must rest, has not so far given me any encouragement to hope that she regards me as anything beyond a mere acquaintance and chance guest. I love her too well, I think, not to be well aware of her feelings towards me, and I cannot flatter myself for a moment by the belief that these are anything warmer than a gentle liking, little removed from in difference." The earl's face was full of thought.

"Catherine's nature is peculiar," he said; "her feelings lie very deep, and are difficult to read; no one can really know what they may be." "I admit that; yet I confess I have little hope-at least in the present." "Whilst I," said Lord MacAlister, quietly, "have little fear." An eager look crossed Edward's face. "You think——"

"I cannot easily explain what I think, but I believe there will be less difficulty with Catherine than you anticipate. She does not yet know her own heart that I admit. She may be startled at first but that is not necessarily against us. Will you let me break this matter to her? Will you let me act as your ambassador? I understand Catherine as you can hardly do. Will you let me see if I cannot plead your cause as expressively as you can do it for yourself? Trust me, it will be better so. My daughter and I understand one another well."

Edward was silent a moment then he said very gravely and seriously- -"If you think that it will be best so, I gladly place myself in your hands. I confess I should find it difficult to approach the subject myself-at any rate at present. But"——he paused a moment, and looked the other full in the face——"pardon me for saying as much-you do not propose putting pressure upon your daughter? Believe me, I would rather never see her face again, than fell that she accepted me as a husband under any kind of compulsion or restraint," Lord MacAlister smiled a smile of approval. "You need not fear," he answered, quietly. Catherine's nature is not one to submit tamely to any kind of coercion, nor am I the man to attempt to constrain her feelings upon a matter so important as this."

"And if," pursued Edward, with quiet resolution, "Lady Catherine declines the proposal made to her on my behalf, I shall request you to join with me in breaking the entail; for I can never consent to be the means of taking from her that which by every moral right is hers. I could not for a moment tolerate the idea of forcing from her the right to style herself, as she has always been styled, the Lady of MacAlister. This is her rightful home, and I shall appeal to you, if my suit fails, to assist me in installing her there for life."

She had given herself to him to love and cherish; surely this great love could accomplish the rest. He drew her gently towards him. She did not resist; she let herself be encircled by his protecting arms.

"I will try to make you very happy," he said, with quiet manly simplicity that meant more than the most ardent protestations could have done. "May I kiss you, Catherine?"

She lifted her down-bent face a little, and he pressed a kiss upon her brow. She made no attempt to return the caress, but he did not expect it. It was enough that she permitted him to worship her. "You have made me very happy Catherine," he said presently, whilst the shadows deepened round them. Will you let me hear you say that you are happy too?" She looked at him at last. He could not read the meaning of the gaze. "I want to make happy, my darling," said Edward, very softly.

Again that strange, earnest gaze. "Make my father and Matthew happy," she said sweetly and steadily, "and I shall be happy too." He did not understand the full drift of those words as he might perhaps have done had he been calmer did not realise as at another moment he might have done their deep significance. He was desperately, passionately in love, carried away inwardly, if not outwardly, by the confusion of his feelings. He did not realise——it was hardly likely that he should-that to secure her father's happiness and the future well-being and happiness of her brother, Catherine had promised to be his wife. She respected him, she liked him, she was resolved to make him a true and faithful wife; she knew so little of the true nature of wedded love that it never occurred to her think of the injury she might be doing to him in giving the without the heart.

She had been moved and disquieted by Matthew's words of a few days back. Her father's appeal to her that day had touched her to the quick. What better could she do with her life than secure with it the happiness of those she loved? How better could she keep her vows towards Matthew than by making the promise asked of her? Catherine thought first of others in this matter, it is true, and yet there was a strange throb akin to joy deep down in her heart, when she thought of the love tendered to her by one she had learned to consider and to trust. Those sweet, sudden glimpses of the golden land of sunshine beyond kept flashing before her eyes, and thrilled her with feelings that made her almost afraid. She did not know what it all meant. She did not know that it was but the foreshadowing of the deep love that was rooting itself, all unknown, in the tenderest fibres of her nature. She never thought she loved Edward MacAlister, but she was conscious of a strange exultation and stress of feeling, which she attributed to the enthusiasm of the sacrifice she had made for those she loved. She did not yet know the secret of her own heart.

Chapter 8

Courted, Married

So, Catherine and her kinsman Edward MacAlister, were engaged, and the neighbourhood, though decidedly astonished at this sudden surrender of liberty on the part of the fair, unapproachable girl, could not but see how desirable was the match from every point of view, and rejoice in the thought that MacAlister would never lose its well-loved Lady.

As for Catherine herself, the days passed by as in a dream—a shifting dream of misty sunshine and sweet, faint fragrance, through which she wandered with uncertain steps, led onward by a sense of brighter light beyond.

She was not unhappy; indeed, a strange new sense of calm and rest had fallen upon her since she had laid her hand in Edward's and promised to love him if she could. A few short weeks ago how she would have rubbed against the restraint's she wore! Now she hardly felt them as restraint's they were neither painful or hurting her. Indeed, after the feeling of uncertainty, of impending change that had hung over her of late, this peaceful calm doubly grateful. It seemed at last as if she had reached the shelter of a safe haven, and pausing there, with a sense of grateful well-being, she felt as if no storm or tempest could ever touch her again.

Catherine's nature was not introspective; she did not easily analyse her feelings. Had she done so now, she might have laid bare a secret deep down within her that would have surprised her not a little; but she never attempted to look into her heart, she rather avoided definite thought; she lived in a vaguely sweet dream, glad and thankful for the undercurrent of happiness which had so unexpectedly crept into her life. She did not seek to know its source it was enough that it was there.

Edward was very good to her, she did not attempt to deny that. Nothing could have been more tender and gallant or courteous than his manner towards her. He claimed none of the rights which an affianced husband might fairly have claimed; he was content with what she gave him; never tried to force her confidence or to win words or promises that did not come spontaneously to her lips.

She was shy with him for some time after the engagement had been confirmed more silent and reserved than she had been before; yet there was a charm in her very silence that went home to his heart, and he felt that she grew nearer to him day by day. "I will win her yet-heart and soul," he would say sometimes, with a thrill of proud joy as he looked into the sweet eyes raised to his, and read a something in their depths that made his throb gladly. "Give me time, only time, and she shall be altogether mine she never shunned him."

She never shunned him. She let him be her companion when and where he would, and she began to look for him, and to feel more satisfied when he was at her side. He was too wise to overdo her with his society, or seem to infringe the liberty in which she had grown up; but he frequently accompanied her on her walks or rides, and he had the satisfaction of feeling that his presence was not distasteful to her; indeed, as days went by, and she grew used to the idea that had been at first so strange, he fancied that there was something of welcome in the smile the greeted his approach. She never spoke of the future when they should be man and wife, and only by a hint here and there did he bring up for discussion the subject or tell of his private affairs. Both were content for the time being to live in the present-that present that seemed so calm and bright and full of promise.

As days and weeks fled by, a colour drawned upon Catherine's cheeks and a light in her eyes; she grew more beautiful every day, or so thought those who loved her, and watched her with loving scrutiny; and Mrs. Pendrill, who was, so to speak, the girl's angel in this crisis of her life, would caress the golden head sometimes, and ask with gentle, motherly solicitude——"my Catherine is happy, is she not?" "I think so, Aunt Jennifer,"

Catherine answered once, speaking out more freely than she had done before. "Other people are happy——the dread and uncertainty about the future seems all gone. MacAlister is not sad any longer——it is my own home again, my very own. I cannot quite express it, but something seems to have come into my life and changed everything. I am happy often now-nearly always, I think." Mrs. Pendrill smiled a little.

"Does your happiness result from the knowledge that you-you and Matthew——I suppose I must include him-need never leave MacAlister, and that you have pleased your father? Tell me, Catherine is that all?"

A faint colour mantled the girl's face. "I know it sounds selfish; but I hardly think any one knows what MacAlister is to us, and what Matthew's welfare is to me."

Then reading the meaning of the earnest glance bent upon her, she added quickly, Ah, yes, Aunt Jennifer, I know there is that too. He is very, very good to me, and I will do everything to make him happy, and to be a good wife when the time comes. Indeed, I do think of him. I know what he is, and what he deserves-only-only I cannot talk about that even to you." "I do not want you to talk, my love, I only want you to feel." And very low the answer was spoken. "I think I do feel."

Certainly things were going well, very well. It seemed as if the course of Edward's true love might run smoothly enough to the very end now. Bruce Pendrill teased him somewhat mercilessly on the easy victory he had obtained over the somewhat difficult subject, and he felt an exultant sense of joyful triumph when he compared his position of today with the one he had occupied a week or two back. Catherine's gentleness and growing dependence upon him were inexpressibly sweet, the dawn of a quiet happiness in her face filled his heart with delight. The victory was not quite won yet, but he began to feel a confidence that it was not far distant. And this hope would in all probability have been realised in due course, had it not been for untoward circumstances, and from the presence of enemies in the camp, one his sworn foe, the other his champion and ally: but despite this, a born mischief-maker and meddlesome.

So long Edward was on the spot all went well. His strong will dominated all others, and his influence upon Catherine produced its own effect. Love like his could not but win its way to the heart of the woman he loved. But Edward could not remain always at MacAlister. Hard as it was to tear himself away, the conventionalities of life demanded his absence from time to time, and other duties called him elsewhere. And it was when it was when his back was fairly turned that the mischief makers began their task of undoing, as far as was possible, all the good that had been accomplished.

Edward had been exceedingly careful to say nothing to Catherine about hastening their marriage. He saw that she took for granted a long engagement, that she had hardly contemplated as yet the inevitable end whither that, engagement tended; and until he had assured himself that her heart was wholly his, nothing would have induced him to ask her to give herself irrevocably to him. When the right moment came she would surrender herself willingly, for Catherine was not one who would do anything by halves. Till that day came, however, he was resolved to wait, and breathe no word of the future before them.

Lady Louise was of a different way of thinking. She had been amazed at Catherine's flexibility in the matter of her engagement, so surprised and so well pleased that, for some considerable time, she had acted with unusual discretion, and had avoided saying anything to irritate or alarm the sensitive feelings of her niece. Possibly she stood in a little unconscious awe of Edward, for certainly so long as he remained she was quiet and discreet enough. But when his presence was once removed, then began a system of petty persecution and annoyance that was the very thing to rouse in Catherine a spirit of opposition and hostility. Lady Louise had set heart upon a speedy marriage, afraid that her niece might change her mind; she took a half-spiteful pleasure in the knowledge that the girl's independence was at last to be curbed, and that she was about to take upon herself the common lot of womanhood. She lost no opportunities of reading homilies of wifely submission and subjection. She bestirred herself over the matter of the trousseau as if the day were actually fixed, and Catherine's indignant protests were laughed at and ignored, as if too childish for serious argument.

The girl began to observe, too, that her father spoke of her marriage as if something speedily approaching, and that he, Lady Louise, and even Matthew, seemed to understand that she would spend much of her time away from MacAlister, when once that ceremony had taken place. Her father and brother spoke cheerfully of her leaving them, taking it for granted that her affianced husband was first in her thoughts, and that they must make her way easy to go away with him, without one regret for those left behind. Lady Louise, with more of feminine insight, had less of kindliness in her method of approaching the subject; but when she found them all agreed upon the point, the girl felt almost as if she had been betrayed. There was no Edward to shield and protect her. She could not put into written words the tumult of her conflicting feelings; she could only struggle and suffer, and feel like a wild thing trapped in the hunter's toils. Ah if only Edward had not left her! But when the poison had done its work, she ceased even to wish for him back. Another enemy to her peace of mind was Sir David MacRae. Catherine was growing to feel a great dislike to this fair-haired, smooth-tongued man, despite the nominal friendship that existed between him and those of her name. She knew that her feelings were changing towards him; but like other young things, she was ashamed of any such change, regarding it as treacherous and ungenerous, especially after the pledge she had given him.

David MacRae thus found opportunities of seeing her from time to time, and set to work with malicious pleasure to poison her mind against her affianced husband. She would not listen to a single direct word against him: that he discovered almost at once, somewhat to his astonishment and chagrin; but "there are more ways of killing a cat than by hanging it," as he said to himself; and a well-directed shaft steeped in poison, and launched with a practised hand, struck home and did its work only too well.

He insinuated that after her marriage MacAlister would never be her home during her father's lifetime, at least, possibly never any more. Edward had property of his own; was it likely he would bury himself and his beautiful young wife in a desolate place like that? Of course her care of Matthew would be a thing entirely put on one side. It was out of the question that she should ever be allowed to devote her to him as of old, when once she had placed her neck beneath the matrimonial yoke. Most likely some excuse would be forthcoming to rid MacAlister of the undesirable presence of the invalid Edward was not a man to be deterred by any nice scruples from going his own way. Words spoken before marriage were never regarded seriously when once the inevitable step had been taken.

Catherine heard, and partly believed-believed enough to make her restless and miserable. Never a word crossed her lips that could show her trust in Edward shaken. She was loyal to him outwardly, but she suffered keenly nevertheless. He was not there to give her confidence, as he could well have done, by his unwavering love and devotion, and in his absence, the influence he had won slowly waned, and the old fear and distrust crept back. It might have vanished had he returned to charm it away; but alas! he only came to make Catherine his wife in sudden, unexpected fashion, before her heart was really won.

Lord MacAlister had been taken dangerously ill. It was an attack similar to those he had suffered from once or twice before, but in a more severe form. His life was in imminent danger; nothing could save him, the doctors agreed, but the most perfect rest of body and mind; and it seemed as if only the satisfaction of calling Edward son, of seeing him Catherine's husband, could secure to him that repose of spirit so absolutely essential to his recovery.

Catherine did not waver when her father looked pleadingly into her face, and asked if she were ready. Her assent was calmly and firmly spoken, and after that she left all in other hands, and did not leave her father's presence night or day.

He was better for the knowledge that the wish of his heart was about to be consummated, and she was so utterly absorbed in him as be all but unconscious of the flight of time. She knew that days sped by as on wings. She absorbed in care for her almost dying father; on the evening of that day Edward stood before her, holding her hands in his warm clasp. "Is this your wish, my Catherine?" She thrilled a little beneath his ardent gaze, a momentary sense of comfort and protection came over her in his presence; but physical languor blunted her feelings; she was too weary even to feel acutely.

"It is my wish," she answered gently. He bent his head and kissed her tenderly and lingeringly, looking earnestly into the pale, sweet face that seemed less responsive than it had done when he saw it last; but he could not read the look it wore. He kissed her and went away, breathing half sadly, half triumphantly, the word "tomorrow." Lady Louise, ever indefatigable and contriving, had managed as if by magic to have all things in readiness; rich white satin and brocade, orange blossom and lace veil-all was in readiness-as if she had weeks for her preparations.

Catherine started and half recoiled as she saw the bridal dress laid out for her adornment, but she was quiet and passive in the hands of her attendants as they arrayed her in her snowy robes, and well she repaid their efforts. Only Lady Louise felt any dissatisfaction.

"Why, child," she said, impatiently, "you look like a snow maiden. You might be a nun about to take the veil instead of a bride going to her wedding. I have no patience with such pale looks. Edward will think we have brought him a corpse for his bride."

Edward was waiting in the little church on the cliff. His heart beat thick and fast; he himself began to feel as if he were living in a dream. He could not realise that the time had come when he was to call Catherine his own. Lady Louise and Mrs. Pendrill were there, and a friend of his own, young Lord MacMurray, who had accompanied him from town the previous day, to play the part of best man at the ceremony. There was a litter rustle and little stir outside, and the Catherine entered, leaning on Bruce Pendrill's arm, and without once lifting her eyes, walked steadily up the church, till she stood beside Edward.

Never, perhaps, had she looked more lovely, yet never, perhaps, more remote and unapproachable, than when she stood before the altar in her bridal robes, to pledge herself for better for worse to the man who loved her, till death should them part. He looked at her with a strange pang and aching at heart; but the moment was not one when hesitation or drawing back was possible. In a few more minutes Catherine and Edward MacAlister were made man and wife.

Chapter 9

Married

The monotonous vibrating throb of the express train seemed ceaselessly repeating that one word. The sound of it was beaten in upon Catherine's brain as with hot hammers, and yet she did not feel as if she understood what it meant, or realised what had happened to her. One thing only was clear to her that she had been torn away from MacAlister, from her father, who though pronounced convalescent, was still in a very precarious state; from Matthew, who, after the anxiety and excitement of the past days, was prostrated by a sharp attack of illness; from everything and everybody she held most dear; and cast it were upon the mercy of a comparative stranger, who did not seem the less strange to her because he had the right to call himself her husband.

What had happened during the three days that had passed since Catherine stood beside Edward in the little cliff church, and pledged herself to him for better or worse? She herself could not have said, but the facts can be summed up in a few words.

When once Lord MacAlister had seen Catherine led by Edward to his bedside in her bridal white, and knew that they were man and wife, a change for the better took place in his condition, very slight at first, but increasing every hour. Little by little the danger passed away, and for the time at least his life was safe.

But Catherine's mind, no sooner relieved on his account, was thrown into fresh misery and suspense by a bad attack of illness on Matthew's part, and the strain upon her was so great, that coming as it did after all the mental conflict she had lately endured, her own health threatened to break down, and this caused no small anxiety in the minds of all about her.

"There is only one thing to be done, and that is to take her right away out of it all," said Bruce Pendrill, with authority. "She will break down as sure as fate if she stays here. The associations of the place are quite too much for her. She will have a brain or nervous fever if she not taken away. You have a house in London, MacAlister? Take her there and keep her quiet but let her have change of scene; let her see fresh faces, and form new habits, and see the world from a fresh stand-point. It will do her all the good in the world. She may rebel at first, and think herself miserable; but look at her now. What can be worse than the way in which she is going on? MacAlister is killing her, whether she knows it or not. Let us see what London can do for her. "No dissentient voice was raised against this suggestion. The Earl, Lady Louise, Edward, and even Matthew, were all in accord, and Catherine heard her sentence with that unnatural quietude that had disturbed them all so much.

She did not protest or rebel, but accepted her fate very quietly, as she had accepted the marriage that had been the preliminary step. How white she looked as she lay back in her corner of the carriage! How lonely, how frail, how desolate! Edward's heart ached for her, for knew her thoughts were with her sick father and suffering brother; knew that it, not unnaturally, seemed very, very hard to be taken away at a crisis such as the present. She could not estimate the causes that made a change so imperative for her. She could not see why she was hurried away so relentlessly. It had all been very hard upon her, and upon him also, had he had thought to spare for himself; he was too much absorbed in sorrow for her to consider his own position over-much.

He was indirectly the cause of her grief, and his whole being was absorbed in the longing to comfort her. She looked so white and sickly as the hours passed by that he grew alarmed about her. He had done before all he could to make her warm and comfortable, and had then withdrawn a little, fancying his close proximity distasteful to her, but she looked so ill at last he could keep away no longer, and came over to her, taking her hand in his. "Catherine," he said gently.

The long lashes stirred a little and slowly lifted themselves. The dark eyes were dim and full of trouble. She looked at him wonderingly for a moment, almost as if she did not know him, and then she closed her eyes with a little shuddering sigh. He was alarmed, and not without cause, for the strain of the past days was showing itself now, and want of rest sleep had worn down her strength to the lowest decline. She was so faint and weary that all power of resistance had left her. She let her husband do what he would, submitted passively to be tended like a child, and heaved a sigh that sounded almost like one of relief as he drew her towards him, so that her weary head could rest upon his broad shoulder. There was something restful and supporting, of which she was dumbly conscious, in the deep love and protecting gentleness of this strong man.

She only spoke once to him, and that was as they neared their destination, and the lights of the great city began to flash upon her bewildered gaze. Then she sat up, though with an effort, and looking at her husband, said gently "You have been very good to me Edward." His heart bounded at the words, but he only asked, "Are you better, Catherine?" She pressed her hand to her brow. "My head aches so," she said and the white strained look came back to her face. She was almost frightened by the flashing lights and the myriads of people she saw as the train steamed into the terminus; and she could only cling to Edward's arm in hopeless bewilderment, as he escorted her to the waiting carriage.

Edward owned a house near to the park, in a pleasant open situation. It had been left to him by an uncle, a great traveller, and was quite a museum of costly and interesting treasures, fitted up in the luxurious fashion that appeals to men who have grown used to oriental ease and splendour.

The young man had often pictured Catherine in such surroundings, had wondered what she would say to it, how she would feel in a place so strange and unlike anything she had ever known. He had fancied that the open situation of the house would please her, that she might be pleased too by the quaint beauty and harmony of all she saw. He had often pictured the moment when he should lead her into her new home and bid her welcome there; yet now when the time had come, she was so worn-out and ill that her heavy eyes could hardly look around her, and all he could do was to support her to her room, to be tended by his old nurse, Lorna, whose services he had bespoken for his wife in preference to those of a youthful and accomplished chambermaid. For some days Catherine was really ill, not with any specific complaint, but prostrated by nervous exhaustion- too weary and worn to have a clear idea of what went on around her, only conscious that everything was very strange, that she was far away from MacAlister, and that strangers were watching over and tending her.

Her husband's care was unremitting. He was always by her side. She seemed to turn to him instinctively amid the other strange face, and to be more quiet and tranquil when he was near. Yet she seldom spoke to him; he was not always certain that she knew him; but that half-unconscious dependence was inexpressibly sweet, and Edward felt hope growing stronger day by day. Surely she was slowly learning to love him; and indeed she was, only she knew it not as yet.

Then a day came when the feverish fancies and distressful exhaustion gave way to more cheering symptoms. Catherine could leave her room, and leaning on her husband's arm, wander slow about the new home that looked so strange to her. The smiles began to come back to her eyes, a faint flush of colour to her cheeks, and when at length she was set down upon a luxurious sofa beside the drawing-room fire, she held her husband's hand between both of hers, and looked up at him with a glance that went to his very heart.

"You have been so very, very good to me Edward, though I have only been a trouble to you all this time. I never thought I could feel like this away from MacAlister. Indeed I will try to make you happy too." He bent down and kissed her, a thrill of intense joy running through him. "Doe's that mean that you can be happy here, my Catherine?" he asked.

She was always perfectly truthful, and paused a little before answering; yet there was a light in her eyes and a little smile upon her lips. "It feels very strange," she said, "and very like a dream. Of course I miss MacAlister of course I would rather be there; but——" and here she lifted her eyes with the sweetest glance of trusting confidence, "I believe that you know best, Edward, I know that you judge more wisely than I can do; and that you always think of my happiness first. You have been very, very good to me all this time, far better than I deserve. I am going to be happy here, and when I may go home, I know you will be the first to take me there."

He laid his hand upon her head in a tender caress. "I will, indeed, my Catherine," he answered; "but, believe me, for the present you are better here. You will grow strong faster away from MacAlister than near it." she smiled a little, very sweetly. "I will try to think so too Edward, for I am very sure that you are wiser than I; and I have learned how good you are to me-always. "That evening passed very quietly, yet very happily. Was this the beginning of better things to come?

Chapter 10

Trouble Makers

"Now that you been a fortnight in town, and have begun to feel settled in your new life," wrote Lady Louise, "I think it is time you should be made aware of a few facts relative to your engagement and marriage, which you are not likely to hear from the lips of your too indulgent husband, but with which, nevertheless, you ought to be made conversant, in my opinion, in order that you may better appreciate the generous sacrifices made on behalf of you and your family, and return him the measure of gratitude he deserves for the benefits he has bestowed."

Catherine was alone when she received this letter, breakfasting in her little boudoir at a late hour, for although almost recovered now, she had not yet resumed her old habit of early rising. She had risen this morning feeling more light at heart than usual. She had chatted with unusual freedom to her husband, had kissed him before he went out to keep an appointment with his lawyer, and had promised to ride with him at one o' clock, if he would come back for her. She had only once been out since her arrival in town, and that was in the carriage. She was quite excited at the prospect of being in the saddle again. She almost told herself that she should yet be happy in her married life——and now came this cruel, cruel letter to dash to the ground all her faint dawning hopes.

Lady Louise had felt very well-disposed, even if a little spiteful, as she penned this unlucky letter; but she certainly was not nice in her choice of words or of expression. Not being sensitive herself, she had little comprehension of the emotion and sensitivity of others, and the impression its perusal conveyed to the mind of Catherine was that Edward had married her simply out of generosity to herself and regard for her father; that the proposal was none of his own making, and that his unvarying kindness arose from his knowledge of her very difficult temper, and a wish to secure for himself by bribes and caresses a peaceful home and an amiable wife. In conclusion it was added that Catherine, in return for all that had been done for her, must do her utmost to please an gratify him. Of course he would wish to show his beautiful wife in the world of fashion to which he belonged. He would wish her to join in the life social festivities to which he was about to introduce her, and any hanging back on her part would be most unbecoming and ungrateful. It possessed her to keep in mind all these facts, to remember the sacrifices he had made for her, and to act accordingly. He had not chosen a wife from his own world, as it was presumable he would have preferred to do. He had consented to the family match proposed to him, and she must do her utmost to make up to him the sacrifice he had made.

A few weeks back such a letter, though it might have hurt Catherine's pride, would not have cut her to the quick, as it did now. The first place, she would then have simply disbelieved it, where as recent circumstances had given her a very much greater respect for the opinions of those who knew the world so much better than she did, and who had forecasted so accurately events that had afterwards fulfilled themselves almost as a matter course. She had begun to distrust her own convictions, to believe more in those of others, who had had experience of life, and could estimate its chances better than she could. She believed her aunt when she told her these things, and the poisoned shaft struck home to her heart. A few days ago she could have borne it better.

Her pride would have been hurt, but the sting would have been less keen. She did not know why the doubt of husband's love hurt her so cruelly; but hurt her it did, and for a moment she felt stricken to the earth. She had said to herself many times that she did not want such a wealth of love, when she had none on her side to bestow; but yet, when she learned that it was not hers after all, but was only the counterfeit coin of a hollow world——the bribe by which her submission and gratitude were to be obtained——the knowledge was unspeakably bitter. She felt she would rather have died than have been forced to doubt.

As she dressed for her ride, pride came to the assistance of her crushed spirit. Lorna the faithful servant who had tended and loved Edward from his infancy, and was ready to love his wife for his sake and her own, was aware of a subtle change in her young mistress that she did not understand, and which she could not well have described. Catherine had been very quiet and gentle since her arrival, and very silent too. She was quiet enough today; but the gentleness had been replaced by a certain, inexplicable behaviour. The pale face wore a glow of warm colour; the dark eyes that had been languid and heavy were wide open and full of fire. Catherine looked superbly handsome in the brilliant radiance of her beauty, and yet the faithful attendant was not certain that she liked the change on her.

Edward detected it the moment he entered the room, and found his wife equipped for the proposed ride. "Why Catherine," he said, smiling, "You have got quite a colour. It looks natural to see you dressed for the saddle."

"Yes," she answered, coolly: "we must turn over a new leaf now, must we not? You will be dying of boredom cooped up at home so long. Let us go out and enjoy ourselves. We must learn to do in Rome as Rome does."

Edward felt one keen pang of disappointment that the first return to health and strength should have brought a return instead of the former coldness and aloofness; but he had gained ground before, and why not now? Could he expect to win his way without a single repulse? So he took courage, and tried to ignore the change he saw in his wife.

He led her down the staircase to the hall door where the horses were waiting, and he saw the sudden flash of joyful recognition that crossed her face. "James!" she exclaimed, "my own little James!" yes, there could be no mistake about it; it was her own little delicate thorough-bred, standing with impatience, his supple limbs trembling with eagerness, as he stepped daintily to and fro upon the pavement. He turned his shapely head at the sound of Catherine's voice, pricked his ears, and uttered a low whinny of joyful recognition. "It was good of you to think of it, Edward," she said, a softer light in her eyes as she turned them towards her husband. "It is like a little bit of home having him."

"I thought you would like him better than a stranger, though I have his counterpart in the stable waiting for you to try. He has been regularly exercised in Piccadilly every morning, and I coaxed him to let me ride him once myself in the park, though he did not much like it. I don't think he will be very troublesome now, and I know you are not afraid of his restive moods; though this is very different from MacAlister." Catherine's eyes grew wistful, and her husband saw it. He guessed whither her thoughts had fled and he let her dream on undisturbed. He exchanged bows with many acquaintances as they passed onwards and entered the row. And many admiring glances were levelled at his beautiful young wife, whose unusual loveliness and perfect horsemanship alike attracted attention; but he attempted no introductions; and Catherine, dreamy and absorbed, noticed, till the sight of David in the row awoke her to consciousness of her surrounding.

David in London! How long had he been there? Did he bring news from MacAlister? She looked almost wistfully at Edward as she returned the young baronet's bow, but his face wore its rather stern expression, and she dared not attempt to speak with her former friend. David however, saw the look, and smiled to himself. "My day will come yet," he said. "Shall we push on, Catherine?" asked Edward. "James is aching to stretch his limbs."

Catherine was only too willing, and they had soon reached the farther end of the row, which was much less full than the other had been. A pretty, dark, vivacious-looking girl, accompanied by a fair-haired young man, rather like her, were approaching with glances of recognition. "Edward, I am angry with you-yes, very angry. You have been a whole fortnight in town——I heard so yesterday-and we have never seen you once, and you have never let me have the pleasure of an introduction to your wife. I call it very much too bad!" "Well, it is never too late to mend," answered Edward, smiling. "Catherine, may I present to you Lady Rebecca Scott, whom I have had the honour of knowing intimately since the days of our early acquaintance, when she wore pinafores and pigtails. Lord Charles MacMurray I think I need not introduce again. You have met before."

The little flush deepened in Catherine's face. She had fancied the face of the brother was not totally unfamiliar to her; but she did not remember until this moment where or when she could possibly have seen him.

"Oh, Charles has been raving about Lady Catherine ever since the auspicious day when he saw her," cried Rebecca happily. I hope your father is quite recovered now?" she added, with a touch of quick sympathy, "since you were able to leave him so soon." "I think he is much better, thank you," answered Catherine, quietly; "but he was still very ill when I left him." "And, Edward, you have not explained away your guilt yet. Why have you been all this time without letting us see you or your wife? I call it shameful!"

"My wife has been very unwell herself ever since we came up," answered Edward. "She has not been fit to see anybody." "You should have made an exception in my favour," persisted Rebecca, bringing her horse alongside that of Catherine, and walking on with her. "You see, I have known Edward so long, he seems almost like a brother. I feel defrauded when he does not behave himself as such. We must be great friends, Lady Catherine, for his sake. He has told us all about you and your delightful Cornish home. I suppose you know all about us too, and what near neighbours we are—near for London, at least."

But Catherine had never heard the name of the girl beside her. She knew nothing of her husband's friends, never having taken the least interest in subjects foreign to all her past associations. She hinted something of the kind in kind in a gently indifferent way, that sincere, without being in the least discourteous.

She was wondering why it was that her husband, who could value his own friends and appreciate their good-will, was so strenuously set against receiving the only acquaintance she possessed in this vast city.

Nevertheless, when, upon midday two days later, at an hour he knew her husband was away, David presented himself in her boudoir, following the man who had brought his card without waiting to be invited, Catherine was conscious of a feeling of distinct displeasure and distrust. She knew very little of the ways of the world, but she felt that he had no right to be there, forcing himself upon her in her private room, when her husband would hardly speak to him or receive him, and that he merited instant dismissal.

But then came a revulsion of feeling. Was he not her childhood's friend? Had she not promised not to turn her back upon him, and help to drive him to despair by her coldness? Had he not come with news of MacAlister and of home? Then in that last eager thought all else was lost, and she met him gladly, almost eagerly.

He told her all she longed to know. He came primed with the latest news from MacAlister. His manner was quiet and gentle. He was very cautious not to alarm or disturb her. "I shall not be able to see much of you in the future, Catherine," he said, "but you will let me call myself still your friend?" She bent her head in a half assent. "And will you let me take a friend's privilege, and ask one question. Are you happy in your new life?" Catherine's face took a strange expression. "It is very bright, very lively. I shall like it better as I get more used to it."

"I see," he answered, very gently, "I understand. And when are you going home again?" "I am at home now," she answered, steadily. I thought MacAlister was to be always home. Has he thrown off the mask so soon?" "I think," said Catherine, with a little gleam in her eye, "that you forget you are speaking of my husband. "David's eyes gleamed too; but she did not see it. Forgive me, Catherine; I did forget. It is all so strange and sudden. Then he makes you happy? Tell me that! Let me have the assurance that at least he makes his captive happy." She started a little; but David's face expressed nothing but the quietest, sincerest good-will and sympathy.

"He is very, very good to me," she said, quietly. "He studies me as I have never been studied before. All my wishes are forestalled: he thinks of everything he does everything. I cannot tell you how good he is. I have never known anything like it before. Did you ever see any one more surrounded by beauty and luxury than I am?" He looked at her steadily. She knew that she had evaded his question––a question he had no right to put, as she could not but feel-and that he knew she had done so.

"Ah!" he murmured, "the gilded cage, the gilded cage; but only a cage, after all. Catherine, forgive me for expressing a doubt; but I know the man so well, and my whole soul revolts at seeing you dragged as it were at his chariot-wheels for all the world to look at and admire. To take you from your wild free home, and bribe you into submission––I hate to think of it!" Catherine's cheek had flushed suddenly; but before she could frame a rejoinder the door opened to admit Edward. He carried in his hand some hot-house flowers, which he had brought for his wife. He stopped short when he saw who was Catherine's guest, and her cheek flamed anew, for she knew he would not understand how she came to receive him in her private room, and she felt that by a want of firmness and presence of mind she had allowed herself to be placed in a false position.

David's exit was effected with more dispatch than dignity, yet he contrived in his farewell words to insinuate that he had passed a very happy morning with his hostess, instead of a brief ten minutes. Edward did not speak a word, but stood leaning against the chimney-piece with a stern look an his handsome face. Catherine was angry with herself and with David, yet she felt half indignant at the way her husband ignored her guest.

"Catherine," said Edward, speaking first, "I am sorry to have to say it; but I cannot receive Sir David MacRae as a guest beneath my roof." You had better give your orders, then, accordingly. "He stepped forward and took her hand. "Surely, Catherine, you cannot have any real liking for this man?" "I do not know what you call real liking. We have been friends from childhood; and I do not easily change. He was always welcomed to my father's house." "Your father did not know his history." "Perhaps not; but I do. At least I know this much: that he has sinned and has repented. Is not repentance enough?" "Has he repented?" "Yes, indeed he has." Edward's face expressed a fine incredulity and scorn. There was no relenting in its lines. Catherine was not going to sue longer.

"Am I also to be debarred from seeing mary his sister, who is married, and not living so very far away? Am I to give her up too my old playmate?"––"I have nothing against Mrs. MacFie, except that she is his sister. I suppose you need not be very intimate?"

Catherine's overwrought feelings vented themselves in a burst of indignation. "I see what you want to do-to separate me from all my friends-to break all old ties-to make me forget all but your world, your life. I am to like your friends, to receive them, and be intimate with them; but I am to turn my back with scorn on all whom I have known and loved. You are very hard, Edward, very hard. It is not that I care for David––I know he has done wrong, though I do believe in his repentance. I liked him once, and Mary too; I should like to know them still. They are not much to me, but they belong to the old life-which you do not, which nothing does here. Can you see how hard it is, and how unjust, to try and cut me off from everything?" He looked at her with a great pity in his eyes, and then gently put the flowers into her hand. "I brought them for you to wear tonight, Catherine. Will you have them? Believe me, my child, I would do much to spare you pain, yet in some things I must be the judge. Some day, perhaps, I shall be able to make my meaning plain; meantime I must ask my wife to trust me." He stooped and kissed her pale brow, and went away without another word.

"Edward, Edward!" she murmured, "if you only loved me I could bear anything; but they all see it-only I am blind––it is the golden cage with its captive, and they know the ways of their world so well, so well! He bribes me with gifts, with kind words, but it is only the peaceful home and the handsome wife that he wants-not me myself, not my heart, my love. Well, he shall have what he craves. I will not disappoint him. I will do his bidding in all things. He has got his prize-let that content him-but for the wifely love, the wifely trust I have struggled so to offer––he does not care for them let them go, like these." She pressed the flowers for a moment to her lips, and then flung them from the open casement. Edward, lost in silent thought standing at a window below, saw the white blossoms as they fell to the earth, and knew what they were and whence they had come.

Chapter 11

The Rift

A little misunderstanding easily arises between two people not yet in perfect accord-so very soon arises, and is so difficult to lay to rest. Edward saw plainly now, that Catherine's late gentleness had been caused simply by exhaustion and ill-health. She had submitted to his caressing care merely because she been too weak to resist, but the first indication of restored health had been the effort to repel him. He was grieved and saddened by this conviction, but he accepted his fate with quiet patience. He would draw back a little, stand aside, as it were, and let her feel her way in the new life; and gain her confidence, if he could, by slow and imperceptible degrees. He did not despair of winning her yet. He had more than one of those rapturous moments when he had felt that she was almost his. He would not give up, but he would be more self-restrained and reserved. He would not attempt too much at once. Catherine was keenly conscious of the change in her husband's manner, though she could not understand why it was that it cut her so deeply. She was conscious of the great blank in her life, and though her face was always calm and quiet, her manner gently cold and tinged with sadness, yet she tried in all things to study her husband's wishes, and to follow out any hints he might let fall as to his tastes and feelings.

She made no effort to see anything of Mary MacFie, her former child-friend, and even when that vivacious little woman sought her out, and tried to strike up a great friendship, she did not respond with any ardour. Mrs. MacFie, indeed, was not all a woman that Catherine would be inclined to cultivate at this crisis of her life; they had almost nothing in common, but the past was a sort of link that could not entirely be broken. Mary appeared to love to talk of MacAlister; she was always eager to hear the latest news from thence, to recall the by-gone days of childhood, and bring back the light and colour to Catherine's face by reminiscences of the past.

But the young wife tried to be loyal to her husband's wishes, and was laughed at by her friend for her for her "old-fashioned" ways. Once when, in course of conversation, David's name was mentioned between them, Catherine asked, in her straightforward way, what it was that he had done to draw upon him censure and distrust. "Why, do you not even know that much? Poor boy! I will tell you all about it. He was very young, and you know we are miserably poor. He got into bad company, and that led him into frightful embarrassments. He got so miserable and desperate at last that I believe his mind was almost unhinged for a time; and in the end," lowering her voice to a whisper, "He forged a cheque in the name of a rich friend. Of course it was a mad thing to do. He paid his debts, but the fraud was discovered within a few weeks, and you know what might have happened. Colonel Ferguson, however, who had been a kind friend to David before, forgave him, and took no steps against him; and the poor boy was so shocked and humiliated that he quite turned over a new leaf, and has been perfectly steady ever since. He was working hard to pay off the debt, but Colonel Ferguson died before he could do so. Edward MacAlister, your husband, my dear, was intimate with the Colonel, and knew all about this. He had always disliked David I suspect they were rivals once in the affections of some Lady, and that he did not get the best of the rivalry-and I always believe it was through him that the story leaked out. At any rate, people did hear something, and poor David got dreadfully cold shouldered. He had always been wild and reckless, and people are so fond hitting a man when he is down. But I call it very unkind and unjust, and I did think that an old friend like you would be above it. It hurts David dreadfully to find you so cold to him. I should have thought you would have liked to help him to recover the ground he has lost."

"That can hardly be my office now," said Catherine, gravely. "But at least you need not be unkind. I do assure you the poor boy has gone through quite enough, as it is." "You have told me the whole truth about his past, Mary?" asked Catherine, after a brief silence. "There is nothing worse you are keeping back?" Mrs. MacFie clasped her hands together with a little gesture of astonished dismay. "Is not forgery bad enough for you, Catherine? What has your husband been telling you? Did you think he had committed a murder?"

Catherine left Mrs. MacFie's presence somewhat relieved in mind. She was glad to know the secret of David's past, the cause of her husband's disdain and distrust of the man. It was natural, she thought, that Edward, as a friend of Colonel Ferguson's should feel deep indignation at the ingratitude and treachery of the fraud, and yet she felt a sense of relief that it was nothing blacker and baser. She had begun to have an undefined feeling, since she had entered somewhat into the tumultuous life of the great world, that there were depths of folly and sin and crime beneath its smooth, polished surface, of whose very existence she had never dreamed before. When she returned home that day, and said from whose house she had just come, she fancied a shade gathered on her husband's brow. "Do you not go there rather often Catherine?"

"We were friends as children," she said. "Am I to give up everything that seems connected with the past-with my home?" "I lay no embargo upon you, Catherine," he said; "or at least only one: I cannot permit Sir David MacRae to visit my wife, nor enter my house. If his sister is your friend, and you wish to continue the friendship, I say nothing against it. You shall be the judge whether or not you visit at a house your husband cannot enter, and run the risk of meeting a man whose hand he can never touch. You shall do exactly as you wish in the matter. I leave you entire liberty." A flush rose slowly in Catherine's face. "I want to do what is right to every one," she said. "You put things very hardly, Edward. You only see one side, and even that you view very harshly. I have heard David's story; it is very painful and shameful; but he has repented––he has indeed, and done all he could to make amends. I have been taught that repentance makes atonement, even in God's sight. I cannot sit in judgment then, and condemn him utterly." Edward looked at her keenly. "Do you know all?" "Yes," she answered steadily, "I know all. It is very bad; but he has repented." "I have seen no signs of repentance." "Have you ever given yourself the chance to do so?" He was still gazing earnestly at her. "Catherine", he said very gravely, "be advised by me, Do not make yourself MacRae's champion." "I do not intend," she answered, coldly, "but neither will I be his judge."

There was silence for a moment, then Edward spoke. "We will discuss this question no further. It is a painful one for me. I can never meet that man in friendship; I could wish that you could be content to forget him too; but he is an old friend. You are not connected with the dark passages in his life, and if his repentance is sincere I will not forbid your meeting him or speaking to him, if you find yourself in his company. It goes against me, I confess, Catherine. But I do not feel I have the right to say more. If you are acquainted with the story of his life, you are able to form your own estimate of his deserts."

The subject ended there, but it left a vague sore constraint in the minds of both. It was almost with a feeling of relief a few mornings later that Edward opened a letter from the bailiff of his scotch estate, requesting the presence of the master for a few days. The young man had been getting his shooting-box renovated and beautified for the reception of his young wife, hoping to prevail upon her in the autumn to come north with him, and his own presence on the spot had become a matter of necessity. Catherine heard of his proposed absence with perfect quietness which, however, hid a good deal of sinking at heart. She did not venture to ask to accompany him, nor did she suggest, as he had half feared, returning to MacAlister. She assented quietly to the proposition, and gave no outward sign of dismay. Edward sighed as he noted her indifference. Once she would have dreaded being left alone in the strange world of London, have begged him not to leave her, but now she was quite happy to see him depart. He was gradually growing sorrowfully convinced that his marriage had been a great mistake, and that Catherine's love might never be his. There had been sweet moments both before and after marriage, but they were few and far between, and the hope he had once so ardently cherished was growing fainter every day.

However, life must go on its accustomed groove, and the night before his departure was spent with Rebecca and her brother, who were giving a select dinner-party. Edward and Catherine seldom spent an evening at home alone now. Rebecca Scott's little parties were very popular. She was an excellent hostess, her endless sparkle and flow of spirit kept her guests well amused, and she treated her numerous admirers with a provoking friendliness and equality that was diverting to witness. Lord Charles MacMurray was a favourite, too, from his good-natured simplicity and frankness; and there was an easy unconstrained atmosphere about there house that made it a pleasant place of resort to its fashion, and felt more at home in her house than in any other. Sometimes when those two were alone together Rebecca would lay aside that brilliant sparkle and flow of spirit, and lapse into a sudden gravity and seriousness that would have astonished many of her friends and acquaintances had they chanced to witness it. Sometimes Catherine fancied at such moments that some kind of tear-stained page, some sad or painful memory; and it was this conviction that had won Catherine's confidence and friendship more than anything else. She could not make a true friend of any one who had never known sorrow.

Tonight Catherine was unusually distraught, sad and heavy at heart, she hardly knew why; finding it unusually difficult to talk or smile, or to hide from the from the eyes of others the melancholy that oppressed her. She felt a strange craving for her husband's presence. She wanted him near her. She longed to return to those first days of married life, when his compassion for her made him so tender, when he was always with her, and she believed that he loved her. Sometimes she had been almost happy then, despite the wrench from the old associations and the strangeness of all around. Now she was always sad and heavy-hearted; and tonight she was curiously oppressed. It was only at this house that she could ever be persuaded to sing, and tonight it was not till the end of the evening that Lord MacMurray's entreaties prevailed with her. She rose at last, crossed over to the piano and sitting down without any music, sang a simple melody.

"When I am dead, my darling, sing no songs for me; plant no roses at my head, no shady cypress-tree. Be the green grass above me, with showers and dew-drops wet; if you will remember-and if you will, forget. "I shall not see the shadows, I shall not feel the rain; no nightingale shall I hear, no pain will I have. No dreaming of twilight, which does not rise or set, I happily will remember––I sadly will forget."

As she sang, the room, the company, all faded from her view and from her mind-all but Edward. One strange longing filled her soul––the longing that she might indeed lie sleeping and at rest in some quiet, wind-swept swept spot her spirit hovering free-to see if her husband ever came to stand beside that grave, to see if he would in such a case remember-or forget. For herself, Catherine knew well that remembrance would be her portion. She never could forget. There was a wonderful sweetness and pathos in her voice as she sang. The listeners held their breath, and sudden tears started to Rebecca's eyes. When the last note had died away, Edward crossed the room and laid his hand upon his wife's shoulder. There was a subdued murmur all through the room, but she only heard her husband's voice.

"That was very sweet, Catherine," he said gently. "I have never heard it before; but you make it sound so unutterably sad." She looked up at him wistfully. "I think sad songs are always sweetest—they are more like life, at least. "His eyes were very full of tenderness; she saw it, and it and it almost unmanned her. "I am so tired Edward; will you take me home? The carriage will be here, but it is such little way. I should like best to walk." A very few moments later they were out in the warm, spring air, under the twinkling stars. She held his arm closely. Her hand trembled a little, he fancied. He drew her light lace wrap more closely round her, thinking she felt chilled. At this little mark of thoughtfulness she looked up at him with a tremulous smile.

"I shall miss you when you are gone, Edward," she said softly. "You will not be long away?" His heart beat high, but his words were very quietly spoken. "No, Catherine, only four or five days." "And you will take care of yourself? You will come back safe-you will not get into any danger?" "Why no, "he answered with a smile. "Danger! What are you thinking about, Catherine?" "I don't know. Sometimes my heart is very heavy. It is heavy tonight. Promise you will take care of yourself-for my sake." Edward did not, after all go away quite comfortless.

Chapter 12

Mrs. MacFie

Edward was gone; and Catherine, left alone in her luxurious London house, felt strangely lost and desolate. Her husband had expressed a wish that she should go out as much as possible, and not shut herself up in solitude during his brief absence, and to do his will was now her great desire. She would have preferred to remain quietly at home. She liked best to sit by her fire upstairs, and make Lorna tell her Edward's childhood and boyish days; his devotion to his widowed mother, his kindness to herself, all the deeds of youthful prowess, which an old nurse treasures up respecting her youthful charges, and delights to repeat in after years. Lorna would talk of Edward by the hour together if she were not checked, and Catherine felt singularly little disposition to check her.

However, she obeyed her husband in everything, and took her morning's ride as usual next day, and was met by Mary MacFie, who rode beside her, with her train of cavaliers in attendance, and pitied the poor darling child who had been deserted by her husband. "I am just in the same sad predicament myself, Catherine," she said plaintively. "My husband has had to go to Paris all of a sudden, and I am left alone too. We must console ourselves together. You must drive with me today and come to tea, and I will come to you tomorrow."

Catherine tried in vain to beg off; Mary only laughed at her. Catherine had not enough tact to parry skilful thrusts, nor insincerity enough to plead engagements that did not exist. So she was monopolised by Mrs. MacFie in her morning's ride, was driven out in her carriage that same afternoon, and taken to several houses where her friend had "just a few words" to say to the hostess. She was taken back to tea, and had to meet David, who received her with great warmth, and had the bad taste to address her by her Christian name before a whole roomful of company, and who ended by insisting on walking home with her. Yet his manner was so quiet and courteous, and he seemed so utterly unconscious of her disfavour, that she was half ashamed of it, despite her very real annoyance.

And the worst of it was that there seemed no end to the attentions pressed upon her by the indefatigable Mary. Catherine did not know how to escape from the manifold invitations and visits that were showered upon her. She seemed fated to be for ever in the society of Mrs. MacFie and her friends. Rebecca Scott and her brother were themselves out of town; Edward was detained longer than he had at first anticipated, and Catherine found herself drawn in an imperceptible way-against which she rebelled in vain--into quite a new set of people and places.

Catherine was a mere baby in Mary's hands. She had not the faintest idea of any malice on the part of her friend. She felt her attentions oppressive; she disliked the constant encounters with David; but she tried in vain to free herself from the hospitable tyranny of the happy little woman. She was caught in some inexplicable way, and without downright rudeness she could not escape.

As a rule, David was very guarded and discreet, especially when alone with her. He often annoyed her by his assumption of familiarity in presence of others, but he was humble enough for the most part, and took no umbrage at her rather pointed avoidance of him. She did not know what he was trying to do: how he was planning a subtle revenge upon his enemy, her husband--the husband she was beginning unconsciously yet very truly to love. She shrank from him without knowing why, but the day was rapidly approaching when her eyes were to be open. Her instincts were so true that it was not easy to deceive her for long. Ignorance of the world and reluctance to suspect evil blinded her for a time; but she was to learn the true nature of her so-called friends before long. There was a small picnic at Richmond one day. Catherine had tried hard to excuse herself from attending, but been laughed and coaxed into consent. It mattered the less what she did now, for her husband was to be at home the following day, and in the gladness of that thought she could almost enjoy the sunshine, the fresh air, the sight of green grass and waving trees, the country sights and sounds to which she had so long been a stranger.

The party, was small, and though David was of the number, he held aloof from Catherine, for which she was glad, for she had felt an increasing distrust of him of late. It was equestrian party, and the long ride was a pleasure to Catherine, who could have spent a whole day in the saddle without fatigue. And then her husband was coming. He would set all right. She tell him everything-she had not felt able to do so in the little brief notes she had written to him-and she would take his advice for the future, and decline friendship with all who could not be his friends too. Everything would be right when Edward came back.

Then Catherine was glad of an opportunity of a little quiet talk with Mary MacFie. The wish for a private interview with her had been one of the reasons which led her to consent to be one of today's party. She had something on her mind she wish to say to her in private, and as yet she had found no opportunity of doing so, it was not until quite late in the afternoon that Catherine's opportunity came; when it did she availed herself of it at once. She and her friend were alone in a quiet part of the park; nobody was very near to them.

Mary," said Catherine, "there is something I wish to say to you now that we are alone together. I am very much obliged to you for being so friendly during my husband's absence-but––but––it is difficult to say what I mean-yet I think you ought not to have had your brother so much with you when you were asking me; or rather I think, as he is your brother, whilst I am only a friend, the best plan would be for us to agree not to attempt to be very intimate. We have drifted apart with the lapse of years, and there are reasons, as you know, why it is not advisable for me to see much of your brother. I am sure you understand me without any more words."

"Oh, perfectly!" said Mrs. MacFie, with a light laugh. "Poor child, what a cruel person he is! Well, at least, we have made the best of the little time he allowed us." Catherine drew herself up very straight. "I do not understand you Mary. Please to remember that you are speaking of my husband." Mrs. MacFie laughed again. "I am in no danger of forgetting, my dear. Please do not trouble yourself to put on such old-fashioned airs with me; as if every one did not know your secret by this time."

Catherine turned upon her with flashing eyes. "What secret?" "The secret of your unhappy marriage, my love. It was obviously a marriage of convenance from the first, and you take no pains to disguise the fact that it will never be anything else. As Edward MacAlister is rather a fascinating man, there is only one rational interpretation to be put upon your persistent indifference."

Catherine stood as if turned to stone. "What?" "Why, that your heart was given away before he appeared on the scene. People like little pathetic romances, and there is something in the style of your beauty, my dear, that makes you an object of interest wherever you go. You are universally credited with a 'history' and a slowly-breaking heart-an equally heart-broken lover in the background. You can't think how interested we all are in you and——"

But the sentence was not finished. Mrs. MacFie's perceptions were not fine, but something in Catherine's face deterred her from permitting her brother's name to pass her lips. It was easy to see that no suspicion of his connection with the "romance" concocted for her by gossiping tongues had ever crossed Catherine's mind. But she was sternly indignant, and wounded to the quick by what she had heard. She spoke not a word, but turned haughtily away and sought for solitude in the loneliest part of the park. She was terribly humiliated. She knew nothing of the inevitable chatter and gossip, half good-humoured, half mischievous, with idle people indulge themselves about their neighbours, especially if that neighbour happens to be a beautiful woman, with an unknown past and apparent trouble upon her. She did not know that spite on David's part, and flighty foolishness on that of his sister, had started rumours concerning her. She only felt that she, by her ingratitude and coolness towards the husband who had sacrificed so much for her, and whom she sincerely respected, and almost loved, had been the means of bringing his name and hers within the reach of malicious tongues, had given rise to cruel false rumours she hated even to think of. If only her husband were with her!——but at least he would soon be with her, and if for very shame she could not repeat the cruel words she had heard, she could show to all the world how false and base they were.

Catherine woke up at last to the fact that it was getting late, and that she was in a totally strange place, far away from the rest of the party. She turned quickly and retraced her steps. She seldom lost her bearings, and was able to find her way back without difficulty, but she had strayed farther than she knew; it took her some time to reach the glade in which they had lunched, and when she arrived there she found it quite deserted. There was nothing for it but to go back to the hotel, whither she supposed the others had preceded her, but when she reached the court-yard no one was to be seen but David, who held her horse and his own, "Ah Catherine! here you are. We missed you just at starting. Did you lose yourself in the park? Nobody seemed to know what had become of you." "I suppose I walked rather too far. Where are the rest?"

"Just started five minutes ago. We only missed you then. I said I'd wait. We shall catch them up in two minutes." As this was Mrs. MacFie's party, and David was her brother, this mark of courtesy could not be called excessive, yet somehow it displeased Catherine a good deal. "Where is my groom?" David looked round innocently enough. "I suppose he joined the cavalcade, stupid fellow! Stablemen are so very gregarious, Never mind; we shall be up with them directly." And Catherine was forced to mount and ride after the party with David.

But they did not come up with the others, despite his assurances, and the fact that they rode very fast for a considerable time. He professed himself very much astonished, and declared that they must have made a stupid blunder, and "I will dispense with your escort. I am perfectly well able to take care of myself alone." He read her displeasure in her face and voice. She had an instinct that she had been tricked, but it was not a suspicion she could put into words. "Sir David!" he repeated, with gentle reproach. "Have I offended you, Catherine?"

"Sir David, it is time we should understand one another," said Catherine, turning her head towards him. "I made you a sort of promise once——a promise of friendship, I believe it was. I am not certain that I ever ought to have given it; but after my marriage with a man you hold as an enemy, it is impossible that I can look upon you as a true friend. I do not judge or condemn you, but I do say that we had better meet as infrequently as possible, and then as mere acquaintances. You have strained your right of friendship, as it is by the unwarrantable and persistent use of my Christian name, which you must have known was not for you to employ now. We were playfellows in childhood, I know, but circumstances alter cases, and our circumstances have greatly changed. It must be Sir David and Lady Catherine now between you and me, if ever we meet in future." His eyes gleamed with that wild beast ferocity that lay latent in his nature, but his voice was well under command. "your will is law, Lady Catherine. It is hard on me, but you know best.

I will accept any place that you assign me." She was not disarmed by his humility. "I assign you no place; and know that what I say is not hard. We are not at MacAlister now. You know your own world well; I am only just beginning to know it. You had no right ever to take liberties that could give occasion for criticism or remark."

He looked keenly at her, but she was evidently quite unconscious of the game he had tried to play for the amusement of his little circle. She only spoke in general terms. "There was a time, Catherine," he said gently. "when you cared less what the world would say." "There was a time, Sir David," she answered, with quiet dignity," when I knew less what the world might say."

Had Catherine felt the least suspicion of what her companion had tried to make it say, she would not now have been riding with him along the darkening streets, just as carriages were rolling by carrying people to dinner or to the theatres. Twice she had imperatively dismissed him, but he absolutely declined to leave her.

"I will not address another word to you if my presence is distasteful to you," he said; "but you are my sister's guest, and in the absence of her husband I stand in the place of your host. I will not leave you to ride home at this late hour alone. At the risk of incurring your displeasure I attend you to your own door."

Catherine did not protest after that, but she hardly addressed a single word to her silent companion. As she rode up to her own house she saw that he door stood open. The groom was there, with his horse. He was in earnest converse with a tall, broad shouldered man, who held a hunting-crop in his hand. Catherine's heart gave a sudden leap. He turned quickly at the sound of her approach—it was her husband. He looked at her and her companion in perfect silence. David took off his hat, murmured a few incoherent words, and rode quickly away.

Edward's hand closed like a vice upon his whip, but he only gave one glance at the retreating figure, then turned quietly to his wife and helped her to dismount. The groom took the horse, and without a word from any one, husband and wife passed together into the house. And this was the meeting to which Catherine had looked forward with so much trembling joy.

Chapter 13

Edward's Story

Edward led his wife upstairs to the drawing-room, and closed the door behind them. It was ten o' clock, and the room was brightly illuminated. Edward was in dinner dress, as though he had been at some time at home. His face was pale, and wore an expression of stern repression more intense than anything Catherine had ever seen there before. She was profoundly agitated-agitated most of all by the feeling that he was near her again; the husband that she had pined for without knowing that she pined. Her agitation was due to a kind of tumultuous joy more than to any other feeling, but she hardly knew this herself, and no one else would have credited it, from the whiteness of her face, and the strained look it wore. As a matter of fact, she was physically and mentally exhausted. She had gone through a great deal that day; she had eaten little, and that many hours ago; she was a good deal prostrated, though hardly aware of it––a state in which nervous tension made her unusually susceptible of impression; and she trembled and shrank before the displeasure in her husband's proud face. Would he look like that if he really loved her? Ah, no! No! She shrank a little more into herself.

Edward did not hurry her. He took off his overcoat leisurely, and laid his whip down upon the table. He looked once or twice at her as she sat, pale and wan in he arm-chair whither he had led her. Then he came and stood before her. "Catherine, what have you to say to me?" She looked up at him with an expression in her dark eyes that moved and touch him. Something of the severity passed from his face; he sat down too, laid his hand upon hers.

"You poor innocent child," he said quietly, "I do not even believe you know that you have done wrong." "I do, Edward," she answered. "I do know, but not as you think––I could not help that. I hated it I hate him; but tonight I could not help myself. Where I was wrong was in not doing as you asked persisting in judging for myself. But how could I know that people could be so cruel, so unworthy, false? Edward, I should like tonight to know that I should never see one of them again!"

She spoke with a passionate energy that startled him. He had never seen her excited like this before. "What have they been saying to you?" he asked in surprise. "Ah! Don't ask me. It is too hateful! It was Mary. She seemed to think it was amusing––a capital joke. Ah! How can people be so unwomanly, so debased"

She put her hands before her eyes, as if to shut out some hideous image. "Yes, I will tell you Edward I will. I owe it to you, because-because-oh, because there is just enough truth to make it so terribly bitter. She said that people knew it was not an ordinary marriage, ours-she called it a marriage of convenance. She said everybody knew we had not fallen in love with one another." Catherine's hand was still pressed over her eyes; she could not look at her husband. "She said I showed it plainly, that I let every one see. I never meant to, Edward, but perhaps I did. I don't know how to pretend. But oh, she said people thought it was because I cared-for some one else-that I had married you whilst I loved some one else-and that is all a wicked, wicked lie!

You believe that, Edward, do you not?" do you not?" She rose up suddenly and he rose too, and they stood looking into each other's eyes. "You believe that at least, Edward?" she asked, and wondered at the stern sorrow visible in every line of his face. "Yes, Catherine, I believe that," he answered, very quietly; yet in spite of all his yearning tenderness there was still some sternness in his manner, for he was deeply moved, and knew that the time had come when at all costs he must speak out. "I too, have heard that false rumour, and have heard-which I hope you have not––the name of the man to whom your heart is supposed to be given. Shall I tell it you? His name is Sir David MacRae."

Catherine recoiled as if he had struck her, and put both her hands before her face. Edward continued speaking in the same concise way. "Let me tell you my tale now, Catherine. I left Scotland early this morning, finishing business twelve hours sooner than I expected. I wired from Durham to you; but you had left the house before my telegram reached. In the train, during the last hour of the journey, some young fellows got in, who were amusing themselves by idle repetition of current gossip. I heard my wife's name mentioned more than once, coupled with that of Sir David MacRae, in whose company she had evidently been frequently seen of late. I reached home-Lady Catherine was out for the day with Mrs. MacFie-presumably with Sir David also. I dined at my club, to hear from more than one source that the world was gossiping about my handsome wife and Sir David MacRae. I came home at dusk to find the groom just returned, with the news that Sir David was bringing his Lady home that he was dismissed from attendance; and in effect the man whose acquaintance I repudiate, whose presence in my house is an insult, rides up to my door in attendance upon my wife. Before I say any more, tell me your story. Catherine, let me hear what you have been doing whilst I have been away." Catherine roused to a passionate indignation by what she heard-an indignation that for the moment seemed to include the husband, who had uttered such cruel, wounding words, told her story with graphic energy. She was grateful to Edward for listening so calmly and so patiently. She was vaguely aware that not all men would show such forbearance and self-control. She knew she had wounded him to the quick by her indiscretion and self-will, but he gave her every chance to exculpate herself. When she had told her story, she stood up very straight before him. Let him pronounce sentence upon her; she would bear it patiently if she could.

"I see, Catherine," he answered, very quietly, "I understand. It is not all your fault. You have only been unguarded. You have been an innocent victim. It is MacRae's own false tongue that has set on foot these idle, baseless rumours. It is just like him."

Catherine recoiled again. "Just like him! But Edward, he is my friend!" A stern look settled upon Edward's face. "Oblige me, Catherine, by withdrawing that word. He is not your friend; and he is my enemy." "Your enemy?" "Yes; and this is how he tries to obtain his revenge." Catherine was trembling in every limb. "I not understand," she said. "Sit down, then and

I will tell you. "She obeyed but he did not sit down. He stood with his back against the chimney-piece, the light from the chandelier falling full upon his stern resolute face, with its handsome features and luminous dark eyes.

"You say you know the story of MacRae's past"? "Yes; he forged a cheque, his sister told me". Edward looked at her intently. "Was that all she told you?" "Yes; she said it was all. He deceived a friend and benefactor, and committed a crime. Was not that enough?" "Not enough for MacRae, it seemed," answered Edward, significantly. "Catherine, I am glad you did not know more, since you have met that man as a friend. Forgiveness is beautiful and noble-but there are limits. I will tell you the whole story, but in brief. The colonel Ferguson of whom you heard in connection with the forgery was MacRae's best and kindest friend. He was a friend of my mother's and of mine. I knew him intimately, and saw a good deal of his protégé at his house and at oxford. I did not trust him at any time. It was no very great surprise when after a carefully concealed course of vulgar dissipation, he ended by disgracing himself in the way you have heard described. It cut Ferguson to the quick. 'Why did not the lad come to me if he was in trouble? I would have helped him,' he said. He let me into the secret, for I happened to be staying with him at the time; but it was all hushed up. MacRae was forgiven, and vowed an eternal gratitude, as well as a complete reformation in his life."

"Did he keep promise?" asked Catherine in a whisper. "You shall hear how," answered Edward, with a gathering sternness in his tone not lost upon Catherine. "From that moment it seemed as if a demon possessed him. I believe——it is the only excuse or explanation to be offered-that there is a taint of insanity in his blood, and that with him it takes, or took, the form of an inexplicable hatred towards the man to whom he owed so much. About this time Colonel Ferguson, till then a bachelor, married a friendless, beautiful young wife, to whom in his very quiet and undemonstrative way he was deeply and passionately attached, as she was to him. But she was very young and very inexperienced, and when that man, with his smooth false tongue, set himself to poison her life by filling her mind with doubts of her husband's love, he succeeded but too well. She spoke no word of what she suffered, but withdrew herself in her morbid jealous distress. She broke the faithful heart that loved her, and she broke her own too. It sounds a wild and foolish tale, perhaps, to one who does not understand the mysteries of a passionate love such as that; but it is all too true. I had been absent from England for some time, but came home, all unconscious of what had happened, to find my friend Ferguson in terrible grief. His young wife lay dying-dying of a rapid decline, brought on, it was said, by mental distress; and worse than all, she could not endure her husband's presence in the room, but shrank from him with inconceivable terror and excitement. He was utterly broken down by distress. He begged me to see her, and to learn, if I could, the cause of this miserable alteration. I did see her. I did get her to tell her story. I heard what David MacRae had done; and I was able, I am thankful to say, to relieve her mind of its terrible fear, and bring her husband to her before the end came. She died in his arms, happy at the last; but she died; and he, in his broken-hearted misery for her loss, and for the treachery of one he had loved almost as a son, did not survive her for long. Within six months my true, brave friend followed her to the grave.

"I was with him to the end. I need hardly say that MacRae did not attempt to come near him. He was plunged in a round of riotous dissipation. Upon the day following the funeral, I chanced to come upon him, surrounded by a select following of his boon companions. Can I bring myself to tell you what he was saying before he knew that I was within earshot? I need not repeat his words, Catherine: they are not fit for your ears. Suffice it to say that he was passing brutal jests upon the man who had just been laid in his grave, and upon the young wife whose heart had been broken by his own base and cruel slanders. Coupled with these jests were disgraceful boastings, as unmanly and false as the lips that uttered them.

"I had in my hand a heavy riding-whip. I took him by the collar, and I made him recant each one of those cruel slanders he had uttered, and confess himself a liar and a villain. I administer, then and there, such a chastisement as I hope never to have to administer to any man again. No one interposed between us. I think even his chosen companions felt that he was receiving no more than his due. I thrashed him like the miserable hound he was. If it had been possible, I would have called him out and shot him like a dog."

Edward's voice had not risen whilst he was speaking. He was very calm and composed as he told his story; there was no excitement in his manner, and yet his quiet, quivering wrath thrilled Catherine more than the fiercest invective could have done.

"My whip broke at last. I flung him from me, and he lay writhing on the floor. But he was not past speech, and he had energy left still to curse me to my face, and to vow upon me a terrible vengeance, which should follow me all my life. He is trying now to keep this vow. History repeats itself you know. He ruined the happiness of one life, and brought about this tragedy, by poisoning the mind of a wife, and setting her against her husband; and I presume he thinks that experiment was successful enough to be worth repeating. There, Catherine, I have said my say. You have now before you circumstantial history of the past life of Sir David MacRae-your friend."

Chapter 14

Storm and Calm

Catherine sat with her face buried in her hands, her whole frame quivering with emotion. Those last words of her husband's smote her almost like a blow. She deserved them, no doubt; yet they were cruel, coming like that. He could not have spoken so if he loved her. He would not stand coldly aloof whilst she suffered, if he held her really dear. And yet, once he had almost seemed to love her, till she had alienated him by her pride and self-will. It was just, she admitted, yet, oh! It was very hard! She sat, crushed and confounded, for a time, and it was only by a great effort that she spoke at all. "I did not know Edward; I did not know. You should have told me before."

"I believe you did know. You told me that you did." "Not that. Did you think I could know that and treat him as a friend? Oh, Edward! How could you! You ought to have told me before." "Perhaps I ought." he said. "But remember, Catherine, I spoke out very plainly, and still you insisted that he was, and should continue to be, your friend-your repentant friend."

Catherine raised her eyes to her husband's face, full of a mute reproach. She felt that she merited the rebuke-which he might have said much more without being really harsh-and yet it was very hard, in this hour of their reunion, to have to hear, from lips that had never uttered till then anything but words of gentleness and love, these reproofs and strictures on her conduct. She saw that he was moved: that there was a repressed agitation and excitement in his whole manner; but she could not guess how deeply he had been roused and stirred by the careless jests he had heard passed that day, nor how burning an indignation he felt towards the man who had plotted to ruin his happiness.

"You should not have left me, Edward, "said Catherine, "If you could not trust me." He went up to her quietly, and took her hands. She stood up, looking straight into his eyes. "I did trust you—I do trust you," he answered, with subdued impetuosity. "Can I look into your face and harbour one doubt of your goodness and truth? I trust you implicitly; it is your judgment, not your heart that has been at fault. "She looked up gratefully, and drew one step nearer. "And now that you have come back, all will be right again, "she said. "Edward, I will never speak to that man again." His face stern; it wore a look she did not understand.

"I am not sure of that," he answered, speaking with peculiar incisiveness. "It may be best that you should speak to him again." She looked up, bewildered. "Edward. Why do you say that? Do you think that, after all, he has repented?" Edward's face expressed an unutterable scorn. She read the meaning of his glance, and answered it as if it had been expressed in words. "Edward, do you believe for a moment that I would permit anyone to speak ill of you to me? Am I not your wife?" His face softened as he looked at her, but there was a good deal of sadness there too.

I do not believe you would deliberately listen to such words from him; but are not poisoned shafts launched sometimes that strike home and rankle? Has no one ever come between you and me, since the day you gave yourself to me in marriage?" He saw her hesitation, and a great sadness came into his eyes. How near she was, and yet how far! His heart ached for her in her loneliness and isolation, and it ached for himself too.

Catherine broke the silence first. "Edward," she said timidly, "no harm has been done to you really? He cannot hurt you; can he?" His face was stern as he answered her. "He will hurt me if he can-through my wife. His threat is still unfulfilled; but he knows where to plant a blow, how to strike in the dark. Yes, Catherine, he has hurt me. "She drew back a pace.

"How?" "It hurts me to know that idle gossip couples my wife's name with his-that he has the credit of being a lover, discarded only from motives of policy. I know that there is not a syllable of truth in these reports-that they have been set afloat by his malicious tongue. Nevertheless, they hurt me. They hurt me more because my wife has given some countenance to such rumours, by permitting a certain amount of intimacy with a man whom her husband will not receive.

Catherine was white to the lips. She understood now, as she had never done before, what Mary MacFie had meant by her flighty speeches a few hours before. They had disgusted and offended her then, now they appeared like absolute insults. Edward saw the stricken look upon her face, and knew that she was cut to the quick.

"Catherine," he said, more gently, "what has been done can be undone by a little patience and self-control. We need not be afraid of a man like Sir David. I have known him and his ways long. He has tried before to injure me without success. He has tried in a more subtle way this time; yet again I say, most emphatically, that he has failed. "But Catherine hardly heard. She was torn by the tumult of her shame and distress. "Edward!" she exclaimed, stretching out her hands towards him: "Edwards, take me home! Oh! Take me home, out of this cruel, cruel, wicked world! I cannot live here. It kills me; it stifles the very life out of me! I am so miserable, so desolate here! Ah! I was happy once!"

"I will take you to MacAlister, Catherine, believe me, as soon as ever I can; but it cannot be just yet. Shall I tell you why?" She recoiled from him once more, putting up her hand with that instinctive gesture of distress. "You are very cruel to me, Edward," she said, with the sharpness of keen misery in her voice. He stood quite still, looking at her, and then continued in the same quiet way—

"Shall I tell you why? I cannot take you away until we have been seen together as before. I shall go with you to some of those houses you have visited without me. We must be seen riding and driving, and going about as if nothing whatever had occurred during my absence. If we meet MacRae, there must be nothing in your manner or in mine to indicate that he is otherwise than absolutely indifferent to us. I dare say he will put himself in your way. He would like to force upon me the part of the jealous, distrustful husband, but it is a role I decline to play at his bidding. I am not jealous, nor am I distrustful, and he and all the world shall see that this is so. If I take you away now, Catherine, I shall give occasion for people to say that I am afraid to trust my wife in any place where she my meet MacRae. Let us stay where we are, and ignore the foolish rumours he has circulated, and we shall soon see them drop into deserved oblivion."

"Edward, I cannot!" cried Catherine, who was now overwrought and agitated to the verge of exhaustion; "I cannot stay here. I cannot go amongst those who have dared to say such things, to believe such things of me. What does it matter what they think, when we are away? Take me back to MacAlister, and let us forget it all. Let me go, if only for a week. I have never asked you anything before. Oh! Edward, do not be so hard! Say that you will take me home!"

"If I loved you less, Catherine," he answered, in a very low, gentle tone, I should say yes. As it is, I say no. I cannot take you to MacAlister yet. "She turned away then left him without a word, passing slowly through the brilliantly-lighted room, and up the wide staircase. Edward sat down and rested his head upon his hand, and a long-drawn sigh rose up from the very depths of his heart. This interview had tried him quite as much as it had done Catherine-possibly even more. "Perhaps, after all MacRae has revenged himself," he muttered, "though not in the way he anticipated. Ah. Catherine! My fair young wife, why cannot you trust me a little more?"

Catherine trusted him far more than he knew. It was not in anger that she had left him. In the depth of her heart she believed that he had judged wisely and well; it was only the wave of home-sickness sweeping over her that had urged her to such passionate pleading. And then his strong, inflexible firmness gave her a curious sense of rest and confidence. She was so torn and rent by conflicting emotions, by bewilderment and uncertainty, that his resolute determination and singleness of purpose were as a rock and tower of defense. She had called him cruel in the keen disappointment of the moment, but she knew he was not really so. Home-sick, aching for MacAlister as she was——irrepressibly as she shrank from the idea of facing those to whom she had given cause to say that she did not love her husband, she felt that his decision was right. It might be hard, but it was necessary, and she would go through her part unflinchingly for his sake. It was the least that she could do to make amends for unconscious wrong she had done him.

She felt humbled to the very dust, utterly distrustful of herself, and quite unworthy of the gentleness and forbearance her husband showed towards her. How much he must be disappointed in her! How hard he must feel it to have married her out of kindness, to be treated thus! She was very quiet and submissive during the days that followed, doing everything he suggested, studying in all things to please him, and make up for the past. In society she was bright and less silent than she had been heretofore. She was determined not to appear unhappy. No one should in future have cause to say that her present life was not congenial to her. Certainly, if any one took the trouble to watch her now, it would easily be seen that she was no longer indifferent to her husband. Her eyes often followed him about when he was absent from her side. She always seemed to know where he was, and to turn to him with instinctive welcome when he came back to her. This clinging to him was quite unconscious, the natural result of her confidence in his strength and protecting care; but it was visible to one pair of keenly jealous eyes; and David MacRae, when he occasionally found himself in company with Edward and his wife, watched with a sense of baffled malevolence the failure of his carefully-planned scheme.

People began to talk now of the devotion of Mr. MacAlister and Lady Catherine with as much readiness and carelessness as they had done about their visible estrangement. It takes very little to set idle tongues wagging, and every one admired the bride and liked the bridegroom, so that the good opinion of the world was not difficult to regain. But Catherine's peace of mind was less easily recovered. At home she was grave and sad, and Edward thought her cold; and the full and entire reconciliation of which, indeed, at that time she would have felt quite unworthy-was not to be yet. Each was conscious of deep love on his or her own side, but could not read the heart of the other, and feared to break the existing calm by any attempt to ruffle the surface of the waters.

They were not very much alone, for Lord MacMurray and his sister spent many evenings with them when they were not otherwise engaged, and the intimacy between the houses increased rapidly. Catherine had never again alluded to the prospective return to MacAlister––the half-promise made by Edward to take her back soon. She did not know what "soon" might mean, and she did not ask. She had grown content now to leave that question in his hands.

Once, when in the after-dinner twilight, she had been talking to Rebecca of her old home, the latter said, with eager vehemence––"How you must long to see it again! How you must ache to be out of this tumult, and back with your beloved sea and cliffs and pine woods! Don't you hate our noisy busy London? Don't you pine to go back?"

Catherine was silent, pondering, as it seemed. She was thinking deeply. When she answered out of the fullness of her heart, her words startled even herself. "I don't think I do. I missed the quiet and rest at first, but, you see, my husband is here; I do not pine when I have him. "Rebecca's eyes grew suddenly wistful. "Ah, no!" she answered. "I can understand that. "Then after a long silence she rallied herself and asked "But is he not going to take you back? Do you not want to see your father and brother again?" "Yes, if Edward is willing to take me; but it must be as he wishes." "He will like what will please you best. "Catherine smiled a little. "No; he will like what is best, and I shall like it too."

Rebecca studied her face intently. "Do you know, Catherine, that you have changed since I saw you first?" Catherine passed her hand across her brow. What a long time it seemed since that first meeting in the park! "Have I?"

"Yes. Do you know I used to have a silly fancy that you did not much care for Edward? It was absurd and impertinent, I know; but Lord MacMurray had brought such a strange account of your sudden wedding, called you the 'snow bride,' and had some how got an idea that it had all been rather cold and had sad-forgetting, of course, that the sadness was on account of your father's health. I suppose I got a preconceived idea; and do you know, when first I knew you I used to think of you as the 'snow bride,' and fancy you very cold to every one-especially to Edward; and now that I see more of you and know you better, it is just as plain that you love him with all your heart and soul."

Catherine sat quite still in the darkness, turning about the ring upon her finger––the pledge of his wedded love. She was startled at hearing put into plain words the secret thought treasured deep down in her heart, but seldom looked into or analysed. Had it come to that? Did she indeed love him thus? Was that the reason she yielded up herself and her future so trustfully and willingly to him?––the reason that she no longer yearned after MacAlister as home, so long as he was at her side? Yes, that was surely it. Rebecca had spoken no more than the truth in what she said. She did love her husband heart and soul; but did he love her too? There lay the sting-she had proved unworthy of him: he must know it and feel it. She had

Graham Lomas

been near to winning his heart; but alas! She had not won it-and now, now perhaps it was too late. And yet the full truth was like a ray of sunshine in her heart. Might she not yet win his love by the depth and tenderness of her own? Something deep down within her said that the land of promise lay, after all, not so very far away.

Chapter 15

A Summons To MacAlister

Edward! Edward! Why did you not take me home when I begged so hard to go? It was cruel! cruel! And now it is too late!" This irrepressible cry of anguish burst from Catherine in the first moments of a terrible, overmastering grief. And open telegram in Edward's hand announced the sudden death of Lord MacAlister. He had just broken to his wife, with as much gentleness as he could, the news of this crushing sorrow. It was hardly unnatural that she should remember, in such a moment, how eloquently she had pleaded a few weeks back to be taken home to MacAlister, yet she repented the words before they had passed her lips, for she saw they had hurt her husband.

He was deeply grieved for her, his heart yearned over her, but his words were few. "Catherine can you be ready for the noon express?" She bent her head in a silent assent, and moved away as one who walks in a dream. "Poor child!" he said softly, "poor child! If only my love could make up to you for what you have lost; but alas! That is not what you want."

It was a strange, sad silent journey, almost as sad as the one in which Edward had brought his bride to London. He was taking her back at last to her childhood's home. Was he any nearer to her innermost self than he had been that day, now nearly three months ago?

He was hopeful that he had made an advance, and yet this sudden recall to MacAlister disconcerted him. Apart from the question of the Earl's death, there was another trouble, he believed, hanging over Catherine's future. Bruce Pendrill had been profiting by her absence to "experiment," as she would have called it, upon Matthew, with results that had surprised even him, though he had always believed the case curable if properly treated. Edward had had nothing to do directly with the matter, but Bruce had written lately, asking him to find out the best authorities on spinal injuries, and get some one or two specialists to come and have a look at the boy. This Edward had done at his own expense, and with the result, as he had heard a few days back, that Matthew was to be sent abroad for a year, to be under a German doctor, whose cures of similar cases had been bringing him into marked repute.

Catherine had been, by Matthew's special wish, kept in ignorance of everything. He was eagerly anxious, even at the cost of considerable suffering, to submit to the prescribed treatment, feeling how much good he had already received from Bruce's more severe remedies; but he knew how Catherine shrank from the idea of anything that could give him pain, how terrible she would consider the idea of parting, how vehemently she would struggle to thwart the proposed plan. So he had begged that she might be kept in ignorance till all was finally settled. Indeed, he had some idea, not entirely discouraged by Bruce, of getting himself quietly removed to Germany in her absence, so that she might be spared all the anxiety misery, and suspense.

Edward could hardly have been acquitted of participation in the scheme, the whole cost of which was to fall upon him, and he wondered what Catherine might think of his share in it. It had been no doing of his that she had not been told from the first. He had urged upon the others the unfairness of keeping her in the dark; Matthew's vehement wish for secrecy had won the day, and he had held his peace until he should be permitted to speak.

And now, what would happen? What was likely to be the result upon Catherine of the inevitable disclosure? Would it not seem to her as if the first act of her husband, on succeeding to the family estate, was to banish from it the one being for whom she had so often bespoken his protection and brotherly care? Might she not be acute enough to see that but for him it never could have been carried out, owing to lack of necessary funds?

Her father might have approved it, but he could not have forwarded it as Edward was able to do. Might it not seem to her that he was trying to rid himself of an unwelcome burden, and to isolate his wife from all whom she loved best? He could not forget some of the words she had spoken not very long after their marriage. Practically those words had been rescinded by what had followed, but that could hardly be so in this case. Catherine's heart clung round Matthew with a passionate, yearning tenderness, that was one of the mainsprings of her existence. What would she say to those who had banded together to take the boy from her?

Edward's pre-occupation and gravity were not lost upon Catherine, but she had no clue to their real cause. She felt that there was something in it of which she was ignorant, and there was a faint sadness and constraint even in the suspicion of such a thing. She was unnerved and miserable, and although she well knew she had not merited her husband's full confidence, it hurt her keenly to feel it was withheld from her. Evening came on, a wild, melancholy, stormy evening——is there anything more sad and dreary than a midsummer storm? It does not come with the wild, resistless might of a winter tempest, sweeping triumphantly along, carrying all before it in the exuberance of its power. It is a sad, subdued, creature, full of eerie sounds of wailing and regret, not wrapped in darkness, but cloaked in misty twilight, grey and ghostlike——a pale, sorrowful, mysterious thing, that seems to know itself altogether out of place, and is haunted by its own melancholy and dreariness.

It was in the fast waning light of such a summer's evening that the portals of MacAlister opened to welcome Catherine again. She was in the old familiar hall that once had been so dear to her——the place whose stern, grim desolation had held such charms for her. Why did she now gaze round her with dilated eyes, a sort of horror growing upon her? Why did she cling to her husband's arm so closely, as the frowning suits of male and black carved faces stared at her out of the husky darkness? Why was her first exclamation one of terror and dismay? "Edward! Edward! This is not MacAlister! It cannot be MacAlister! Take me home! Ah, take me home!"

There was a catch in her breath; she was shaken with nervous agitation and exhaustion. It seemed to her that this ghostly place was altogether strange and terrible. She did not know that the change was in herself; she thought it was in her surroundings. "What have they done to it? What have they done to MacAlister? This is not my old home!" Edward took her in his arms, alarmed by her pale looks and manifest disquietude. "Not know your old home, Catherine?" he said, half gravely, half playfully. "This is the only MacAlister I have ever known. It is you that have half forgotten, you have grown used to something so very different."

Catherine looked timidly about her, half convinced, yet not relieved of all her haunting fears. What a strange, vast, silent place it was! Voices echoed in it, resounding as it were from remote corners. Footsteps sounded hollow and strange as they came and went along the deserted passages. The staircase stretched upwards into black darkness, suggesting lurking horrors. All was intensely desolate. Was this truly the home she had loved so well?

But Lady Louise appeared from one direction, and Bruce Pendrill from another. Catherine dropped her husband's arm and stood up, her calm, quiet self again. Food was awaiting the travellers, and as they partook, or tried to partake of it, they heard all such particulars of the Earl's sudden death as there were to hear. He had been as well as usual; indeed, during the past week he had really appeared to gain in strength and activity. He had been out of doors on all fine days, and only yesterday had sat out for quite a long time upon the terrace. He had gone to bed apparently in his usual health; but when his man had gone to him in the morning he found him dead and cold. Bruce Pendrill had come over at once, and had remained for the day, relieving Lady Louise from all trouble in looking after things, and thinking what was to be done. It was his opinion that the Earl had died in his sleep, without a moment's premonition. It was syncope of the heart, and was most likely almost instantaneous. There had been no struggle and no pain, as was evident from his restful attitude and expression.

The next days passed sadly and heavily, and the Earl was laid to rest amongst his forefathers in the family vault. Lady Louise took her departure, glad, after the strain and sorrow of the past days, to escape from surroundings so gloomy, and to solace herself after her long stay at MacAlister, by a retreat to an atmosphere more congenial to her.

Catherine was glad to see her go. She shrank from her sharp words and sharper looks. She longed to be alone with her husband that she might try to win back his heart by her own deep love that she hid away so well. But it was not easy even then to say what was in her heart. Edward was busy from morning till night over the necessary business that must ensue upon the death of a landed proprietor. Bruce Pendrill, who had been much with the Earl of late, remained to assist his successor; and both the men seemed to take it for granted that Catherine would gladly be spared all business discussions, and devote herself to Matthew, from whom she had so long been separated.

Catherine, very gentle and submissive, accepted the office bestowed upon her, and quietly bided her time. Despite the loss she had just sustained, she was not unhappy. How could she be unhappy when she had her husband? when she felt that every day they were drawing nearer and nearer together? She looked wistfully into his face sometimes, and saw the old proud, tender look shining upon her, thrilling her with wonderful gladness. Some little shadow still hung over them, but it was rolling slowly away the dawn was breaking in its golden glory––the time was drawing very near when each was to know the heart of the other wholly and entirely won.

She never shrank from hearing the new Lord MacAlister called by his title; but looked at him proudly and tenderly, feeling how well he bore the dignity, how nobly he would fulfill the duties now devolving upon him. She watched him day by day with quiet, loving solicitude. She saw his care for her in each act or plan, knew that he thought for her still, made her his first object, although she had disappointed him so grievously once. Her heart throbbed with joy to feel that this was so; the sunshine deepened round her path day by day. Just a little patience-just a little time to show him that the old distrust and insubordination were over, and he would give to her-she felt sure of it now––the love she prized above all else on earth. Catherine's face might be pale and grave in these days, yet it wore an added sweetness as each passed by, for her heart was full of strange new joy. She loved her husband––he loved her––their heart were all but united.

<center>~~~</center>

Chapter 16

<center>~~~</center>

Changes

"Matthew!"

"Aha! My Lady! You didn't expect that, did you? Now look here!"

Matthew, who was sitting up in an arm-chair——a thing Catherine had never seen him do since that terrible fall from the cliffs years ago-now pulled himself slowly into a standing position, and by the help of a stout stick, shuffled a few paces to his couch, upon which he sank breathless, yet triumphant, though his drawn brow betrayed that the achievement was made at the cost of some physical pain.

"Matthew, don't! You will kill yourself!" "On the contrary, I am going to cure myself-or rather, Bruce and his scientific friends are going to cure me," answered Matthew, panting a little with the exertion, but very happy and confident. "Do you know, Catherine, that for the last three months I have been at Bruce's tender mercies, and you see what I can do at the end of that time! Edward paid no end of money, I believe, to send down two big swells from London to overhaul me; and now-now what do you think is going to happen?" "What?" "The day after tomorrow I am going to start for Germany-for a place where there are mineral springs and things; and I am going to stay there for a year, with a doctor who has cured people worse than me. Edward is going to pay——isn't he just awfully good? And in a year, Catherine, I shall come back to you well-cured! What do you think of that? Haven't we kept our secret well? Why, Catherine, don't look like that! Aren't you pleased to think that I shall not be always a cripple?" But Catherine was too utterly astounded to be able to realise all at once what this meant.

"Matthew, I don't understand," she said at length. "You seeing doctors-you going to Germany! Whose doing is it all?" "Whose? Edward's practically, I suppose, since he finds the money for it." "Why was not I told?"

"That was my doing. I felt that if you knew you would dissuade me. But you can't now, for in two days I shall be gone!" "Was Edward willing to keep a secret from me about you?" asked Catherine slowly. "No, he didn't like it. He wanted you to be told; but I wouldn't have it, and he gave in. I wanted to tell you myself when everything was fixed. Can you believe I am really going?" "No, I can't. Do you want to go, Matthew-to leave MacAlister?" "I want to get well," he answered eagerly. "If you had been lying on your back for years, Catherine, you would understand," "I do understand," answered Catherine, clasping her hands. Only-only——" "Oh! Yes, I know all that. It won't be pleasant. But I'd do more for a good chance of getting well. So now it's all settled, and I'm off the day after tomorrow!" "You've not given much time for my preparations."

Matthew laughed outright. "Oh, you're not going-did you think you were? Why, you're Lady MacAlister now——a full-blown countess. It would be too absurd, your tying yourself to me. Besides"——with a touch of manly gravity and purpose——"I wouldn't have you, Catherine, not at any price. I can stand things myself, but I can't stand the look in your eyes. Besides, you know, it would be absurd now-quite absurd. You're married, you know, and that changes everything." Catherine's face was hard to read. "I should have thought that even married, I might have been allowed to see you placed safely in the hands of this new doctor, after having been almost your only nurse all these years." He stretched out his hand and drew her towards him, making her kneel down beside him, so that he could gaze right into her face. "you must not look like that, you sweet, sensitive sister," said Matthew, caressingly. "You must not think I have changed, because I wish to go away, and because I will not have you with me. I love you the same as ever. I know that you love me, and if you want a proof of this you shall have it, I am going to ask a favour of you——a very great favour."

Catherine smoothed his hair ward with her hand. "A favour, Matthew?——Something that I can grant? You know have only to ask." "I want you to lend me Edward," he said, with a little laugh, as if amused at the form of words he had chosen. "I want to know if you can spare him for the journey. Bruce is going to take me, but somehow, Bruce-well, he is very clever and kind, but he does hurt me, there's no denying, and I don't feel quite resigned to be entirely at his mercy. But Edward is different. He is immensely strong, he moves me twice as easily, and he is so awfully kind and gentle; he stops in a moment if he thinks it hurts. He has been here a good bit with Bruce since he got back, and can't think how different his handling is. I don't like to take him away from you. You must miss him so awfully: he is such a splendid fellow!" "Have you said anything to Edward about it?" Oh, no. I couldn't till I'd asked. I do fell horrid to suggest such a thing; but you've made me selfish, you know, by spoiling me. It will take us three days to go; but he could come back much quicker. Bruce is going to stop on for a bit, to study cures with this old fogey; so I shall have somebody with me. I'll not keep Edward a day after I get landed there, but I should like him for the journey uncommonly."

Catherine stooped and kissed him. "I will arrange that for you," she said quietly, and went away without another word. She went slowly downstairs to the study, where her husband was generally to be found. She was dazed and confused by the astounding piece of news she had heard: hurt, pleased, hopeful, grieved, anxious, and half-indignant all in one. Her indignation was all for Bruce Pendrill, whom she had always regarded, where Matthew was concerned, something in the light of a natural foe. For her husband's quiet generosity and goodness she had nothing but the warmest gratitude. He would not be led away by professional enthusiasm, or wish to inflict suffering upon Matthew just for the sake of scientific inquiry. He would not wish to send him from MacAlister unless he believed that some great benefit would result from that banishment. She smiled proudly as she thought of David's old prediction fulfilling itself so exactly now. Once she would have felt this deed of his a crushing blow, aimed at the very foundation of her love and happiness; now she only saw in it a new proof of her husband's single-minded love and strength. He would do even that which he knew would cause present pain, if he felt assured it were best to do so. He had proved his strength like this before, and she knew that he had been in the right. Should she distrust him now? Never again! Never again! She had done with distrust. She loved him too truly to feel a shadow of doubt. Whatever he did must be true and right. She would find him now, and thank him for his goodness towards her boy.

She went to the study, full of this idea. Her eyes were shining strangely; her face showed that her feelings had been deeply stirred. But when she opened the door, she paused with a start expressive of slight discomfiture, for her husband was not alone-Bruce Pendrill was with him. They had guidebooks and a continental bradshaw open before them, and were deep in discussions and plans.

They looked up quickly as Catherine appeared, and Edward, seeing by her face that she knew all, nerved himself to meet displeasure and misunderstanding. Catherine could not say now what she had rehearsed on the way. Bruce was there, and she was not sure that she quite forgave him, although she believed he acted from motives of kindness; but certainly she could not speak out before him. The words she had come prepared to utter died away on her lips, and her silence and whole attitude looked significant of deep-lying distress and displeasure. "You have heard the news, Catherine?" said Bruce, easily. "Yes, I have heard the news," she answered, very quietly. "Is it true that you take him away the day after tomorrow?" "Quite true," answered Bruce, looking very steadily at her. "Do you forgive us, Catherine?" she was silent for a moment; a sort of quiver passed over her face. "I am not quite sure if I forgive you," she answered in a low even tone.

She had not looked at her husband all this time, nor attempted to speak to him. She was labouring visibly under the stress of subdued emotion. Edward believed he knew only too well the struggle that was going on within her.

"Catherine," he said-and his voice sounded almost cold in his effort to keep it thoroughly under control "I am afraid this has been a shock to you. I am sure you will feel it very much. Will you try to believe that we are acting as we believe for the best as regards Matthew's future, and pardon the mystery that has surrounded our proceedings" Catherine gave him one quick look-so quick and transient that he could not catch the secret it revealed. She spoke very quietly. Everything has been settled, and I must accept the judgment of others. Results alone can quite reconcile me the idea;

but least I have learnt to know that I do not always judge best in difficult cases. Matthew wishes to go, and I will not stand in his way. There is only one thing that I want to ask," and she looked straight at her husband. "What is that, Catherine?" "I want you to go with him, Edward." "You want me to go with him?" "Yes, to settle him in his new quarters, and to come and tell me all about it, and how he has borne the journey. Bruce will not be back for weeks––and I dont know if I quite trust Bruce's truthfulness. Will you go too, Edward? I shall be happier if I know he is in your keeping as well."

He looked at her earnestly. Did she wish to get rid of him for a time? Was his presence distasteful to her after this last act of his? He could not tell, but his heart was heavy as he gave the required assent. "I will do as you wish, Catherine. If you do not mind being a few days alone at MacAlister, I will go with Matthew. It is the least I can do, I suppose, after taking him away from you." "Thank you, Edward," she said, with one more of those inexplicable glances. "I need not be alone at MacAlister. Aunt Jennifer will come, I am sure, and stay with me!" and she went quietly away without another word. "I say, MacAlister, you have tamed my Lady pretty considerably," remarked Bruce, when the men were alone together. "I expected no end of a shine when she found out, and she yields the point like a lamb. Seems to me you've cast a pretty good spell over her during the short time you've had her in hand."

Edward pulled thoughtfully at his moustache as he turned again to the papers on the table. He did not reply directly to Bruce's remark, but presently observed, rather as if it were the outcome of his own thoughts–– "All the same, I would give a good deal if one of my first acts after coming into the property were not to banish Matthew from MacAlister for a considerable and indeterminate time."

"Oh, rubbish!" ejaculated Bruce, taking up bradshaw again. "Why, even Catherine would never put a construction like that upon this business." That day and the next flew by as if on wings. There was so much to think of, so much to do, and Catherine had Matthew so much upon her mind, that she found no opportunity to say to Edward what she had purposed doing in the heat of the moment. Speech was still an effort to her; her reserve was too deep to be easily overcome. She was busy and he was pre-occupied. When he returned she would tell him all, and thank him for his generous goodness towards her boy.

"Catherine," said Matthew, as she came to bid him good-night upon the eve of his journey——he had had a soothing draught administered, and was no longer excited, but quiet and drowsy——" Catherine, you will be quite happy, will you not, with only Edward now? You love him very much, don't you?" She bent head and kissed him. "Yes Matthew," she answered softly. "I love him with all my heart."

"Just as he loves you," murmured Matthew. "I can see it in his face, in every tone of his voice, especially when he talks of you-which is pretty nearly always we both like it so much. I am so glad you feel just the same. I thought you did. I shall like to think about you so-how happy you will be!

The next day, after Matthew had been placed in the carriage that was to take him away from MacAlister, and Catherine had said her last adieu to him, and turned away with pale face and quivering lips, she felt her hands taken in her husband's strong warm clasp. "Catherine." he said tenderly, "good-bye. I will take every care of him. You shall hear everything, and shall not regret, if I can help it, trusting him to me" Catherine looked up suddenly into his face, and put her arms about his neck. She did not care at that moment for the presence of Bruce or of the servants. Her husband was leaving her-she had only thoughts for him.

"Take care of yourself, Edward," she said, her voice quivering, and almost breaking. "Take care of yourself, and come back to me as quickly as you can. I shall miss you, oh so much, till I have you safe home again. Good-bye, dear husband, good-bye!"

He held her for a moment in his arms. His heart beat with excitement; for an instant everything seemed to recede, and leave him and his wife alone in the world together; but it was no time to indulge in raptures. He kissed her brow and lips, and gently unloosed her clasp. "Good-bye, my wife," he said gently. God bless and keep you always. "The next moment the carriage was rolling rapidly away along the road, Catherine gazing after it, her soul in her eyes.

"Ah! My darling," said Mrs. Pendrill, coming and taking her by the hand, "it is very hard to part with him; but it was kind to Matthew to spare him and it is only for a few days." "I know, I know." answered Catherine, passing her hand across her eyes. "I would not have kept him here. Matthew wanted him so much——I can understand so well what he felt——it would have been selfish to hold him back. But it feels so lonely and desolate without him; as if everything were changed and different. I can't express it; but oh! I do feel it all so keenly." Mrs. Pendrill pressed the hand she held. "You love him, then, so very much?" "Ah, yes," she answered; "how could I help it?" "It makes me very happy to hear you say that. For I was sometimes rather afraid that you were hurried into marriage before you had learned to know your own heart."

Catherine passed her hand across her brow. "Was I hurried?" she asked dreamily. "It is so hard to remember that now. It seems as if I had always loved Edward––as if he had always been the centre of my life. "And Mrs.

Pendrill was content. She said no more, asked no more questions. "You know, Edward," said Matthew to his kindest of nurses and attendants, as he lay in bed at night, after rather a hard day's travelling, "I don't wonder that you've so completely cut me out. I shouldn't have believed it possible once, but it seems not only possible, but natural enough, now that I know what kind of a fellow you are.

"What do you mean, my boy?" asked Edward. Mean? Why, what I say, to be sure. I understand why you've so completely cut me out with Catherine. I only hold quite a subordinate place in her affections now. It is quite right, and I shall never be jealous of you, old fellow; only mind you always let me be her brother. I can't give up that. You may have all the rest, though. You deserve it, and you've got it too, by her own showing. "Edward started a little involuntarily. "What do you mean?" "Mean? Why, that she loves you heart and soul, of course. You must know it as well as I, and I had it from her own lips."

"My wife, my wife!" said Edward, as he paced beneath the starry heavens that night. "Then I was not deceived or mistaken-my wife-my Catherine-my very own-God bless you, my darling, and bring me safe home to you and to your love!"

Chapter 17

United

During the days that followed Catherine lived as in one long, happy dream. The clouds all seemed to have rolled away, letting in the sunshine to the innermost recesses of her heart. Why was she so calmly and serenely happy, despite the real sorrow hanging over her in the recent death of a tenderly-loved father? Why did even the loss of the brother, to whom she had vowed such changeless devotion, give her no special extreme pain? She had felt his going much, yet it did not weigh her down with any load of sorrow. She well knew why these things were. The old love had not changed nor waned, but it had been eclipsed in the light of the deep wonderful happiness that had grown up in her heart, since she had come to know how well and faithfully she loved Edward, and to believe at last in his love for her.

Yes, she no longer doubted that now. Something in the very perfectness of her own love drove away the haunting doubts and fears that had troubled her for so long. He had her heart, and she had his, and when once she had him home again the last shadow would have vanished away. How her heart beat as she pictured that meeting! She counted the hours till she had him back! Only once was she disturbed in her quiet, dreamy time of waiting. Once, as she was riding through the loneliest part of the lonely pine wood, David MacRae suddenly stood in her path. Gazing earnestly at her with a look she could not fathom.

Her face flushed and paled. She regarded him with a glance of haughty displeasure. "Let me pass, Sir David." He did not move; he was still fixedly regarding her. "I told you how it would be, Catherine," he said, "I told you Matthew would be sent away." She smiled a smile he did not understand. "Let me pass," she said again. His eyes began to glow dangerously. Her beauty and her scorn drove him to a sort of fury. "Is this the way you keep your promise? Is this how you treat a man you have promised to call your friend?" "My friend!" Catherine repeated the words very slowly, with an inflection the meaning of which could be misunderstood; nor did his affect to misunderstand her. "Lady Catherine," he said, "you have heard some lying story, I, perceive, trumped up that scoundrel you call your husband." He was forced to spring on one side then, for Catherine had urged her horse forward, regardless of his presence, and the flash in her eye made him recoil for moment; but he was wild with rage, and sprang at her horse, catching him by the bridle.

"You shall hear me!" he cried. "You shall, I say! You have heard his story, now hear mine. He has given false reports. I knew him long ago. He is my enemy. He has poisoned others against me before now. Lady Catherine, upon my word of honour——" "Your honour!"

That was all. Indeed, there was no more to be said. Even David felt that, and his grasp upon the reins relaxed. Catherine was not in the least afraid of him. She looked steadily over as she moved quietly onward, without the least haste or flurry. Her quiet courage, her lofty scorn of him, stung him to madness.

"Very good Lady Catherine——I beg your pardon-Lady MacAlister, I should say now. Very good. We understand each other excellently well. You have made a promise, only to break it——I will show you how a vow can be kept. I too have made a vow in my time. I make another now. I have vowed to ruin the happiness and prosperity of Edward MacAlister's life; now I will do more. I will destroy your peace and happiness also!" He was following Catherine as he spoke, and there was a deep, steady malevolence in every tone of his voice, and in each word that he uttered, which gave something of sinister significance to threats that might well have been mere idle bravado. Catherine paid not the slightest heed. She rode on as if she did even hear; but she wished had her husband beside her. She was not afraid for herself, only for him; and in his absence it was easy to be haunted by vague yet terrible fears.

The days sped by; news Germany was good. Edward's task was accomplished, and he was on his way home; no, he would be there almost as soon the letter which announced him. He did not specify exactly how he would come, but he bid her look for him about dusk that very day.

How her heart throbbed with joy! She could not strenuously combat Mrs. Pendrill's determination to return home at once, so that husband and wife should be alone on his return. She wanted Edward all to herself. She hungered for him; she hardly knew how to wait for the slowly crawling hours to pass.

She drove Mrs. Pendrill to St. Maws, and on her return wandered aimlessly about the great lonely house, saying to herself, in a sort of ceaseless cadence "He is coming. He is coming. He is coming." Dusk was falling in the dim house. The shadows were growing black in the gloomy hall, where Catherine was restlessly pacing. The last pale gleam of sunlight flickered and faded as she watched and waited with intense expectancy.

A man's firm step upon the terrace without—a man's tall shadow across the threshold. Catherine sprang forward with a low cry. "Edward" "Not exactly that, Lady MacAlister!" She stopped short, and threw up her head like some beautiful wild creature at bay. "Sir David, how dare you! Leave my husband's house this instant! Do you wish him to find you here? Do you wish a second chastisement at his hands?"

David's face flushed crimson, darkening with the intensity of his rage, as he heard those last words. He had been drinking deeply; his usual caution and cowardice were merged in a passionate desire for revenge at all costs. And what better revenge could he enjoy at that moment than to be surprised by the master of the house upon his return in company with his wife? Catherine had asked him if he wished Edward to find him there—it was just that wish which had brought him.

"Catherine!" he cried passionately, "You shall hear me. I will be heard! You shall not judge me till I can plead my own cause. The veriest criminal is heard in his defense." He advanced a step nearer, but she recoiled before him, and pointed to the door. "Go, Sir David, unless you wish to be expelled by my servants. I will listen to nothing. "She moved as if to summon assistance, but he sprang forward and seized her hand holding her wrist in so fierce a grasp that she could neither free herself nor reach the bell. She was a prisoner at his mercy.

But Catherine was a true MacAlister, and a stranger to mere physical fear. The madness in his gleaming eyes, the ferocity of his whole aspect, were sufficiently alarming. She knew in this vast place that it would be in vain to call for help, no one would hear her voice; but she faced her enemy with cool, inflexible courage, trusting to her own strong will, and the inherent cowardice of a man who could thus insult a woman alone in her husband's house. "Let me, loose Sir David!" she said. "Not until you heard me." "I will not hear you. I know as much of your story as there is any need I should. Let me, loose I say! Do you know that my husband will be here immediately? Do you wish him to expel you from his house?"

David laughed wildly, a sort of demoniac laugh that made her shudder in spite of herself. Was he mad? Yes, mad with drink and with fury- not irresponsible, yet so blind, so crazed, so possessed with thoughts of vengeance, that he was almost more dangerous than a raving maniac would have been. His eyes glowed with sullen fire. His voice was hoarse and strained. "Do I wish him to find me here? Yes, I do——I do!" he laughed wildly. "Kiss me, Catherine-call me your friend again! Yourself in his absence.

Catherine recoiled with a cry of horror; but the strength of madness was upon him. He held her fast by the wrist. It was unspeakably hideous to be alone in that dim place with this terrible madman. "Catherine, I love you-you shall-you must be mine!" Was that another step without? It was——it was! Thank heaven he had come! Edward! Edward! Edward!"

Catherine's voice rang out with that sudden piercing clearness that bespeaks terror and distress. The next moment David was hurled backwards, with a force that sent him staggering against the wall, breathless and powerless. Before he could recover himself he was lifted bodily off his feet, shaken like a rat, and literally thrown down the terrace steps, rolling over and over in the descent, till he lay at the foot stunned, bruised and shaken. He picked himself slowly up, muttering curses as he limped away. Little were his curses heeded by the two he had left behind.

Catherine, white, trembling, unnerved by all she had gone through during the past minutes, held out her arms to her husband. "Edward! Oh, Edward!" He clasped her close to his heart, and held her there as if he never meant to let her go. He bent his head over her, and she felt his kisses on her cheek. He did not doubt——he did not distrust her! His strong arms pressed her ever closer and closer. She lay against his chest, feeling no wish ever to leave that shelter. Oh, he was so true and noble——her own loving, faithful husband! How she loved him she never known until that supreme moment. At last she stirred in his arms and lifted her face to his.

"Edward, you must never leave me again," she said. "I cannot bear it——I cannot." "I will not, my dear wife," he answered. "Never again shall aught but death thee and me." she clung to him, half shuddering. "Ah! Do not talk of death, Edward. I cannot bear it——I cannot listen." He pressed a kiss upon her trembling lips. "Does my wife love me now?" he asked very gravely and tenderly. "Let me hear it from your own lips, my Catherine." "Ah, Edward, I love, I love you;" she lifted her eyes to his as she spoke. There was something almost solemn in their deep, earnest gaze. "Edward, I do not think any but your wife could know such a love as mine." "Not your husband?" he asked, returning her look with one equally full of meaning. "Catherine, you may love as well, but I think you cannot love more than I do." She laid her head down again. It was unspeakably sweet to hear him say so, to feel his arms about her, to know that they were united at last, and that nothing could part them now.

"Not even death," said Catherine to herself; "for love like ours is stronger than death." "How came that scoundrel?" asked Edward, somewhat later as they stood together on the terrace, watching the moonlight on the sea. "I think he came to frighten me-perhaps to try and hurt us once more by his wicked words and deeds. Edward is he mad? He looked so dreadful today. He was not the old David I once knew. It was terrible-till you came."

"I believe at times he is mad," answered Edward, "with a sort of madness that is not actual insanity, though somewhat akin to it. It is the madness of ungovernable passion and hatred that rises up in him from time to time against certain individuals, and becomes, as it seems, a sort of monomania with him. It was so with his friend and benefactor Colonel Ferguson, when once he felt himself out. Ever since the horsewhipping I administered to him, I believe he has felt vindictively towards me. Our paths led us wide apart for several years, but as soon as we met again the old enmity rose up once more. He tried to hurt me through my wife." Edward looked down at her with a proud smile upon his handsome face. "I need not say how utterly and miserably he has failed."

Catherine glanced up at him, a world of loving confidence in her eyes;

yet the clinging clasp of her hands tightened upon his arm. He fancied she trembled a little. "What is it, my Catherine?" She pressed a little more closely towards him. "Edward, do you think he will try to hurt you now-try to do you some injury?" The husband smiled reassuringly at her. "Hurt me? How, Catherine?" "Oh, I don't know; but he has spoken such cruel, wicked words. He said he had vowed to ruin our happiness—he looked as if meant it-so vindictive, so terrible!" she shivered a little. He took her hands, and held them in his warm, strong clasp. "Are you afraid of what that bad man says, Catherine—a man who is a coward and a scoundrel of the deepest dye? Are you afraid of idle threats from his lips?

How could he ruin our happiness now?" She looked up at him, still with a vague, undefined trouble in her eyes.

"He might hurt you, Edward," she half whispered. "What hurts you, hurts me. If—if he were to take you away from me—" Edward laid his hand smilingly upon her lips. "My darling, you are unnerved by the fright he gave you. When was Catherine troubled by idle fears before?" "I don't know what I fear, Edward; but I have feelings sometimes-premonitions, presentiments, and I cannot shake them off. Ever since David came, I felt a kind of horror of him, even though I tried to call him friend. Sometimes I think it must mean something." "No doubt it does," answered Edward. It is the natural shrinking of your pure soul from his evil, vicious nature. I can well understand it. It could hardly be otherwise. He could not deceive you long." She looked gravely out before her.

"No, I do not think he really deceived me long not my innermost self of all. But I was very self-willed. I wanted to judge for myself, and I could not judge him rightly. I believe him. I did not want to be unjust-and he deceived me." Edward smiled, and laid his hand caressingly upon her shoulder. She looked up with a smile. "That is right, Catherine. You must put away these sad, wistful looks. We must not let this evening's happiness be marred by any doubts and fears. You have your husband again. Is not that enough?" She turned and laid her head against his shoulder. His arm was fast about her in a moment. She drew a long breath, almost like a sigh. "Edward, I think that moments like this must be a foretaste of heaven." He kissed her, and she added, low and dreamily "Only there, there will be no fear of parting. Death could not part us there."

"Death could not sunder our hearts even here, my Catherine," said

Edward. "Some love is for eternity." "Yes." she answered, looking out over the wide sea with a deep smile that seemed as if it were reading the future in the vast, heaving expanse of moonlit water. "Our love is like that-not for time alone, but for eternity.

He caught the gravity of her mood. Some subtle sympathy drew them ever closer and more close together. "And so," he added gravely and tenderly, "we need fear nothing; for nothing can alter that one great thing. Nothing can change our love. We belong to one another always-always." She stood very still and quiet. "Yes," she said, "for ever and ever. Edward, if we could both die tonight I think it would be a happy thing for us." "Why?" Because then there would be no parting to fear." "And now?" "Now I do fear it. I fear it without knowing why. He will part us if he can." Edward strained his wife close to his heart. "If he can! Catherine, look up; put away these idle fears, my love. Can I not take care of you and of myself? Let us put him for ever out of our lives." "Ah! If only we could!" breathed Catherine.

Chapter 18

A Shadow

The days that followed were very full of happiness and peace for Catherine and her husband. They were alone to together in the dim old Castle, far away from the busy whirl of life they had so gladly left behind, free to be with each other every moment of the flying hours, learning to know and to love one another with a more perfect comprehending love with each succeeding day.

Not one tiny cloud of reserve or distrust dimmed the sunshine of their horizon. Catherine had laid before Edward that unlucky letter of Lady Louise's, had listened with a mingling of delight and indignation to his comments on the composition-delight to hear that he had always loved her from the first, that in gratifying her father's desire he had but been gratifying the dearest desire of his own heart-indignation towards the mischief-making relative, who had tried to deceive and humiliate her, who had told her one half of the story and concealed the other. But indignation was only a momentary feeling. Catherine was too happy to cherish resentment. Her anger was but a passing spark.

"I should like to speak my mind to Lady Louise," remarked Edward, as he tore the paper into small fragments and tossed them over the cliff. "I always distrusted her wisdom, but I did not look for deliberate malice like that. Why did you not show me that letter when it came, Catherine, and let me see what I had to say to it?" She looked up with a smile. "Because I was so foolish and distrustful in those days. I did long to once, but then came the thought suppose it should be true?" At that they both smiled. There was a charm and sweetness in thus discussing the past, with the light of the happy present shining upon it. "But she meant to be your friend, Edward. We must not forget that. I suppose she thought that you would tell me of your love, but that she ought to inform me of your generosity. Poor Aunt Louise! We should get on better now. In those days, Edward, I think I was very difficult——very willful and unapproachable. I used to think it would kill me ever to leave MacAlister. I think now that it would have been the ruin of me to stay. It is not good to grow up in one narrow groove, and to gain no knowledge of anything beyond,"

"That is quite true, Catherine. Does that mean that you will be willing to leave MacAlister by-and-by?" "I shall be willing to do anything that you wish, Edward. You know I would go anywhere with you. Do you want to take me away again?" "Presently I think I do. I should like to take you to Scotland in August, to stay a month or two at my little shooting-box there. You would like the free, roving life you could lead there, amongst that world of heather. And then there are things to be done at MacAlister. Catherine, will you be able to reconcile yourself to changes here?" "Changes?" "Yes. I should like to see MacAlister restored to what it must have been a century ago. The glory has departed of late years, but you have only to look round to see what the place once was. I want to restore that faded glory-not to introduce glaring changes, but to make it something like what it must have been when our ancestors lived there long years ago. Would you like that, Catherine? It would not go against you, would it, to see MacAlister look so? I want it to be worthy of the mistress who will preside there. It is a wish that has haunted me ever since I entered its precincts and met you there."

Catherine was glad to enter into any plan proposed by her husband. She was willing he should restore MacAlister in any way that he wished; but she preferred that he should make his own arrangements about it, and let her only judge by the result. She could not yet enter with any sense of realisation into projects for making the castle other than she had known and judgment, and let him plan and settle everything as he would.

She was ready to leave home whenever he wished it, the more so that David MacRae still occupied a suite of rooms in his half-dismantled house, and hung about the neighbourhood in an aimless and irresponsible fashion. How he spent his time no one seemed to know, but he must have developed roving tendencies, for Catherine was constantly seeing him in unexpected places, down by the rocky shore wandering over the trackless downs, or crouching in the heather or behind a tree, as she and her husband passed along in their daily walks or rides

He never met them face-to-face. He appeared to endeavour always to keep out of sight. Edward, as a matter of fact, seldom saw him, and paid no heed, when he did, to the vindictive scowl upon the yet beautiful face. But Catherine seemed haunted by this persistent watching and waiting. She was ever on the look-out for the crouching figure in some place of concealment, for the glitter of the fierce blue eyes, and the cruel sneer of the pale lips. She felt intensely nervous and timid beneath that sense of espionage; and she was glad when August came, and she was to leave MacAlister and its specter behind. Accounts from Germany were very good. Matthew wrote little pencil notes every week, informing Catherine that he was getting on "like a house on fire," and singing the praises of Bruce, who had stayed so long with him, "like the good fellow he was," and would have remained longer only it really wasn't worth while. "I'm afraid I've been very unjust to Bruce," said Catherine, "I want to tell him so when comes back. May we wait till he does? I want to hear all about Matthew at first hand, as I may not go to see him yet."

So they waited for the return of the traveller. Catherine did sincerely wish to hear about Matthew, but she had something else to report to Bruce as well. She had the greatest confidence in his acuteness and penetration, and could sometimes say to him what she would have despaired of communicating intelligibly to any one else.

There was no difficulty in securing a private interview when once he had come back. Every one knew how anxious Catherine would be to hear every detail of Matthew's present life, so Bruce resigned himself, and told his tale with all possible fullness and accuracy. Catherine listened with an absorbed look upon her face. When he told all, she said simply—

—"Thank you, Bruce, for all your goodness to him. I am very sorry I ever misunderstood you, and said such hard things of and to you. You have got the best of it in the end, by heaping coals of fire upon me."

He smiled slightly. "My dear Catherine, you don't suppose I troubled my head over your Ladyship's righteous wrath. I found it very amusing, I assure you." "I believe did," assented Catherine, smiling in turn; "which made things a little trying for me. Bruce, I believe you have always been my friend, even when we have seemed most bitterly opposed." The sudden earnestness of her manner made him look at her keenly, and spoke without his usual half-mocking intonation.

"I hope so, Catherine. I wish to have the right to call myself your friend. "He looked steadily at her, knowing there was more to follow. She was silent for a time, and then came a sudden and most unexpected question, one apparently quite irrelevant. "Do you know Sir David MacRae?" "I used to know him when he was child. I knew him slightly at oxford. He has made no attempt to renew the acquaintance since he has been down here; and judging by what I have heard, I should not be inclined to encourage him if he did."

"But there would be nothing extraordinary in your visiting him?" "possibly not; but I cannot say I have any wish to try the experiment." "You know his history. Perhaps?––the dark stain." "I heard of it at the time it happened-not from MacAlister, though. It's a sort of story that doesn't make one yearn to renew acquaintance with the hero." For a few moments Catherine sat very still and silent. Then she asked quietly––"Do you think he is the kind of man to be dangerous?" "Dangerous?" "Yes––if he had taken a vow of vengeance. Do you think––? "Well, what?" "Think he would try very hard to accomplish such a vow? Do people never in these days try to do an injury to a man they hate?" Bruce began to understand her vow.

"Well, one cannot lay down hard-and––fast lines; but it is not now customary for a man to attempt the sort of vengeance that he would have done a century or so back. He tries in these days to hurt an enemy morally by injuring his reputation; and I think no one need stand in much awe of MacRae, least of all a man like your husband. It is necessary to possess a reputation of one's own to undermine that of another with much success. MacRae certainly has a reputation, but not the kind that makes him dangerous as an enemy."

Catherine heard this dictum in silence. She did not appear much relieved, and he saw it. "Now you anticipate," he continued, quite quietly and unemotionally, "that he will make a regular attack upon MacAlister one these days?" "I am afraid so sometimes," answered Catherine. "It may be very foolish; but with such an evil look in his eye. Bruce, I sometimes think that he is going mad." The young man's face changed slightly.

"That, of course, would put a new colour on the matter. Have you any reasons upon which to base your suspicions?"

"Nothing that you would perhaps call reasons, but they make me suspicious. Edward spoke of a touch of insanity that he had fancied lurked in his brain. At least, when he hates he seems to hate with a ferocity that suggests the idea of madness. Bruce, if you were to see him, should you know?" Bruce mused a little.

"I might be able to hazard a shrewd guess, perhaps. Why do you want so much to know?" Without answering, Catherine propounded another question. "If he were mad, he would be much more dangerous, would he not?" "Yes and if really dangerous, could be placed under proper control." A look of relief crossed Catherine's face. "Could that be done"?

"Certainly, if absolute madness could be proved. But you know in many cases this is most difficult to establish; and MacRae's independent position it might be exceedingly hard to get the needful evidence." Her face clouded again. "But you will see him, Bruce? You will try to find out?" Hesitated a little. To tell the truth he did not care about the job. He had a hearty contempt for the man himself, did not attach much weight to Catherine's suspicions, and thought her fears far-fetched But her pleading face prevailed.

"Well, Catherine, if you particularly wish it, I will endeavour to meet him, and enter into a speaking acquaintance. I don't promise to force myself upon him if he avoids me pointedly, I will do what I can in a casual sort of way to find out something about him. But it is not all likely he will prove mad enough to be placed under restraint." "I believe he drinks," said Catherine softly. "He used not to, but I believe he does now."

"Well, if he has a screw loose and drinks as well, he may make an end of himself in time. At any rate, if it will relieve your mind, I will find out what I can about him." "Thank you Bruce; I am very much obliged to you; and if you cannot do much, at least you can keep your eye upon him, and let me know how long he stays here. I-I-it may be very foolish; but I don't want Edward to come back till he has gone." Bruce's eyebrows went up. "Then you really are afraid?" She smiled faintly. "I believe I am." "Well, it sounds very absurd; but I have a sort of faith in your premonitions. Anyway, I will keep your words in mind, and do what I can; we will try and get him off the field before you are ready to return to it. I should not think the attractions of the place will hold him long." So Catherine went off to Scotland with a lightened heart; and yet the shadow of the haunting fear did not vanish entirely even in the sunshine of her great happiness.

Chapter 19

In Scotland

"An empty sky and a world of heather." Such was the scene that met Catherine's eye as she stepped out into the clear morning sunshine, and gazed out over the wide expanse of moorland that lay in a kind of purple glory all around her. Edward's shooting-box was situated in a very lonely, yet wonderfully picturesque spot. It seemed as if it had just been dropped down upon its little craggy eminence amid this rolling sea of billowy heather, and had anchored itself without more ado. There was no attempt at park or garden, or enclosed ground of any kind. The moor itself was park and garden in one, and the heather and gorse grew right up to the wide terrace walk upon which south windows of the little house opened. A plantation of pine and fir behind gave protection from the winter winds, and shade from the summer sun; but save for this little wood-an oasis in a blooming desert—the moor stretched away in its wild freedom on every hand, the white road alone, glimpses of which could be seen here and there, seeming to connect it with the great world beyond. MacAlister was lonely and isolated enough, but it almost seemed to Catherine, as she gazed over the sunny moorland that glorious summer morning, as if she had never been so utterly remote from the abode of man as she was today.

There was a step behind her, and a hand was laid upon her shoulder. "Well, Catherine?" She turned to him with lips that quivered as they smiled. "It is all so exquisite, Edward-so perfect. You did not tell me half." "You like it, my Catherine?" "Like it! It seems as if you and I were just alone in the world together." He bent his head and touched her brow with his lips. "And that contents you, Catherine?" She looked up with eloquent eyes. "Need you ask that question now?" He smile expressed an unspeakable happiness; he put his arm about her, saying softly--"There are some questions one never tires of hearing answered, sweet wife. Ah, Catherine! When I think of the past, I feel as if it were almost necessary to have lived through that, to know what such happiness as ours can be. It is the former doubt that makes the present certainty so unutterably sweet. Do you ever feel that yourself, my darling?" He spoke gravely and gently, as they stood together in the golden sunshine. She looked up into his face with deep love and reverence, yet he felt her slight form quiver in his clasp. He looked at her smilingly.

"What is it, Catherine?" "Nothing-only a strange feeling I have sometimes. I know what you mean, Edward. You are quite, quite right-only do not let us today think of the sorrow that went before. Let us be happy with one another."

"We will, my Catherine. You are quite right. This is our bridal holiday, of which circumstances cheated us at the outset, and as such we will enjoy it. Come in to breakfast now; and then we will have the horses out, and you and I will explore our new world together, and forget there is any other before or behind us."

The shadow fled from Catherine's brow, the happy light came back to her eyes, came back and took up its abode there as if never to depart again, what happy, happy days were those that followed! No one invaded the solitude which was such bliss to the two who had sought it; no foot crossed the threshold of the peaceful home that Edward had made ready with such care for the reception of his bride. And yet, as everything must end at last, pleasure as well as pain, joy as well as sorrow, a day came at last when it was needful to leave this happy seclusion, and mingle once again with the busier stream of life that flowed onwards, ever onwards the walls of their retreat.

Engagements had been made before, pledges given to various friends that visits should be paid during that period so dear to the heart of man, "the shooting season." Little enough did Edward care for sport in his present mood; far rather would he have spent longer time alone with his wife in happy isolation; but his friends became urgent, letters persecuted them with increased vehemence, and Catherine, casting away her first reluctance, roused herself to say at last that she thought they ought to go. "We shall be together still, Edward" she said, with a little laugh. "It is not as if we should not have one another. No one can separate us now, and we ought to be able to be happy anywhere together." And yet, when the time came, it was very hard to go. Edward came upon Catherine the last evening at sunset, watching the glorious pageantry of the sky, with something of old wistfulness upon her face. "You are sorry to be leaving then, Catherine?" She started, and turned to him, almost as if for protection.

"Yes, I am sorry. We have been so very, very happy here. Edward, is it very foolish? Sometimes I feel as if such happiness were too great for this world-as if it could not go on always so. It seems almost too beautiful, too perfect. Do you ever feel the same?" "I know what you mean, sweet wife. Yet I am not afraid of our happiness or of the future. It is love that brings the brightness with it, and I think nothing now can change our love."

Ah, no, no" she cried impetuously; "nothing can change that. You always understand. Edward, you are so strong, so good, so patient. Ah! What should I do without you now?" "You have not got to do without me, Catherine. A husband cannot be set aside by any one or anything. You must not let nervous fears get the better of you. Tell me, is anything troubling you tonight?"

"No, no; only that the old feeling will sometimes come back. It is foolish, I know; but I cannot quite rid myself of it." "The old feeling?"

"Yes, that some trouble is coming upon me-upon us. I cannot explain; but I feel it sometimes––I feel as if it were coming nearer." He did not laugh at her fears. He only said, very gently and tenderly––

"I pray God, my sweet wife, that trouble may be very far away from you; yet if it come, I know it will be bravely, nobly borne, and that the furnace of sorrow will only bring out the gold more bright and pure."

She glanced at him, and then over the purple moorlands and into the glorious western sky. A look of deep, settled purpose shone out of her eyes, and her face grew calm and resolute. She thought of that moment often in days to come, and of her husband's words, It was a recollection always fraught with much of strengthening comfort. The round of inevitable visits to be paid proved less irksome than Catherine had anticipated.

Edward's friends were agreeable, well-bred people, with whom it was easy to get on, and to make things more pleasant for Catherine, Rebecca Scott and her brother were not infrequently numbered among the house party they were invited to meet. Both the young earl and his sister were devoted to Catherine, and their presence added much to her enjoyment of the different visits that they paid together. Lord Charles MacMurray was her constant attendant wherever her husband could not be with her, and his frank, boyish homage was accepted in the spirit in which it was offered. Catherine, though much admired and liked, was not "popular" in the ordinary sense of the term. She did not and liked, was not "popular" in the ordinary sense of the term. She did not attract round her a crowd of amused admirers, as Rebecca did, and most young men, however much they might admire her stately beauty, found her somewhat difficult to get on with. With elderly people she was more at ease and a great favourite from her gentleness and peculiar refinement of thought and manner; but for the most part, during the happy doings of the day, she was left to the attendance of Edward or MacMurray, and no arrangement could have been to her own liking. Yet once trifling incident occurred to disturb her peace of mind, although she thought she possibly dwelt upon it more than the circumstance warranted. She was at a large luncheon party, to which her hostess and guests had alike been invited to meet many other parties from surrounding houses.

A grand battue in the park had drawn away most of the sportsmen, and ladies were lunching almost by themselves. Catherine's surprise was somewhat great to find in her right-hand neighbour none other than Mary MacFie, with whom her last interview had been anything but agreeable.

Mrs. MacFie, however seemed to have forgotten all about that. "It is really you, Catherine. I hoped I should meet you somewhere; I heard you were staying about; I know I've behaved badly. I ought to have written to you when your father died. I was awfully sorry, I was indeed. We were always fond of the Earl, David and I. He was so good to us when we were children. It was horrid of me not to write a letter of condolence. I hope you're not very angry with me."

"Indeed, no," answered Catherine. "Indeed, I never thought about it." "I knew you wouldn't care to hear from me," pursued the lively little woman. "I didn't behave nicely to you, Catherine, and I've repented of listening to David's persuasions; but I'm so easy-going, I thought it all fun. I'm sorry now, I really am, for I've got shaken in my confidence in Master David. I believe he'll go to the dogs still, all his professions. By-the-bye, did you ever see him after you got back to MacAlister?" "Once or twice. I believe he was living in his house down there." "That dreadful old barn! I can't think how he can exist there. He will take to drink, and go mad, I do believe, if he stays six months in such a place. Catherine, I don't want to frighten you——I may be silly to think such a thing, but I can't believe he's after any good there." Catherine shivered a little instinctively. "What do you mean?" "I don't quite know what I do mean. If you weren't such a old friend, of course I couldn't say a word; but you know perhaps that there's something rather odd sometimes about David."

"Odd?" "Yes——I know he's always bad enough; it's when he had his odd fits on that he's worse. I don't believe he is always altogether responsible. He's given way, and now he can't always help himself, I do think. He isn't mad, of course, but he can be very wild at times," and she glanced at her companion with something of significance. "Why do you say all this to me?" asked Catherine, with a sort of apprehension. Mrs. MacFie laughed a little. "Why can't you see? Don't you know how he hates your husband?" Catherine's face blanched a little. "But you don't mean——" No, no, of course not," with a short laugh that had little of mirth in it. "I don't mean anything only I think, if ever David is lurking about in his wild moods, that Lord MacAlister had better keep a sharp look out. Your woods and cliffs are nasty lonely places, and its always well to be on the safe side".

Catherine sat pale and silent; Mrs. MacFie laughed again in that half-uneasy way. "Now, don't look like that, and keep your own counsel. I'm a silly woman, as you know, and nobody minds what I say, but I can't be quite comfortable without just warning you. For mischief is sometimes done in a moment between two angry men that never can be undone so long as the world lasts. Now don't go and get frightened, Catherine it may be all a ridiculous fancy; but just keep your eyes open. "Open." "Thank you, MacFie," said Catherine quietly. "I will."

Chapter 20

A visit to Matthew

"Are you getting tired of this sort of thing, Catherine?" asked Edward, about three days later. He had fancied he detected traces of weariness at times-weariness or anxiety, he could hardly have told which—in the lines of her face; and he thought that possibly some trouble was resting upon her. He was very quick to note the least change in one he loved so well.

Her smile, however, was very re-assuring. "I think I should never be really tired of any life you shared, Edward; but I like being alone together best."

"I, too," he responded, with great sincerity. "Catherine, as we have done our duty by society now, shall we indulge ourselves once more, leave the world to wag on its own way, and forget it again for a few more happy weeks?" Her face was bright and eager. "Go back to the moorland shooting-box, Edward?" "No; not that quite. The season is getting a little late for remaining up in the North. I have a better plan in my head for you."

"Are we going back to MacAlister, then?" "MacAlister is not ready for us; it will be some time before it is. Can you think of nothing else you would like to do?——of nobody you want to see?" A flush rose suddenly into Catherine's face: her eyes shone with happiness.

"Oh, Edward! Are you going to take me to see Matthew?" "You would like to go?" "Above everything." Then the thing is done. We will start next week. I talked about it to the doctor when I saw him, and he advised three months of entire quiet and seclusion whilst he settled down to the new life. After that, he believed there would be no reason at all against his seeing friends from home. I wrote again last week to put the question definitely, and the answer is entirely satisfactory. If you want to go, Catherine, the matter is settled." She came close up to him, clasping her hands upon his shoulder, and looking up with loving gratitude and delight.

"You think of everything, Edward. You are so good to me. It is just the the one thing to make my happiness complete: to see my boy again, and make sure with my own eyes that he is well cared for and content with his life. I want to be able to picture him where he is. I want to hear him say that he is happy: that he does not pine after MacAlister."

"I think you will have your wish, Catherine, for, from what I can gather, he is very pleased with his quarters, and improved health makes life pleasant and full of zest. He has the natural love of change that you never knew, and your inherited love for your old home is not really shared by him to any great extent now that he has tried another life. MacAlister is not woven into the very fibres of his heart as into yours. I think the home-sickness passed off quickly with him."

"Yes, I daresay. I believe I was foolish myself about MacAlister, and taught him to be foolish too. Why is it that the younger we are, and the less we know, the more we are convinced we are always right? I have made so many, many mistakes. Once I thought you did not love me, Edward." It was sweet to him still to hear her speak thus, with the intonation that always thrilled him through with the look upon her so much more eloquent then any words. It was sweet to fell her loving confidence and dependence. Again and again he vowed deep down in his heart that she should never know a trouble from which he could save her.

The journey was approved by both. It would take them away once again from the round of social duties and pleasures-of which for the time being they had had enough-and leave them practically alone together, to be all in all to one another, as was now their greatest happiness. "It is too bad of you to run away, Catherine," Rebecca grumbled, when she heard the news. "Your brother can't want you more than we do here. And if you go, you'll vanish no one knows for how long, as you did before, and then you will go and bury yourselves in your enchanted castle away by the sea, and nobody will hear of you anymore. I call it too bad: just as we were getting to be friends and learning to know you."

Catherine smiled at the imputation of vanishing so entirely. "You shall hear of us sometimes, I promise you," she answered. "And if you and your brother will not find the 'enchanted castle' too dull, I hope you will come and see us there when we go back in the autumn. There are not a great many attractions, I am afraid, but there is some shooting and hunting. I should like to show you MacAlister some day, Rebecca, though I believe it will be good deal changed from the place I have sometimes described to you.

"It is sure to be perfect, whatever it is like," was the quick response. "I should think we would come MacMurray and I—if ever we get an invitation. I always did long to see MacAlister, and I am sure he does the same, though he is no hand at pretty speeches, poor old boy!" MacMurray smiled, and coloured a little, but answered frankly enough,

"Lady MacAlister does not want pretty speeches, as you call it, made to her, Rebecca. She knows quite well what a pleasure it would be to visit her and Edward at MacAlister." "I should like my husband's oldest friends to see the place," she answered, smiling. "So we will call the matter settled when we really do get home; though I do not quite know when that will be." Next day Edward and Catherine said good-bye to Scotland, and began their journey southward. They were in no great haste, and travelled by easy stages. Matthew was to be told nothing of the prospective visit, which was to be kept as a surprise till the last moment. Catherine was never a very good correspondent, even where Matthew was concerned, and if she posted a letter to him, last thing before leaving England, he would not be surprised at a silence of a fortnight or more, by which time at latest she would be with him.

So they took their time over their journey, and the strangeness of all she saw possessed a curious charm for Catherine, when viewed beneath her husband's protecting care, and in his company. He took her to a few quaint Norman towns, with their fine old churches and picturesque streets and market-places; then to Paris, where a few days were passed in seeing the sights, and watching the vivid, hurrying, glittering life of that happy capital. Steering an erratic course turning this way and that to visit any place of interest, or any romantic spot that Edward thought would please his wife, they approached their destination, and presently reached the pretty, picturesque little town, hardly more than a village, which was only just rising to springs lately discovered.

One good-sized hotel and the doctor's establishment, both of which stood at the same end of the village, and a little distance from it, testified to the rising importance of the place. Edward had secured comfortable rooms in the hotel, where they arrived late one evening.

Catherine liked the place; it was not in the least like what she had pictured, far more pretty, more primitive, and more country-like. Wooded hills surrounded the valley in which it lay. A broad rapid stream ran through it, spanned by more than one grey stone bridge, and the irregularly-built village was quite a picture in its way, with its quaint old houses, with their carved gables and little wooden balconies, the spire of its church rising above the surrounding trees. Viewed by moonlight, as she saw it first, it was a charming spot; and the charm did not vanish with the more prosaic light of day.

The interview with the doctor was most satisfactory. He was a kindly, simple-minded man, much interested in his patient from a professional standpoint, and of the lad for his own sake. Catherine's beauty and sweetness were evidently not lost upon him. He heard much of her from the young Herr, he explained and could understand well the feelings he had so often heard expressed. No, the invalid had not been told of the expected arrival. He did not know but that Lord and Lady MacAlister were in England. Did the noble Lady wish to go to him? He would honour himself by leading the way.

Catherine followed him with a beating heart. The went up a wide carpetless staircase, and on the first landing her guide paused, and indicated a certain door. "He is up; madam can go straight in. A joyful surprise will but do him good." Catherine turned the handle, and entered, as quietly and calmly as if this had been the daily visit to the old room at MacAlister. Matthew was lying with his back to the door. He was reading, and did not turn his head, fancying it was the servant entering, as he heard the rustle of a dress. Catherine came and stood behind him, laying her hand upon his head.

"Matthew!" she said softly. Then he started as if he had been shot. He sat up with an energy that showed a decided increase of strength, holding out his hands in eager welcome, Catherine! Catherine!" he cried, in a sort of rapturous excitement. It is Catherine herself!" She bent over him and kissed him again, and again and would have made him lie down again; but was too excited to obey.

"Catherine! My own Catherine! When did you come? What does it all mean? Oh, this is too splendid! Where's Edward?" "Here," answered the familiar voice, just within the door. "Well, my boy, how are you getting on? Like a house on fire, eh? Catherine and I are on our wedding trip, you know. We thought we would finish it off by coming to have a look at you. Well, you look pretty comfortable up here, and have made fine progress, I hear, since I saw you last. Like everything as much as you make out in your letters, eh?"

"Oh! I'm all right enough. Never mind me. Tell me about yourselves. Whose idea was this? I call it just splendid!" "Edward's idea, answered Catherine. "All the good ideas are his now, Matthew. We have come to stay a whole fortnight with you; and when I have seen everything with my own eyes, and am quite convinced that everybody is treating you well, I shall go home content to MacAlister, to wait till you can join us there."

"I mustn't think of that just yet," answered Matthew, cheerfully. "My old doctor says it will be a year perhaps two-before I shall really be on my legs again; but he is quite sure he going to cure me, which is all that matters. I am awfully comfortable here, and there are jolly little children of his, who come and amuse me by the hour together. Oh yes! I have capital times. I couldn't be more comfortable anywhere; and if you and Edward come sometimes to see me, I shall have nothing left to wish for."

Certainly Matthew was surrounded by every luxury that wealth could bestow. There was none of the foreign bareness about his rooms that characterised its other apartments. Edward had ordered everything that could possibly add to his comfort, and make things home-like for him, even to the open fire place, and in cold weather did valuable service in keeping an even temperature in the room.

Matthew's visitors had made him gradually understand how much more sumptuously he was lodged than others patients, and he well knew to whom he owed the luxuries he enjoyed. He explained all this to Catherine, and in her own sweet way she thanked her husband for his tenderness towards her boy. "Always feel as if Matthew were a sort of link between us, Catherine," he said. I am sure he was in those old days, when we were strangers to each other. I owe him a great deal that he knows nothing about. Were it only for that, I must always love him, and feel towards him as towards a brother." Quickly and happily the days slipped by, and the pleasant visit drew to its close. It lengthened out into nearly three weeks; but at last the news came that MacAlister was ready for its master and mistress, and Matthew bid a brave farewell to those who had done so much for him, and settled himself with cheerful readiness to his winter with his new friends. A visit next spring and summer was confidently promised and he saw his guest go with an unselfish brightness that was in no way assumed.

Catherine was quite happy about him now, and though the parting was a little hard, she was as brave as he. She turned her face homeward with a light heart. Only one little cloud of anxiety lay upon her heart. What was David MacRae doing? Was he still lurking about MacAlister? Even that question was destined to be answered in a satisfactory manner before many days had passed. They travelled rapidly homewards, as the season was advancing, and they were anxious to be once more at MacAlister.

They were in a train, which had stopped at some station, when another train from an opposite direction steamed up and also stopped. Catherine, leaning back in her corner seat, noticed nothing for a time, but was roused to the consciousness that she was being intently regarded by a passenger in the opposite train, whose face was pressed close against the glass. For some seconds she resisted the impulse to look; but as she felt the glance withdrawn, she presently turned her eyes in the direction of the half-seen face, and then she started violently. David MacRae, his face pale and sharp, wearing a frightfully malevolent expression was gazing or rather glaring, at her husband, with eyes like those of a wild beast, in their fiery, hungry hate. Edward, seated opposite her, reading the paper, was perfectly unconscious of the proximity of his foe; but Catherine recoiled with a feeling of horror she could hardly have explained. The next moment the train had moved on. At least, it was some comfort to know that they were being rapidly carried in opposite directions. Yet it was long before she could forget the vindictive hatred of the gaze she had seen directed towards her husband. Would David MacRae ever do him the deadly injury he had vowed?

Chapter 21

Back At MacAlister

"Edward! Can this really be MacAlister?" The young countess stood in all her radiant loveliness upon the threshold of her old home, and turned her happy face towards the husband who stood beside her, watching with a smile in his eyes for the effect to be produced by his labour of love.

"Can this really be MacAlister?" You seem destined never to know your old home again when you have been banished from it, Catherine," he answered, smiling. "Well, is it as much changed as you expected?" "It is perfect," said Catherine simply; adding, after another long look round her——"if only my father could have seen this-could have lived to witness the realisation of his dream!"

But he would not let her indulge one sad thought that should cloud the brightness of this happy home coming. He kissed her gently in token of his sympathy, and then drew her towards the blazing fire, whose dancing flames were illuminating the great hall. "Does it realise your dream too, my Catherine?" he asked softly. She looked up in his face, deep feeling welling up in the glance of her soft dark eyes. "To be with you is my dream, Edward. That is enough for me."

He saw that she was moved, and knew that the associations of MacAlister, the old home, were crowding upon her. Without speaking, he led her towards a door, which in old days led to a room vast and empty, save for the odds and ends of lumber that gradually accumulated there. Catherine glanced up in questioning surprise as he turned the handle. Why was he taking her there?

She paused on the threshold, and looked about her in mute amaze. The floor was of polished parquetry work; the panelled walls, quaintly and curiously carved, shone with the care that had been bestowed upon them; the vaulted roof had been carefully restored, and was a fine specimen of mediaeval skill and beauty. The mullioned window to the west had been filled with rich stained glass, that gave back a dusky glimmer through its tinted panes, though the daylight was failing fast. Near to the window stood the one great feature of the room, an organ, which Catherine's eyes saw at once was a particularly fine and perfect instrument. An organ of her very own! It was just like Edward to think of it! She gave him one sweet glance of gratitude, and went up to it in the dim, dusky twilight.

"How good you are to me!" she said softly. He heard the little quiver in her voice, and bent his head to kiss her; but he spoke in a lighter tone. "Do you like it? I am so glad! I thought your home ought not to be without its music-room. See, Catherine, your organ will be a sort of friend to whom you can confide all your secrets: for you want nobody to blow it for you. You can set the bellows at work by just turning this handle, and nobody need disturb your solitude when you want to be alone." She looked up gratefully. He never forgot anything-not even her old love for solitude. "I never want to be alone now Edward," she said. "I always want you." "And you generally have me, sweet wife. I think we have hardly been separated for more than a few hours at a time since that happy, happy day that made you really mine." "I want it always to be like that," said Catherine, dreamily; "always like that." He looked at her, and carried the hand that he held to his lips.

"Will you play, Catherine?" She sat down and struck a few dreamy chords, gradually leading up to the theme that was in her mind. Edward leaned against the mullioned window-frame and watched her. He could see, even in the darkness, the pure, pale outline of her perfect profile, and the crown of her golden hair that framed her face like an aureole. "Another dream realised, Catherine," he said softly, as she turned to him at length. "What dream, Edward?" "A dream that came to me once, in the little cliff church where we were married, as I watched you little as you knew it-sitting at the organ, and playing to yourself, one sunny afternoon. But this is better than any dream of pictured saint or spirit my Catherine, my own true wife."

She looked up at him, and came and put her arms about his neck-an unusual demonstration, even now, for her, and they stood very close together in the gathering darkness that was not dark to them. Catherine paid an early visit to St. Maws to see her friends, and to confide to Mrs. Pendrill a little of the wonderful happiness that had flooded her life with sunshine. Then, too, she wanted to see Bruce, and to ask him the result of the mission he had half promised to undertake. So far she had learned nothing save that MacRae had not been seen near MacAlister for many weeks, and was supposed to have gone abroad.

"Did you see him, Bruce?" she asked, when she had found the opportunity she desired. "Yes, once or twice. I had a good look him, I should not call him exactly mad, though in a decidedly peculiar mental state. We merely met, as it were, by chance, and talked on indifferent subjects for the most part. Once he asked me, in a sort of veiled way, for professional advice, describing certain unpleasant symptoms and sensations. I advised him to give up the use of spirits, and to try what travelling would do for him. He seemed to think he would take my advice, and shortly afterwards he disappeared from the neighourhood; but where he has gone I do not know."

Catherine knew that this advice had been followed. "He may go anywhere he likes, if he will only keep away from hear," she said. "I am very much obliged to you, Bruce, for doing as I asked." "Pray don't mention it." "I must mention it, because it was very good of you. Bruce, will you come and stay at MacAlister next week? We have one or two people coming for the pheasants, and we want you to make one of the party, if you will."

"Oh, very well; anything to please. I have had no shooting worth speaking of so far. I should like a week's holiday very well." So that matter was speedily and easily arranged. Bruce did not ask who were the guests he was to meet, and Catherine did not think of naming such entire strangers, Lord MacMurray and Lady Rebecca Scott. She forgot that Bruce and the young Earl had met once before on a different occasion. Those two were to be the first guests. Perhaps later on they would ask more, but Catherine was too entirely happy in her present life to wish it in any way disturbed, and Edward by no means cared to be obliged to give up guests those happy hours that heretofore he had always spent with Catherine. But Rebecca and her brother had already been invited. They were his oldest friends, and were Catherine's friends too. She was glad to welcome them to her home, and the rapturous admiration that its beauties elicited would have satisfied a more exacting nature than hers.

Rebecca was, as usual, radiant, bewitching, and delightful. Catherine wished that Bruce had come in time to see her arrival, and listen to her sparkling flow of talk. Bruce professed to be a woman-hater, or next door to it but she thought that even he would have to make an exception in favour of Lady Rebecca Scott. She went upstairs with her guest to her room at length, when Rebecca suddenly turned towards her, with quite a new expression upon her face. "Catherine," she said, looking straight into her eyes, "you are changed-you are different from what you were in London-different even from what you were in Scotland, though I saw a change then. I don't know how to express it, but you are beatified glorified. What is it? What has changed you since I first knew you?"

Catherine knew right well; but some feelings could not be translated into words. "I am very happy," she said quietly. "If there is any change, that must be the cause." "Happier than you have ever been before?" "Yes; I think every week makes me happier. I learn to know my husband better and better, you see." A sudden wistful sadness flashed into the eyes so steadily regarding her. Catherine saw it before it had been blotted out by the arch drollery of the look that immediately succeeded.

"And it does not wear off, Catherine? Sometimes it does, you know-after a time. Will it ever, in your case, do think." "I think not," she answered. "And I think too," answered Rebecca. "Ah me! How happy some people are!" She laughed, but there was something of bitterness in the tone. Catherine looked at her seriously. "Are you not happy Rebecca?" The girl's audacious smile beamed out over her face. "Don't I look so?" "Sometimes-not always."

One must have variety before all things, you know," was the happy answer. "It would never do to be always in the same style––it lacks piquancy after a time. Now let me have time to beautify myself in harmony with this most charming of old places, and come back for me when you are dressed; I feel as if I should lose my way, or see bogies in these delightful corridors and staircases." So Catherine left her guest as desired, coming back half-an-hour later, to find her transformed into the semblance of some pictured dame of a century or two gone by, in stiff amber brocade, quaintly cut about the neck and sleeves, and relieved here and there by dazzling scarlet blossoms. Rebecca never at any time looked like anybody else, but tonight she was particularly, strikingly original.

"Ah, you black-robed queen, you will just do as a foil for me!" was the greeting Catherine received. "Whenever I see you in any garb, no matter what it is, I always think it is just the one that suits you best of everything. Are you having a dinner-party tonight?" "Not exactly. A few men are coming, who have asked Edward to shoot since we came back. You and I are the only ladies." And then they went down to the empty drawing room a good half-hour before any one else was likely to appear.

Rebecca chatted away very brightly. She seemed in happy spirits, and had a great deal to tell of what had passed since their farewell in Scotland a mouth or two ago. She moved about the drawing-room, examining the various treasures it contained, and admiring the beauty of the pictures. She was standing half concealed by the curtains draping a recessed window, when the door opened, admitting Bruce Pendrill. He was in dinner dress, having arrived about an hour previously. "You have come then, Bruce," said Catherine. "I am glad. I was afraid you meant to desert us after all."

The wish being further from the thought, I presume," answered Bruce, shaking hands. "By the by, here is a––letter from Matthew's doctor I've brought to show you. He gives a capital account of his patient. Can you read German writing, or shall I construe? He writes about as crabbedly as––" And here Bruce stopped short, seeing that Catherine was not alone. "I beg your pardon," he added, drawing himself up with ceremoniousness quite unusual with him. "Not at all," answered Catherine, quietly." Let me introduce you to Lady Rebecca Scott-Mr. Bruce Pendrill."

They exchanged bows very distantly. Catherine became suddenly aware, in some subtle, inexplicable fashion, that these two were not strangers to one another that this was not their first meeting. Moreover, it appeared as if their former acquaintance, such as it was, could have been by no means agreeable to either, for it was easy to see that a covert antagonism existed between them which neither of them took over much pains to conceal. Bruce's face assumed its most sharply cynical expression, as he drew at once into his hardest shell of distant reserve and sarcastic politeness. Rebecca opened her feather fan, and wielded it with a sort of aggressive negligence. She dropped into a seat beside Catherine, and began to talk to her with an air of studied affectation utterly at variance with her ordinary manner, ignoring Bruce as entirely as if no introduction had passed between them, and that with an assumption of hauteur that could only be explained by a deeply-seated antipathy.

Catherine tried to include Bruce in the conversation; but he declined to be included, returned an indifferent answer, and withdrew to a distant corner of the room, where he remained deeply engrossed, as it seemed, in the study of a photographic album. Catherine was perplexed. She could not imagine what it all meant. She had never heard the Pendrills speak of Lady Rebecca Scott, and she was sufficiently acquainted with Bruce's history to render her perplexity the greater. She was certain Mrs. Pendrill had heard the name of her expected guest, and it had aroused no emotion in her. Yet she would presumably know the name of a Lady towards whom her nephew cherished so great an antipathy. Catherine could not make it out. But one thing was plain enough: those two were sworn foes, and intended to remain so-and they were guests beneath the same roof.

Chapter 22

An Enigma

It was a relief when the other men came in, and when dinner was announced. Edward evidently knew nothing of any disturbing element in the party as he handed Rebecca in to dinner, and again made an attempt to introduce her to Bruce, who was seated opposite, not knowing that Catherine had already had an opportunity of performing that little ceremony. "You are two of my oldest friends, you know," said their host, in his pleasant, easy fashion, "and you are both my guest now, so you will have a capital opportunity of expatiating together upon my many perfections."

"No need for that, Edward," answered Rebecca, happily. "They speak too loud for themselves, and your wife's eyes tell too many tales of them. You know I never could bear paragons. If you turn into one, I shall have more to say to you." "You are very cutting, Rebecca; almost as much so as Bruce here. It is really rather a trying position to be hedged in between a clever woman and a clever man."

"If you call me a clever woman again, Edward, I'll never forgive you. I abominate the whole race!" cried Rebecca, hotly; "and as for clever men––I detest them!" This was said so heartily as elicit a guffaw of laughter from a ruddy-face young gentleman of sporting tastes, who was her neighbour on the other side. She turned to him with one of her most sparkling glances.

"Now you. I am quite certain, agree with me. Your face tells me you do. Don't you think that it is the clever people who make the world an intolerable place?" "They're the greatest nuisance out," assented that young gentleman, cordially. "I always did say so. I was never clever. I was plucked three times, I think, for my little-go."

"Then you and I are sure to be great friends," said Rebecca, laughing. "I am quite, quite sure I should never have passed any examination if I had been a man. I was at oxford once, long ago; and oh! You know, the only men that were any good at all were those who had been 'plucked,' as they call it, or fully expected to be clever, good, precocious boys were-oh! Well, let us not think of them. It takes away one's appetite!" The sporting gentleman laughed, and enjoyed this summary verdict; but Edward just glanced across at his wife. He too was aware that there was something odd in Rebecca's manner. He detected the covert vein of bitterness in her tone; and he was as much at a loss to understand it as Catherine had been. Bruce's face and his impenetrable silence puzzled him likewise.

Dinner, however, passed smoothly enough. Rebecca was very lively, and her witticisms kept all the table alive. Her young neighbour lost his heart to her at once, and she flirted with him in the most frank and open fashion possible. She could be very fascinating when she chose, and tonight, after the first adge had been taken off sallies, she was undoubtedly, exceedingly attractive.

If there was something a little forced in her mirth, at least nobody detected it, save those who knew her very well, and not even all of those, for MacMurray was obviously unconscious that anything was wrong, and talked to Catherine in the most unconcerned fashion possible. What Bruce thought of all it all nobody could hazard an opinion. At length Catherine gave the signal to her animated guest, and they two withdrew together. Rebecca laughed happily, as she half walked half waltzed across the hall, humming a dance turned the while.

"What a lovely place this would be for a dance!" she exclaimed, "a masked, or, better still, a fancy dress ball. Shouldn't we look charming in these panelled rooms, flitting about this great baronial hall, and up and down that delightful staircase? Catherine, you and Edward mustn't get lazy; you must live up to your house. It is too beautiful to be wasted. If you don't know how to manage matters, I must come and teach you!"

And so she rattled on, first on one theme, and then on another, in restless, aimless fashion, as people do who are talking against time, or talking with a purpose, determined not to let silence fall between them and their companions. It was easy to see that Rebecca wished to avoid any confidential conversation wished to escape from any kind of questioning, or from quiet talk, of whatever description it might be. When at length she did let Catherine go back to the drawing-room, it was not any idea of silence. She went straight to the piano, and began playing stormily.

Presently, after dashing off fragments, vocal and instrumental, in a confused medley, Catherine growing dreamy as she listened to the succession of changing harmonies, she began once again with more of purpose and passion in her voice——indeed, there was so much of pain and passion, that Catherine was aroused to listen.

Smile's.

"There are smiles that make us happy there are smiles that make us blue there are smiles that see away the teardrop's as the sun beats through the morning dew. There are smiles that have a tender meaning that the eyes of love alone may seem and the smiles that my heart with sunshine are the smiles that you gave to me. There are smiles that have a tender feeling the eyes of love alone can see and the smiles that fill my heart with sunshine are the smiles, smiles, smiles that you gave me."

And then the singer's voice failed utterly; a dismal discordant chord broke the eager harmonies that had followed one another so rapidly. Rebecca broke into a sudden of tears, and hurried from the room without a word.

Catherine sat aghast and bewildered. What could it all mean? Was she by chance to come upon the secret sorrow of Rebecca's life?——the sorrow she had half suspected sometimes, but had never heard in any way explained. Was it to be explained to her now? Was Bruce Pendrill connected with that sorrow? If so, what part had he taken? Could they ever have been lovers? Did she not remember, long ago, hearing something of a suspicion on Mrs. Pendrill's part that Bruce had been "jilted" by the woman he loved? Was there not a time, long ago, when he was not the reserved, cynical man he affected now to be; but was genial, brilliant, the pleasantest of companions? Yes, Catherine was sure of it-was certain that he had changed, and changed somewhat suddenly, many years since; but she had paid but little heed to the matter then, as it was about that time when every faculty was absorbed in watching over Matthew, who long lay hovering between life and death. Changes after that passed almost unheeded. Had not her whole life been changed too?

She did not follow Rebecca, however, to try and comfort her, or attempt to force her confidence. She treated her as she would wish herself to be treated in similar case; and shortly after the gentlemen had joined them, had the satisfaction of seeing Rebecca come back as brilliant and full of vivacity as ever, and there was no need after her appearance, to wonder how the evening should be passed, it seemed quite sufficient entertainment for the company to sit in a circle round her, and hear Rebecca talk. Bruce Pendrill was the one exception. He did not attempt to join the magic ring. He took Catherine a little apart, and talked over with her the latest news from Germany.

When the guest had departed, and Rebecca, as well as her brother and Catherine, had gone upstairs, Bruce turned his face towards Edward with its hardest and most cynical look. "Tell you what, MacAlister, don't you ask that poor young fellow Stewart here again, so long as that arrant flirt is a guest under your roof." Edward simply smiled. "The 'arrant flirt,' as you are polite enough to call my guest, is one of my oldest friends. Kindly keep that fact in mind in talking of her to me." "I am not talking of her. I am talking of poor young Stewart." "It seems to me that poor young Stewart, as you call him, is very well able to take care of himself." "Oh, you think that, do you? Shows how much you know! Can't you see she was doing her very best to enslave his fancy, and that he was falling under the spell as fast as ever he could?"

"Oh! Nonsense!" answered Edward; "they were just exchanging a little of the current coin that is constantly passing in a happy society. Young Stewart is not a green-horn. They understand their game perfectly." "She does, of course-no one better; but it's a question if he does." "Well, he's a greater fool than he looks, he does not!" answered Edward. "Does he expect a girl like Rebecca Scott to be enslaved by his charms in the course of a few hours? The thing's a manifest absurdity!" "Possibly; but that woman can make a man think anything." Edward looked at his friend with some attention. "You seem to have formed very exhaustive conclusions about Lady Rebecca Scott." It almost seemed as if Bruce coloured a little as he turned impatiently away. Next day Rebecca appeared to have regained her even flow of spirits. She met Bruce at breakfast as she would meet any quest under the same roof, and neither courted nor avoided him in any way. He seemed to take his cue from her; but his face still wore the thin-lipped cynical expression that betrayed a certain amount of subdued irritation. However, sport was the all-prevailing topic of the hour, and as soon as breakfast was concluded, the men departed, with the dogs and keepers in their wake.

"What would you like to do, Rebecca?" asked Catherine when the sportsmen had disappeared. "We have the whole day before us." "Like to do? why, everything must be delightful in this lovely out-of-the-world place. Catherine, no wonder you are just yourself-not one bit like any one else-brought up here with only the sea, and the clouds, and the sunshine for companions and playmates. I used to look at you in a sort of wonder, but I understand it all now. You ought always to live at MacAlister-never anywhere else. What should I like to do? Why, anything. Suppose we ride. I should love to gallop along the cliffs with you. I want to see the strange little church Lord MacMurray described to me, where you were married, and the picturesque little town where——where Edward and he put on the eve of that day. I want to see everything that belongs to your past life, Catherine. It interests me more than I can express."

Catherine smiled in her tranquil fashion. "Very well; you shall gratify your wish. I will order the horses at once. If we go to St. Maws, I ought to go and see Aunt Jennifer-Mrs. Pendrill that is, aunt to Matthew, and to Bruce Pendrill and his brother. She is sure to want us to stay to luncheon with her if we do. She will be all alone; Bruce here, and Johnathon on his rounds. Would you dislike that, Rebecca? She is a sweet old Lady, and seems more a part of my past life than anything else I can show you, though I could not perhaps explain why." A curious light shone in Rebecca's eyes. "Dislike it! I should like it above everything. I love old ladies. They are so much more interesting than young ones. I often wish I were old myself-not middle-aged, you know, but really old, with lovely white hair, and a waxen face all over tiny wrinkles, like my own grandmother——the most beautiful woman without exception that I ever saw. Yes, Catherine, let us do that. It will be delightful. Why did you never mention the Pendrills to me before?"

She put the question with studied carelessness. Yet Catherine was certain it was asked with effort. "Did I not? I thought I used to tell you so much about my past life." "So you did; but I never heard that name." "You knew Matthew was a Pendrill"? "Indeed I did not, He was always Matthew to you. I wonder I never asked his surname; but somehow I never did. I had a vague idea that some such people as these Pendrills existed; but I never heard you name them." "Perhaps you heard, and forgot it? Suggested Catherine tentatively. "That I am sure I never did," was the very emphatic answer.

Rebecca was delighted with her morning's ride. It was a beautiful autumn day, and everything was looking its best. The sea flashed and sparkled in the sunlight; the sky was clear and soft above them; the horses, delighted to feel the soft turf beneath their feet, pranced and curveted and galloped, with that easy elastic motion that is so peculiarly exhilarating. The girl herself looked peculiarly and vividly beautiful, and Catherine was not surprised at the affectionate interest Mrs. Pendrill evinced in her from the first moment of introduction.

But she was a little surprised at the peculiar sweetness of Rebecca's demeanour towards the old Lady. Whilst retaining all her arch brightness and vivacity, the girl managed to infuse into her manner, her voice, and her words something gentle and deferential and winning that was inexplicably fascinating; all the more so from its evident unconscious sincerity. Mrs. Pendrill was charmed with the beauty and sweetness of the girl, and it seemed as if Rebecca on her side was equally fascinated. When the time came to say good-bye, and the old Lady held both her hands, and gazed into her bright face, as she ask for another visit very soon, she stooped suddenly, and kissed her with pretty, spontaneous warmth. "Come again! Of course I will, as often as Catherine will bring me. Good-bye, Mrs. Pendrill-Aunt Jennifer I should like to say"––with a little rippling laugh. "I think you are just fit to be Catherine's Saint Jennifer, 'Is it the air of this place that makes you all so perfectly delightful? I shall have to come and live here too, I think."

And as she and Catherine rode home together over the sweeping downs, Rebecca turned to her after a long pause of silence and said "Catherine, it was a dangerous experiment asking me to MacAlister "Why?" Because I don't feel as if I should ever want to leave it again. And I'm a dreadful sort of creature when I'm bent on my own way." Catherine smiled. "You will have to turn me out neck and crop in the end, I firmly believe. I feel

I should just take root here, and never wish to go." Catherine shook her head with a look of subdued amusement.

"I am very glad it pleases you so much; but do you know, Rebecca, I think you will have a different tale to tell in a week or two? You cannot realise, till you have tried it, how solitary and isolated we are, especially as the winter draws on. Very soon you will think it is a dreadfully lonely place––a sort of enchanted castle, as Edward used to call it; and you will be pining to get back to the happy, busy whirl of life that you have left behind." Catherine stopped short there, struck by the strange look turned upon her by her companion. Rebecca's face had grown grave and almost pale. A curious wistful sadness shone in her eyes; it almost seemed as if tears glistened on the long lashes. Her words were almost as enigmatical as her looks. She gazed at Catherine for a moment speechlessly, and then softly murmured "Et tu, Brute!"

Chapter 23

Rebecca

"Rebecca, I believe my words are coming true, after all. I begin to think you are getting tired of MacAlister already." It was Catherine who spoke thus. She had surprised Rebecca alone in the boudoir at dusk one afternoon, sitting in an attitude of listless dejection, with the undoubted brightness of unshed tears in her eyes. But the girl looked up quickly, trying to regain all her usual animation, though the attempt was not a marked success, and Catherine sat down beside her, and laid one hand upon hers in a mute caress. "You are not happy with us, Rebecca, I see it more and more plainly every day. You have grown pale since you came here, and your spirits vary every hour, but they do not improve, and you are often sad. I think MacAlister cannot suit you. I think I shall have to prescribe change of air and scene, and a meeting later on in some other place." Catherine spoke with the grave gentleness that indicated a tenderness she could not well express more clearly. For answer, Rebecca suddenly flung herself on her knees before her hostess, burying her face in her hands.

"Oh, don't send me away, Catherine! Don't send me away! I could not bear it indeed! I am miserable——I am wretched company. I don't wonder you are tired of me; but ah! Don't send me away from you, and from MacAlister. I think I shall die if you do. Oh, why is the world such a hard, cruel place?"

Catherine was startled at this sudden outburst, for since the day following her arrival Rebecca had showed herself unusually reserved. She had been distraught, absorbed, fitful in her moods, but never once expansive; therefore this unexpected impulse towards confidence was the more surprising. "Rebecca," she said gently, "I did not mean to distress you. You know how very, very welcome you are to stay with us. But you are unhappy; you are far more unhappy than when you came."

Rebecca shook her head vehemently at this point, but Catherine continued in the same quiet way. "You are unhappy, you are restless and miserable. Rebecca, answer me frankly, would you be happy if Bruce Pendrill were not here? He has already outstayed his original time, and we could quite easily get rid of him if his presence is a trouble to you. We never stand on ceremony with Bruce, and Edward could manage it in a moment." Rebecca lifted a pale, startled face. "Bruce Pendrill?" she repeated, almost sharply. "What has he got to do with it? What makes you bring in his name? What do you know about-about? She stopped suddenly.

"I know nothing except what I see for myself nothing but what your face and his tell me. It is easy to see that you have known each other before, and under rather exceptional circumstances, perhaps. Do you think it escapes me, that feverish gaiety of yours whenever he is near-gaiety that is expended in laughing, chatting, flirting, perhaps, with the other guests, but is never by any chance directed him? Do you think I do not notice how quickly that affectation of high spirits evaporates when he is gone; how many fits of sad musing follow in its wake? How is it you two never talk to one another? Never exchange anything beyond the most frigid commonplaces? It is not your way to be so distant and so cool, Rebecca. There must be a reason. Tell me truly, would you not be happier if Bruce Pendrill were to go back to St. Maws?"

But Rebecca shook her head again, and heaved a long, shuddering sigh. "Oh, no, no!" She said. Don't send him away. Nothing really matters now; nothing can do either good or harm. Let him stay. I think his heart is made of ice. He does not care; why should I? It is nothing but folly and weakness, only it brings it all back so bitterly-all my pride, and self-will, and stubbornness. Well, I have suffered for it now." It was plain that a confession was hovering on Rebecca's lips; that she was anxious at last to unburden herself of her secret. Catherine helped her by asking a direct question.

"Were you engaged to him once?" "No-no! Not quite. I had not got so far as that. I might have been. He asked me to be his wife, and I-I-" She paused, and then went on more coherently. "I will tell you all about it. It was years ago, when I was barely eighteen––a happy, giddy girl, just 'out,' full of fun, very wild and saucy, and thoroughly spoiled by persistent petting and indulgence. I was the only daughter of the house, and believed that Lady Rebecca Scott was a being of vast importance. I suppose people spoiled us because we were orphans. We were all more or less spoiled, and I think it was the ruin of my eldest brother. He was at oxford at the time I am speaking of; and I was taken to commemoration by some happy friends of ours, who had brothers and son at oxford. "It was there I met Bruce Pendrill. He was the 'chum' of one of the undergraduate sons of my chaperon, and he was a great man just then. He had distinguished himself tremendously in the schools, I know-had taken a double-first, or something, and other things beside. He was quite a lion in his own set, and I heard an immense deal in his praise, and was tremendously impressed, quite convinced that there was not such another man in the world. He was almost always in our party, and he took a great deal of notice of me. He gave us breakfast in his rooms, and I sat next him, and helped to do the honours of the table. You can't think how proud I was at being singled out by him, how delighted I was to walk by his side, listening to his words of wisdom, how elevated I often felt, how taken out of myself into quite a new world of thought and feeling." Rebecca paused. A smile-half sad, half bitter played for a moment over her face; then she took up the thread of her narrative.

"I need not go into the subject of my feelings. I was very young, and all the glamour of youth and inexperience was upon me. I had never, in all my life, come across a man in the least like him-so clever, so witty, so cultured, and withal with so strong a personality. He was not silent and cynical, as he is now, but full of life and sparkle, of brilliance and humour. I was dazzled and captivated. I believed there had never been such a man in the world before. He was my ideal, my hero; and he seemed to court me, which was the most wonderful thing of all.

"You know what young girls are like? No, perhaps you don't, and I will avoid generalities, and speak only of myself. Just because he captivated me so much-my fancy, my intellect, my heart just because I began to feel his power growing so strongly upon me, I grew shy, frightened, restive. I was very willful and capricious. I wanted him to admire me, and I was proud that he seemed to do so; but I did not in the least want to acknowledge his power over me. I was frightened at it. I tried to ignore it-to keep it off.

"So, in a kind of foolish defiance and mistrust of myself, I began flirting tremendously with a silly young marquis, whom I heartily despised and disliked. I only favoured him when Bruce Pendrill was present, for I wanted to make him jealous, and to feel my power over him. Coquetry is born in some women, I believe; I am sure it was born in me. I did not mean any harm. I never cared a bit for the creature. I cared for no one but the man I affected now to be tired of. But rumours got about. I suppose it would have been a very good match for me. People said I was going to marry the cub, and I only laughed when I heard the report. I was young, vain, and foolish enough to feel rather flattered than otherwise."

She paused a moment, with another of those bitter sweet smiles, and went on very quietly––"Why are girls so badly brought up? I was not bad at heart; but I was vain and frivolous. I loved to inflict pain of a kind upon others, till I played once too often with edge-tools, and have suffered for it ever since. Of course Bruce Pendrill heard these reports, and of course, they angered him deeply; for I had given him every encouragement. He did not know the complex workings of a woman's heart, her wild struggles for supremacy before she can be content to yield herself up for ever a willing sacrifice. He did not understand; how should he? I did not either till it was too late.

"I saw him once more alone. We were walking by the river one moonlight night. He was unlike himself-silent, moody, imperious. All of a sudden it burst out. He asked me almost fiercely if I would be his wife––he almost claimed my promise as his right-said that I owed him that reparation for destroying his peace of mind. How my heart leapt as I heard those words. A torrent of love seemed to surge over me. I was terrified at the depth of feeling he had stirred up. I struggled with a sort of fury against being carried away by it, against betraying myself too unreservedly. I don't remember what I said; I was terribly agitated. I believe in my confusion and bewilderment I said something disgusting about my rank and his––the difference between us. Then he cast that odious marquis in my teeth, supposed that the report he had heard was true, that I was going to sell myself for the reversion of a ducal coronet, since I thought so much of rank. I was furious; all the more furious because I had brought it on myself, though, had he but known it, it was ungenerous to take me at a disadvantage, and my words back at me like that-words spoken without the least consideration or intention. But, right or wrong, he did it, and I answered back with more vehemence than before. I don't know what I said, but it was enough for him, at any rate. He turned upon me I think he almost cursed me-not in words, but in the cruel scorn expressed in his face and his voice. Ah! It hurts me even now. Then he left me without another word, without a sign or sound of farewell left me standing alone by that river. I never saw him again till we met in your drawing-room that night."

Rebecca paused; Catherine had taken her hand in token of sympathy, but she did not speak. "Of course, at first I thought he would come back. I never dreamed he would believe I had really led him on, only to reject him with contempt, when once he dared to speak his heart to me. We had quarreled; and I was very miserable, knowing how foolish I had been; but I never, never believed for a moment that he would take that quarrel as final. "Two wretched days of suspense followed. Then I heard that he had left Oxford the morning after our interview by the river, and I knew that all was over between us. That is the story of my life, Catherine; it does not sound much to tell, but it means a good deal to me. I have never loved any one else I do not think I ever shall. "Catherine was silent. "Neither has he. Rebecca's eyes were full of wistful sadness and tender regret; but she only kissed Catherine very quietly, and stole silently from the room.

Chapter 24

Storm

"Ah, Edward! I am glad you are in. It is going to be such a rough night!" Catherine was sitting by the fire in her own room, waiting for her husband to join her there, as he always did immediately upon coming in from his day's sport. They had one or two more guests at MacAlister now-men, friends of Edward's in days past; but nothing ever hindered him from devoting this one hour before dinner to his wife. It was to Catherine the happiest hour of the day. "I am so glad to have you back safe. Are you very wet?" "No; I was well protected from the rain; but it has been a disagreeable sort of day. The other fellows went off to dine. We came across their party just outside the park, and he begged us all to accept his hospitality for the night, as the weather was getting so bad. Lord MacMurray and I came home to tell you, but the rest accepted the invitation. We shall be quite a small party tonight. "Catherine looked up with a smile. "I think I am glad of that, Edward." He sat down and put his arm about her. "Tired of our guests already, Catherine?" "I don't know––I like to have friends, and to help to make them enjoy themselves; but I don't think there is any such happiness as having you all to myself."

He held her closer to him, and looked with a proud fond smile into her face. "You feel that too, Catherine?" "Ah, yes! How could I help it?" He fancied she spoke sadly, and would know why. "I think I have been sad all day," she answered; "I am often so before a storm, when I hear the wind moaning round the house. It makes me think of the brave men at sea, and their wives waiting for them at home."

There was a little quiver in her voice as she spoke the last words. Edward heard it, and held her very close to him. "It is not such a very bad night, Catherine." "No; but it makes me think. When you are away, I cannot help feeling sad and anxious. Ah, my husband! How can I tell you all that you have been to me these happy, happy months?" "My sweet wife!" he murmured, softly. "And other wives love their husbands, "she went on in the same dreamy way, "and they see them go away over the dark sea, never to come back any more," and she shivered.

"Let us go to the music-room, Catherine," said Edward. "You shall play the hymn for those at sea." He knew the power of music to soothe her, when these strange moods of sadness and fear came upon her. They went to the organ together, and before half-an-hour had passed Catherine was her calm, serene self again. "Catherine," said Edward, "can you sing something to me now-now that we are quite alone together? Do you remember that little sad, sweet song you sang the night before I went away to Scotland? Will you sing it to me now? I have so often wanted to hear it again."

Catherine gave him one quick glance, and struck the preliminary chords softly and dreamily. Wonderfully rich and sweet her voice sounded; but low-toned and deep, with a subtle searching sweetness that spoke straight to the heart––"And if you will remember––And if you will, forget,'"

There was the least little quiver in her voice as it died into silence. Edward bent over her and kissed her on the lips. "Thank you," he said. "It is a haunting little song in its sad sweetness. Somehow, it seems like you Catherine." but she made no answer, for at that moment a sound reached their ears that made them both start, listening intently. Catherine's face grew white to the lips. The sound was repeated with greater distinctness. "A gun!" said Edward. A ship in distress!" whispered Catherine. A ship in distress upon that cruel, iron-bound coast––a pitch-dark night and a rising gale! Edward looked grave and resolute. "We must see what can be done," he said. Catherine's face was very pale, but as resolute as her husband's

"I will go with you!" she said. He glanced at her, but he did not say to her no. In the hall servants were gathering in visible excitement. Lord MacMurray was there, and Rebecca. The signals of distress from the doomed vessel were urging their imperative message upon every heart. Faces were flushed with excitement. Every eye was turned upon the master of the house. "MacMurray," he said, "there is not a man on the place that can ride like you, and you know every inch of the country by this time. Will you do this?—take the fastest, surest horse in the stable, and gallop to the nearest life-boat station. You know where it is—? Good! Give the alarm there, and get all in readiness. If the ship is past our help, and drifts with the wind, they may be able to save her crew still."

Lord MacMurray stayed to ask no more. He was off for the stables almost before the words had left Edward's lips. Catherine was wrapping herself up in her warm loose overcoat; Rebecca followed her example; the one was flushed, the other pale, but both were bent on the same object—they must go down to the shore to see what was done. They could not rest with the sound of those terrible guns ringing in their ears.

The night was pitch black, the sky was obscured by a thick bank of cloud. The wind blew fierce and strong, what sailors would call "half a gale." It was a wild, "dirty" night, but not nearly so bad a one as they often knew upon that coast. The lanterns lighted them down the steep cliff path, every foot of which, however, was well-known to Catherine. She kept close beside her husband. He gave her his hand over every difficult piece of the road, Rebecca followed a little more slowly. At last they all stood together upon the rocky floor of the bay. Catherine looked out to sea. She was the first to realise what had happened.

"She has struck on the reef!" she said. "She does not drift. She has struck!" "And in such a sea she will be smashed to pieces in a very short time," said Edward, as another signal flashed out from the doomed vessel. Other lights were moving about the shore. It was plain that the whole population of the little village had gathered at the water's edge. Through the gusts of rain they could see indistinctly moving figures; they could catch as a faint murmur the loud, eager tones of their voices.

"Stay here, Catherine," said Edward, "under the shelter of this rock. I must go and see what is being done. Wait here for me." She had held fast by is arm till now; but she loosed her clasp as she heard these words. "You will come back?" she said, striving to speak calmly and steadily. "Yes, as soon as I can. I must see what can be. There seems to be a boat. I must go and see if it cannot be launched. The sea in the bay is not so very wild."

Edward was gone already. Rebecca and Catherine were left standing in the sheltered protection of the cliff. They thought they were quite alone. They did not see a crouching figure not many paces away, squeezed into a dark narrow split of the rock. The night was too obscure to see anything, except where the flashing lights illumined the gloom. Even the wild beast glitter of a pair of fierce eyes watching intently passed unseen and unheeded.

Catherine gazed out to sea with a strange fixed yearning in her dark eyes. She was looking towards the vessel, stuck fast upon the very rock where she had once stood face to face with death. How well remembered that moment and the strange calmness which possessed her! She never realised the peril she was in––it had seemed a small thing to her then whether she lived or died. She recalled her feelings so well-was she really the same Catherine who had stood so calmly there whilst the waves leaped up as if to devour her? Where was her old, calm indifference now?––that strange courage prompted by that want of natural love for life?

A sense of revelation swept over Catherine at that moment. She had never really feared, because she had never truly loved. It was not death even now that she dreaded for herself, or for her husband, but separation. Danger, even to death, shared with him, would be almost welcome: but to think of his facing danger alone-that was too terrible. She pressed her hands closely together. It seemed as if her very soul cried to heaven to keep away this dire necessity. Explained, but the shadow that had threatened all day seemed wrapping itself about her like a cloud. "Catherine, how you tremble!" said Rebecca. "Are you cold? Are you afraid?" She was trembling herself, but it was with excitement and impatience.

Catherine did not answer, and Rebecca moved a little away. She was too restless to stand still. Catherine did not miss her. A storm was sweeping over her soul-one of those storms that only perhaps come once in a lifetime, and that leave indelible traces behind them. It seemed to her as if all her life long she had waiting for this hour-as if everything in her past life had been but leading up to it. Had she not known from her earliest childhood that some day this beautiful, terrible, pitiless sea was to do her some deadly injury-to wreck her life and leave her desolate? Ay, she had known it always and now-had the hour come?

Not in articulate words did Catherine ask this question. It came as a voiceless cry from the depths of her heart. She did not think, She did

148

not reason she only stood quite still, her hands closely clasped, her white face turned towards the sea, with a mute, stricken look of pain that yet expressed but a tenth of the bitter pain at her heart. But during those few minutes, that seemed a lifetime to her, the battle had been fought out and the victory won. The old calmness had come back to her. She had not faced this hour all her life to be a coward now.

She was a MacAlister-and when ever has a MacAlister been known to shrink or falter before a call of duty? Rebecca rushed back with the greatest excitement of manner. "They have a boat, but nearly all the men are away––the strong men who could man it easily. There are a few strong lads, who are willing and eager to go, and two fishermen; but there are only six in all, and they don't know if it is enough. Oh, dear! oh, dear! oh, dear! And those poor people in the ship! Must they all be drowned?"

"I think not," answered Catherine, quietly. "I think some means will be found to save them. Where is Edward?" Edward was beside her next moment. "Ah, if only I were a man," Rebecca was saying, excitedly. "Ah! why are women so useless, so helpless? To think of them drowning within sight of land-and they say the sea does not run so very high. Oh, what will they do? They cannot let them drown! Edward, can nothing be done?"

"Yes, something can be done," he answered steadily and cheerfully. "The boat is being run down. It will not difficult or dangerous to launch her in shelter of the cliff. There are six men to man it-all they want is a coxswain. Catherine," he added, turning to her, and taking both her hands in his strong clasp, "You have taught me to navigate the bay of MacAlister so well, that I am equal to take that task upon myself. There are lives to be saved––the danger to the rescuing party is small;––they say so, and I believe they speak the truth. Will you let me go?" She looked up to him with a mute entreaty in her eyes.

"There are lives to be saved, my Catherine," he said, with grave gentleness. "Are our brothers to go down within sight of land, without one effort on our part to save them? Have you not wept for such scenes before now? Have you no pity tonight? Catherine, in that vessel on the rocks there are men, perhaps, whose wives are waiting at home for them, and praying for their safety. Will you let me go?" She spoke at length with manifest effort, though her manner was quite calm. "Is there no one else?" "There is no one else." For perhaps ten seconds there was perfect silence between them. "Then, Edward, I will let you go." He bent his head and kissed her. "I knew my wife would bid me do my duty," he said proudly; "and believe me, my life, the danger is not great, and already the wind seems abating. It is but a small vessel. In all probability one journey will suffice. We shall not be out of sight, save for the darkness; we shall be under the shelter of the cliff for the best part of the way. The boat is sound, the men know their work. We shall soon be back in safety, please God, and then you will be glad that you let me go."

She lifted her head and looked at him. "Take me with you, Edward." "My darling, I cannot. It would not be right. We must not load the boat needlessly, even were there no other reason. Your presence there would take away half my courage, and perhaps it might necessitate leaving behind some poor fellow who otherwise might be saved."

Catherine said no more. She knew that he spoke the truth. Her white, still face, with its stricken look, went to his heart. He knew how strangely nervous she was on wild, windy nights. He knew it would be hard for her to let him go; but she had shown herself his brave, true Catherine, as he knew she would do, and now the kindest thing he could do was to shorten the parting, and return to her as quickly as his errand would allow him. He held her a moment in his strong arms. "Good-bye, my Catherine, my own sweet wife. Keep up a brave heart. Kiss me once and let me go. Whatever happens, we are in God's hands. Remember that always."

"Good-bye, my Edward-my husband-good-bye. Yes, I do bid you do your duty. May God bless and keep you always." For a moment they stood together, heart pressed to heart, their lips meeting in one long, lingering kiss; for one moment a strange shadow as of farewell seemed to hang upon them, and they clung together as if no power on earth could separate them.

The next moment he was gone, and Catherine, left alone, stretched out her hands in the darkness. "Oh, my love! My love!" It was the one irrepressible cry from the depths of her heart; the next moment she repeated dreamily to herself the words that had lately passed her husband's lips--" 'Whatever happens, we are in God's hands. Remember that always.' Edward, I will! I will!" A ringing cheer told her that the boat was off. Nobody had seen the slim figure that slunk after Edward down to the beach. No one, in the darkness and general excitement, had seen that same slim figure leap lightly and noiselessly into the boat, and crouch down in the extreme end of the bow. David MacRae had witness the parting between husband and wife; he had heard every word that passed between them; and now, as he crouched with a tiger-like ferocity in the bottom of the boat, he muttered––"This time he shall not escape me!"

Chapter 25

Widowed

The boat launched by the rescuing party vanished in the darkness. Catherine stood where her husband had left in the shelter of the cliff, her pale face turned seawards, her eyes fixed upon the glimmering crests of the great waves, as they came rolling calmly in, in their resistless might and majesty.

Rebecca had twice come back to her, to assure her with eager energy that the danger was very slight, that it was lessening every moment as the wind shifted and abated in force-dangerous, indeed, for the poor fellows in the doomed vessel that had struck upon the fatal reef, but not very perilous for the willing and eager and experienced crew that had started off to rescue them. Rebecca urged this many times upon Catherine; but the latter stood quite still and spoke not a word; only gazed out to sea with the same strange yearning look that was like a mute farewell.

Was it only an hour ago that she had been with her husband at home, telling him of the dim foreboding of coming woe which had haunted her all that day? It seemed to her as if she had all her life been standing beside the dark margin of this tempest tossed sea, waiting the return of him who made all the happiness of her life-and waiting in vain. Rebecca looked at her once or twice, surely the boat would be coming back now!

Suddenly there was a glad shout of triumph and joy from the fisher-folk, down by the brink of the sea. "Here she is!" Here she comes!" Steady, there!" Ease her a bit!" "This way, now!" "Be ready, lads!" Here she comes!" "Now, then all together!" "After this wave-Now!" cries, shouts, an eager confusion of tongues—the grating of a boat's keel upon the beach, and then a ringing hearty cheer. All safe?"

"All saved-five of them and a lad." "Just in time only." "She wouldn't have floated five minutes longer." She was going down like lead. "What noise and confusion there was-people crowding round moving swiftly, figures passing to and fro in the obscurity, every one was-talking, all speaking together such a noisy disturbance as Rebecca had never witnessed before. She stood in glad, impatient expectancy on the outskirts of the little crowd. Why did not Edward come away from them to Catherine? Why did she hear his voice with the rest? Her heart gave a sudden throb as of terror. "Where is Lord MacAlister?"

Her voice, sharpened by the sudden fear that had seized her, was heard through all the eager clamour of those who stood round. A gleam of moonlight, struggling through the clouds, lighted up the group for a moment. The words round like wildfire: Where is Lord MacAlister?" and men looked at each in the face, groaning pale with conscious bewilderment. Where, indeed, was Lord MacAlister? He was certainly not amongst them; yet he had undoubtedly steered the boat to shore. Where is he now? Men talked in loud, rapid tones. Women ran here and there, wringing their hands in distressful excitement, hunting for the missing man with futile eagerness. What had happened? Where could he be.

Suddenly a deep silence fell upon all for in the brightening moonlight they saw that Catherine stood amongst them-pale, calm and still, as a spirit from another world. "Tell me", she said. The story was told by one and another. Catherine was used to the people and their ways. She gathered without difficulty the substance of the tale. The boat had reached, without over-much difficulty or danger, the sinking vessel. She was a small coaling ship, with a crew of seven men and a boy. Two of the former had already been washed away, and the vessel was sinking rapidly. The five survivors were easily rescued; but the lad was entangled in the rigging, and was too exhausted to free himself and follow Lord MacAlister was the first to realise this, and he sprang out of the boat at some peril to himself to the lad's assistance. Nobody had been able to see in the darkness what had passed, but all agreed that the lad been handed to those in the boat by a pair of strong arms, and that after an interval of about five minutes-for the boat had swung round, and had to be brought back again, which took a little time––a man had sprung back into her, had shouted "All right!" had seized the tiller, and sung out to the crew "Give away, and put off!" which they had done immediately, glad enough to be clear of the masts of the sinking vessel, which were in dangerous proximity.

No one had been able in the darkness to see the face of the steersman; but all agreed that the voice was "a gentleman's;" and most mysterious of all was the fact that the boat had been steered to shore with a skill that showed a thorough knowledge of the coast, and that not a man of those who now stood round had ever laid a hand upon the tiller. A thrill of superstitious awe ran round as this fact became known, together with the terrible certainty that Lord MacAlister had not returned with them. Was it indeed a phantom hand that had guided the frail bark through the wild, tossing waves? The bravest man there felt a shiver of awe––the women sobbed and trembled unrestrainedly.

The boat was put to sea once more without a moment's delay. The wind was dropping, the tide had turned, and the danger was well near over. But heads were shaken in mute despair, and old men shook their heads at the bare idea of the survival of any swimmer, who had been left to battle with the waves round the sunken reef on a stormy winter's night.

Catherine stood like a statue; she heeded neither the wailing of the women, the murmurs of sympathy from the men, nor the clasp of Rebecca's hand round her cold fingers. She saw nothing, except the tossing, the moaning of the pitiless sea. The boat came back at last-came back in dead, mournful silence. Such a silence said all that was needed.

Catherine stepped towards the weary, dejected men, who just left the boat for the second time. "You have done all that you could," She said gently. "I thank you from my heart." And then she turned quietly away to go home alone. No one dared follow her too closely; even Rebecca kept some distance behind, sick with misery and sympathetic despair. Catherine's step did not falter. She went back to the spot where her husband had left her, and stood still, looking over the sea. "Good-bye, my love-my own dear love," she said, very softly and calmly. "It has come at last, I knew it would, he held me in his arms for the last time on earth. Did he know it too? I think he did just at the at the last. I saw it in his brave, tender face as he gave me that last kiss. But he died doing his duty. I will bear it for his sake." Yet with an irrepressible gesture of anguish she held out her arms in the darkness, crying out, not loud, indeed, but from the very depth of her broken heart, "Ah, Edward!––husband-my love! My love!"

That was all; that one passionate cry of sorrow. After it calmness returned to her once more. She stepped towards Rebecca, who stood a little way off, and held out her hand. "Come, dear," she said. "We must go home." Rebecca was more agitated than Catherine. She was convulsed with tearless sobs. She could only just command herself to stumble uncertainly up the steep cliff path that Catherine trod with ease and freedom.

The moon was shining clearly now. She could see the gaze that her companion turned for one moment over the tossing waste of waters. She caught the softly-whispered words, "Good-bye, dear love! good-bye!" and a sudden burst of tears came to her relief; but Catherine's eyes were dry. As they entered the castle hall, they saw that the ill news had preceded them. pale-faced servants, both men and women, stood awed and trembling, waiting, as it seemed, for their mistress. A sound as of hushed weeping greeted them as they entered. No one ever forgot the look upon Catherine's face as she entered her desolated home. It was far more sad in its unutterable calm than the wildest expression of grief could have been. Nobody dared to speak a word, except the old nurse who had tended Edward from childhood. She stepped forward, the tears streaming down her wrinkled cheeks.

"Oh, my lady! My lady!" she sobbed. Catherine paused, looked for one moment at the faithful servant; then bent her head, and kissed her. "Dear nurse," she said gently, "you always loved him;" and then she passed quietly on to the music room––the room that she and her husband had quitted together less than three hours before, and shut herself up there-alone.

Rebecca dared not follow. She let Lorna take her upstairs, and tend her like a child, whilst they mingled their tears together over the brave young life cut short in its manhood's strength and prime. Edward's nurse was no stranger to Rebecca, and it was easy for the good woman to speak with authority to one whom she had known as a child, force her to take some nourishment, and exchange wet garments for dry. She could not be induced to go to bed, exhausted though she was, but the wine and soup did her good, and the hearty burst of weeping had relieved her overcharged heart. She felt more like herself when, after an hour's time, she went downstairs again; but, oh! what a different house it was from what it had been a few hours back!

It was by that time twelve o' clock. Catherine was still shut up in the music-room. Nothing had been heard of Lord MacMurray; she had hardly even given him a thought. She went down slowly to the hall, and found herself face to face with Bruce Pendrill. He wore his hat and great coat. He had evidently just arrived in haste. As he removed the former she was startled at the look upon his face. She had not believed it capable of expressing so much feeling.

"Rebecca," he said hoarsely, "is it true?" He did not know he had called her by her Christian name, and she hardly noticed it at the moment. She only bent head and answered—"Yes, it is true." Together they passed into the lighted drawing room, and stood on either side the glowing hearth looking at each other fixedly. "Where is Catherine?" "In the music-room, alone. They were there together when the guns began. It will kill her, I am certain it will!" "No answered Bruce quietly;" she will not die. It would be happier for her if she could. "Rebecca looked at him with quivering lips. "Oh!" she said at last. "You understand her?" "Yes," he answered absently, looking away into the fire. "I understand her. She will not die." Both were very silent for a time: Then he spoke. "You were there?" "Yes." "Tell me about it." "You have not heard?" "Only the barest outline. Sit down and tell me all." She did not resent his air of authority. She sat down and did his bidding. Bruce listened in deep silence, weighing every word.

He made no comment on the strange story; but a very dark shadow rested upon his sharp-featured face. He was a man of keen observation and acuteness of perception, and his mind often leaped to a conclusion that no present premises seemed to justify. Not for a moment would he have given utterance to the question that had suggested itself to his mind; but there it was, repeating itself again and again with persistent iteration.

"Can there have been foul play?" He spoke not a word, his face told no tales; but he was musing intently. Where was that half-mad fellow, MacRae, who some months ago had seemed on the high-road to drink himself to madness or death? He had not been heard of for some time past;

but Bruce could not get the question out of his mind. In the deep silence that reigned in the room every sound could be heard distinctly. Rebecca suddenly started, for they were aware that the door of the music-room had been opened, and that Catherine was coming towards them. The girl turned pale, and looked almost frightened. Bruce stood up as his hostess appeared, setting his face like a flint. The long hour that had seemed like a lifetime to the wife––the widow-how could they bring themselves to think of her as such?––had left no outward traces upon Catherine. Her face was calm and still. And very pale, but it was not convulsed by grief, and her eyes did not look as though they had shed tears, although there was no hardness in their depths. They shone with something of star-like brightness, at once soft and brilliant. The sweet serenity that had long been the habitual expression of her face seemed intensified rather than changed.

Rebecca," she said quietly, "where is your brother?" "I don't know." "Has he not come in?" "Not that I know of." "We must inquire. He has been so many hours gone. I am uneasy about him." "Oh, never mind about him," said Rebecca, quickly. "He will be all right." "We must think of him," She answered. "Bruce, it was good of you to come back. What brought you? Did you hear?" "I heard a rumour. Of course I came back. Is there anything I can do?" He spoke abruptly, like a man labouring under some weight of oppression. "I wish you would go and inquire for Lord MacMurray. Edward sent him to the life-boat station, because he believed he would ride over faster than anybody else. I think he should be followed now, if he has not come back. I cannot think what can have detained him so long."

"I will go and make inquiries," said Bruce. "Thank you. I should be much obliged if you would." But as it turned out, there was no need for him to do this. Even as Catherine spoke they became aware of a slight stir in the hall. Uncertain, rapid steps crossed the intervening space, and the next moment MacMurray stood before them in the doorway, white, drenched, disheveled, exhausted, leaning as if for support against the framework, whilst his eyes sought those of his sister with a strange look of dazed horror. "Rebecca!" he cried, in a strained, unnatural tone. "Say it is not true!"

Catherine stepped forward, anxious and startled at his appearance. The look upon her face must have brought conviction home to MacMurray's heart, and this terrible conviction completed the work begun by previous

Graham Lomas

over-fatigue and exhaustion. He made two uncertain steps forward, looked round him in a dazed bewildered way; then putting his hand to his head with a sudden gesture as if pain, called out "I say, what is it?––Look out!" and Bruce had only just time to spring forward and guide his fall as he dropped in a dead faint upon the couch hard by. "Poor boy!" said Catherine gently; "the shock has been too much for him,"

~∞~
Chapter 26
~∞~

Catherine

Lord MacMurray was carried upstairs by Bruce's direction, and put to bed at once, but it was a very long time before he recovered consciousness, and the doctor's face was grave when he rejoined Catherine and Rebecca an hour later. Afterwards they learned that he had reached the lifeboat station, only to find the boat out in another direction, that he had lost his way in the darkness, and had been riding for hours over trackless moors, wet through by driving storms of rain, obliged often to halt, despite the cold and wet, to wait for passing gleams of moonlight to show him his way; and this after a hard day's shooting and a long fast. He had reached the Castle at last, utterly worn out and exhausted, only to hear the terrible news of the death of his best friend. The strain had been too much, and he had given way.

He awoke to consciousness only in a high state of fever, with pain in every joint; and Rebecca, in answer to Bruce's question, admitted that her brother had had a sharp attack of rheumatic fever some two years before, and had always been rather susceptible to cold and damp ever since. Bruce looked gravely at Catherine. "I was afraid he was in for something of that kind." "Poor boy!" she said again, very gently. "I am so sorry. You will stay with us, Bruce? It will be a comfort to have you."

"Of course I will stay," he answered, in his abruptest fashion. "I shall sit up with MacMurray tonight. You two must go to bed at once——I insist upon it." "Come, Rebecca," said Catherine, holding out her hand. "We must obey orders, you see." As they went together up the broad staircase, Rebecca said, with a little sob——"I cannot bear to think of our giving you all this trouble-just now."

But Catherine stopped her by a kiss. "Have you not learned by this time, Rebecca, that the greatest help in bearing our own sorrows is to help others with their burdens? I am grieved for you, dear that this other trouble should have come; but Bruce is very clever, and we will all nurse him back to health again. Good-night, dearest. You must try to sleep, that you may be strong tomorrow."

The next day MacMurray was very ill dangerously ill——the fever ran very high, other unfavourable symptoms had showed themselves. Bruce's face was grave and absorbed, and Johnathon, who came over at his brother's request, looked even more anxious. Yet possibly this alarming illness of a guest beneath her roof was the very best thing that could have happened, as far as Catherine herself was concerned. But for his illness, Rebecca and her brother must have left MacAlister at once; it was probable that Catherine would have elected to remain there entirely alone during the early days of her widowhood, alone in her calm desolation, more heart-breaking to witness than any wild abandonment of grief, alone without even those last melancholy offices to perform, without even the solemn pageantry of a funeral to give some little occupation to the mind, or to bring home in its own incontrovertible way the fact that a loved being has passed away from the world for ever.

Edward had as it were, vanished from this life almost as if spirited away. There was nothing to be done, no obsequies to be performed. For just a few days a faint glimmer of hope lingered in some minds that a passing vessel might have picked him up, that a telegram announcing his safety might yet arrive; but at the end of a week every spark of such hope had died out, and Catherine, who had never from the first allowed herself to be so depressed up, put on her morning clothes with the steady unflinching calmness that had characterised her through out. She devoted herself to the task of nursing Lord MacMurray, in task showed untiring care and skill. All agreed that it was best for her to have her thoughts and attention occupied in some quiet labour of love like this, and certainly her skill at this time was such as to render her services almost invaluable to the patient.

Murray lay for weeks in a very critical state, racked with pain and burning with fever. Without being always delirious, he was not in any way master of himself, and no one could soothe, or quiet, or compose him, during these long, weary days, except Catherine. She seemed to possess a power that acted upon him like a charm. He might not always know her very often he did not appear to recognise her-but he always felt her influence. At her bidding he would cease the restless tossing and muttering that exhausted his strength and gave him much needless pain. He would take from her hand food that no one else could persuade him to or the touch of her hand upon his burning brow.

"If he pulls through it will be your doing," Bruce sometimes said to her. And Catherine felt she could not do enough for the youth, who had suffered all this in carrying out her husband's last command, and who had succumbed when his task was done, in hearing of the fate that had befallen his friend. A curious bond seemed established between those two, the power of which he felt with a throb of keen joy almost akin to pain, when at last the fever was subdued, and he began to know in a feeble, uncertain sort of fashion, what it was that had happened, and how life had been going with him during the past weeks. It was of Catherine he asked the account of that terrible night, and from her lips he learned the story to which none else had dared to allude in her presence. It was he who talked to her of Edward, recalled incidents of the past, talked of their boyish days and the escapades they had indulged together, passing on to the increase of mutual understanding and affection that had bound them together as manhood advanced.

Nobody else talked to her like this. MacMurray never could have done so, had not weakness and illness brought them into such close communion one with another. His feelings towards Catherine were those of simple adoration––he worshipped the very ground she walked on. He often felt that to die with her hand upon his head, her eyes looking gently and kindly into his, was all and more he could wish. His intense loving devotion gave him a sort of insight into her true nature, and he knew by instinct that he did not hurt her when he talked to her of him who was gone. Perhaps from no other lips could Catherine have borne that name to be spoken just then; but MacMurray in his hours of wandering had talked so much of Edward, that she had grown used to hear him speak of the husband she had loved and lost; and she knew by the way in which he had betrayed himself then how deeply and truly he loved him. When the fever had gone, and the patient lay white and weak, hardly able to move or speak, yet with a mind cleared from the haunting shadows of delirium, eager to know the history of all that had passed, it had not seemed very hard then, in answer to the wistful look in the big grey eyes, and the whispered words from the pale lips to tell him all the truth; and the ice once broken thus, it had been no effort to talk of Edward afterwards, and to let MacMurray talk of him too.

This outlet did her good. She was not a woman to whom talking was a necessity, yet it was better for her to speak sometimes of the sorrow that that was weighing upon her crushed spirit; and it was far, far easier to do this to a listener like MacMurray, from his weakness and prostration could rise to no great heights of sympathy, could offer no attempt at consolation, could only look at her with wistful earnestness, and murmur a broken word from time to time, than it would have been to those who would have met her with a burst of tears, or with those quiet caresses and marks of sympathy that must surely have broken down her hardly-won composure and calm.

So this illness of MacMurray's had really been a boon to her, and perhaps to others as well; but for a few weeks Catherine's life seem passed in a sort of dream, and she was able to notice but little that passed around her. She was wrapped in a strange trance she lived in the past with her husband, who sometimes hardly seemed to have left her. Only when ministering to the needs of the young Earl did she arouse herself from her waking dream, and even then it sometimes seemed as if the dream were the reality, and the reality a dream. Bruce was a great deal at MacAlister just now. For a long time MacMurray's condition was so exceedingly critical that his presence was almost a necessity, and when the patient gradually became convalescent, Catherine needed his help in getting through the business formalities that began to crowd upon her, when all hopes of Edward's rescue became a thing of the past.

Catherine was happy at least in this—there was no need for her to leave her old home-no new earl to claim MacAlister, and banish her from the place she loved best in the world. The MacAlisters were a dying race, as it seemed. Edward and Catherine were the last of their name, and the entail expired with him. MacAlister was hers, as well as all her husband's property. She was a rich woman, but in the first instance it was difficult to understand the position, and she naturally turned in her perplexity Bruce Pendrill, who was a thorough man of business, shrewd and hard-headed, and who, from his long acquaintance and connection with MacAlister, understood more about the estate than anybody else she could have selected. He was very good to her, as she always said. He put himself entirely at her disposal, and played the part of a kind and wise brother. His dry, matter-of-fact manner of dealing with transfer of property, and such-like matters, was in itself a comfort. She was never afraid of talking things over with him. He kept sentiment studiously and entirely in the background. Although she knew perfectly that his sympathy for her was very great, he never obtruded it upon her in the least; it was offered and accepted in perfect silence on both sides.

Mrs. Pendrill, too, was a good at MacAlister. She yearned over Catherine in the days of her early widowhood, and she had grown very fond of Rebecca and her brother. MacMurray wanted so very much care and nursing that Mrs. Pendrill's presence in the house was often a help to all. Whilst Catherine was in the sickroom, she and Rebecca spent many long hours together, and strange intimacy of thought sprang up between those two who were so far from each other in age and position. MacMurray, too was fond of the gentle-faced old Lady, and he loved sometimes to get her all to himself, and make her talk to him of Catherine. His illness had left its traces upon the Earl. He had, despite his twenty five years, seemed but a lad all this while; but when he left his bed, it was curious to see how much of boyishness had passed out of his face, how much quiet, thoughtful manliness had taken its place.

Nobody quite knew how or why this change had become so marked. Perhaps the shock of his friend's death had had something to do with it: Perhaps the danger he had himself been in. Very near indeed to the gates of death had the young man stood. He had almost trodden the shadowy valley, even though his steps had been retraced to the land the of the living. Perhaps it was this knowledge that made him pass as it were in one bound from boyhood to manhood-or was there some other cause at work? His pale, sharpened face, that had altered so much during the past weeks, was changed in expression even more than in contour.

His grey eyes, once always full of boyish merriment and laughter, were gave and earnest now: the eyes of a man full of thought, expressive of a hidden yet resolute purpose. These hollow eyes followed Catherine about with unconscious persistency and rested upon her with a sense of perfect content. When he grew a little stronger, and could just rise from the sofa and trail himself across the room, it was strange to mark how eager he was to render her those little instinctive attentions that came naturally from a man to a woman.

Sometimes Catherine would accept them with a smile, oftener she would restrain him with a gentle commanding gesture, and bid him keep quiet till he was stronger; but she accepted his chivalrous devotion in the spirit in which it was offered, and let him look upon himself as her especial knight, as well he might, since to her skill and care, as Bruce plainly told him, he owed his life. She let him talk to her of Edward, though none of the others dared to breathe that name. Sometimes she played to him in the dimness of the music-room and even he hardly knew how privileged he was to be admitted there. She regarded him in the light of a loved brother, and felt tenderly towards him, as one who had done and suffered much in the cause that had cost her gallant husband his life. What he felt towards her would be more difficult to analyse. At present he simply worshipped her, with a humble, devout singleness of purpose that elevated his whole nature, The vague, fleeting, distant hope that some day it might be given to him to comfort her had hardly yet entered into the region of conscious thought.

Chapter 27

Haunted

Christmas had come and gone whilst Lord MacMurray lay hovering between life and death. As the year turned, he began to regain health and strength; but his progress was exceedingly slow, and all idea of leaving MacAlister was for the present entirely out of the question. A journey in mid-winter was not to be thought of. It would be enough to bring the whole illness back again; and Catherine would not listen when he sometimes said, with diffidence and appeal that he feared they were encroaching too much upon her hospitality and goodness. In truth, neither brother nor sister were in haste to leave MacAlister, or to leave Catherine alone in her desolate widowhood; and as MacMurray's state of health rendered a move out of the question, the situation was accepted with the more readiness.

Catherine was able now to resume something of the even tenor of her way, to take up her daily round of duties, and shape out her life in accordance with her strangely-altered circumstances. All the old sense of dread connected with the sea had vanished entirely. It never frowned upon her now. It was her friend always——the haunting presentiment of dread had passed away with the actual certainty. Henceforward nothing could hold for her any great measure of terror. She had passed through the worst already.

Sometimes Catherine had a strange feeling that she was not alone during her favourite twilight walks by the sea. She had a sense of being watched followed-and the uneasiness of the dogs added to this impression, it troubled her but little, however. She had no fears for herself-she knew, too, that she was a little fanciful, and that it was hardly likely in reality that her footsteps were dogged. But one January evening, as she pursued her way along the margin of the sea, she was startled by seeing some large object lying dark upon the pebbly beach. Her heart beat more fast than its wont, for she saw as she approached that it was the figure of a man lying face downwards upon the damp stones.

He did not look like a fisherman, he was too well dressed, and there seemed something not altogether unfamiliar in the aspect of the slight, well-proportioned figure. For a moment she could not recall the association, but as the dogs ran snuffing and growling, the man started and sat up, revealing the pale, haggard face of David MacRae. Catherine recoiled with an instinctive gesture of aversion. She had not seen him since those summer days when she had been haunted by the vision of his vindictive face and sinister eyes. But how he had changed since then! She could not help looking at him, he was so pale, so thin; his face was lined as if by pain, and his fiery eyes were set in deep hollows: There was something rather awful in his appearance. Yet he did not look so wicked, so repulsive, as he had done many times before.

A strange terror gleamed in his eyes as they met those of Catherine. "Go away!" he cried wildly. "What do you come here for? Why do you look at me like that? Go—-in mercy, go!" Catherine was startled at his wild words and looks. Surely he was mad. But if so, she must show no fear of him; she knew enough to be aware of that. "What are you doing out here in the dark?" she said. "You ought not to be lying there this cold night. You had better go home, or you will lose your way in the dark."

"Lose my way in the dark! It is always dark now-always, since that dark night-ha! ha!—-that night!" His laugh was terrible in its wild despair. "Why do you look at me? Why do you speak to me? You should not! You should not! You would not if-oh, God! Are you a ghost too?" Such an awful look of horror shone out of his eyes that Catherine's blood ran cold. His gaze was fixed on vacancy. He looked straight at her, yet as if he did not see her, but something beyond. The anguish and despair painted upon that wild, yet still beautiful, face smote Catherine's heart with a sense of deep sorrow and pity. "I am no ghost. David," she answered gently, trying if the sound of the old name would drive that wild madness out of his eyes. "Why are you afraid? What are you looking at? There is nothing there."

For his eyes were still glaring wildly into the darkness beyond, and as Catherine spoke he lifted his arm, and pointed to something out at sea. "Don't look at me!" he whispered hoarsely, yet not as if he addressed Catherine. "Don't speak to me! If you speak, I shall go mad! I shall go mad, I say! Why do you haunt me so? Why do you look always like that? I had a right——all is fair in love and war and hate! Why did you give me the chance? I had a vow——a vow in heaven——or hell Ah! ha! Revenge is sweet, after all!" and he burst into a wild discordant laugh, dreadful to hear.

Catherine shuddered, a sense of horror creeping over her. She did not catch the whole of his words, lost that hoarse whisper was sometimes in the sullen plash of the advancing waves. The words were not addressed to her, but to some imaginary object visible only to the eye of madness. She attached no meaning to what she heard. She had no clue by which to unravel the workings of his disordered mind. Yet it was terrible to see his terror-stricken face, and listen to the exclamations addressed to a phantom foe. She tried to recall him to himself. "David, there is no one here but ourselves. You have been dreaming."

David turned his wild eyes towards her, but continued to point wildly over the sea. "Can you not see him? There-out there! His head-his eyes-ah, those eye!——as he looked then——then! Ah, those eyes!——as he looked then——then! Ah, don't look so at me, I say! You will kill me!" He buried his face in his hands and shuddered from head to foot. Catherine, despite the shiver of horror that crept over her, felt, more strongly than anything else, a deep pity for one whose mind was so visibly shattered. Much of the past could be condoned to one whose metal faculties were so terribly unstrung. She came one step nearer, and laid her hand upon his arm.

"You should not be out here alone," she said. "You had better go home. It is growing dark already. If you will come with me to the lodge, I will see that you have a lantern; or, if you like, I will send a servant with a lantern with you." She felt, indeed, that he was hardly in a condition to be out alone. She wished Bruce Pendrill could see him now. But at the touch of her hand David sprang back as if she had struck him. His eyes were full of shrinking horror. "Go away!" he said fiercely, "your hand burns me——it burns me, I say! How can you look at me or touch me? What have I done that you come here day by day to torment me? Is it not enough that he leaves me no peace night or day?––that he brings me down to this cursed place, whether I will or no, but you must haunt me too? Ah, it is too much––it is too much, I say!"

She could not catch all these rapidly-uttered words, but she read the hopeless misery of his face. "I do not wish to distress you. David. Will you go home quietly now? You are not well; you should not be out here alone. Have you anybody there to take care of you?" He laughed again, and flung his arms above his head with a wild gesture of despair. "You say this to me––you! you! It only wanted this. My God, this is too much!" He turned from her and sprang away in the darkness. She heard his steps as he dashed recklessly up the cliff path-so recklessly that she half expected to hear the sound of a slip and a fall-and then, he reached the summit and turned inland, they died away into silence.

Catherine drew a long breath of relief when she found herself alone. There was something expressibly awful in talking to a madman in the dimmest of the dying day, in hearing his wild words addressed to some phantom shadow seen only by his disordered vision. She shivered a little as she turned landwards. She could stay no longer in that lonely place. She met Bruce looking out for her on her return. He said something about her staying out too long in the darkness. She laid her hand upon his arm, and pacing up and down the dark avenue, she told him of her adventure with the madman.

"Bruce, I am certain he ought to see a doctor. Will you not see if you can do something for him?" She could not see the expression of Bruce's face. Had she been able to do so, she would have been startled. His voice was very cold as he answered "I am not a lunacy commissioner, Catherine." She was surprised, and a little hurt. "You are very hard, Bruce you saw him once before, why not again?" "If he, or his friends for him, require medical advice, I suppose they are capable of sending for it," he said, adding with sudden fierceness, as it seemed to her, "Catherine, David MacRae, ill or well, is nothing to you. It is not fit you should waste a single thought upon that scoundrel again!"

She was surprised at his vehemence; it was so unlike Bruce to speak with heat. What had there been in her account of the meeting to discompose him so greatly? Before she could attempt to frame the question, he had

asked one of her-asked it abruptly, as it seemed, irrelevant. "How long
has MacRae been in these parts?" I don't know. I have never seen him
till tonight, nor heard of him at all." "Nor I. Go in, Catherine. It is too
late for you to be out." "And you?" "I will come presently." "And you will
think about what I asked you?" "I will think about it-yes." The tone was
enigmatic. She could not make Bruce out at all, she went in at his bidding.
She knew that he wish to be alone, that he had something disturbing upon
his mind, though what it was she could not divine.

Bruce, as it turned out, had no choice in the matter; for his brother sent
to him next day a message to the effect that MacRae's servant had been to
see him with a very sad account of his master, who seemed to be suffering
under an acute attack of delirium tremens. Johnathon thought his brother,
who had seen him once before, had better go the next day in a casual sort
of way, and see if he could do anything. MacRae was furious at the idea of
having a doctor near him; but possibly he would not regard Bruce in that
light, and the servants would do all they could to abstain for him access to
their master. They were terrified at his ravings, and half afraid he would
do himself or them an injury if not placed under proper control.

So Bruce, upon the following afternoon, started for the old dilapidated
house, without saying a word to one as to his destination, and was eagerly
admitted by a haggard-looking servant, who said that his master was
terrible bad today——it was awful like to hear him go on," and expressed it as
his opinion that he was almost past knowing who was near him, he was so
wild and delirious. He had kept his bed for the past two days, having been
very ill since coming in, wet and exhausted, on the night Catherine had
seen him. Between the attacks of delirium he was as weak as a child; and
with this much of warning and explanation, Bruce was ushered upstairs.

An hour later he left that desolate house with a quick, firm tread,
that broke, as he turned a corner and was concealed from view, almost to
a run. His face was very pale; it looked thinner and sharper than it had
done an hour before, and his eyes were full of an unspeakable horror.
Now and again a shudder ran through his frame; but no word passed his
tightly-compressed lips. He hurried through the tangled park as if some
deadly malaria lurked there. He hardly drew his breath until he had left
the trees and brake behind, and plunged into the wild trackless moor; even
then, goaded by his thoughts, he plunged blindly along for a mile or more,

until at last, breathless and exhausted, he sank face downwards upon the heather, trembling in every limb. How long he lay there he never knew. He was roused at last by a touch upon his shoulder, and raising himself with a start, he looked straight into the startled eyes of Rebecca Scott.

Chapter 28

Lovers

Bruce sprang to his feet, and the two stood gazing at one another for a moment in mute surprise. "You are ill," said Rebecca; "You are as white as a sheet. What is the matter?" She spoke anxiously. She looked half frightened at his strange looks; he saw it, and recovered himself instantly. It was perhaps the first time he had ever been taken unawares, and he was not altogether pleased that it had happened now.

"What are you doing out here all alone?" he asked peremptorily. "What are you doing lying on the ground on a cold January evening?" she retorted. "Do you want to get rheumatic fever too?" "Answer my question first. What are you doing out here, miles away from home. With the darkness coming on too?" "I lost my way," she answered carelessly. "I never can keep my bearings in these strange, wild places, where everything looks alike."

"Then I must take you home," said Bruce shortly. "You said you were going to dine at St. Maws tonight," she objected. "I shall take you home first," he said. "It will be ever so much out of road. Just show me the way. I shall find it fast enough." "I dare say-after having lost it in broad daylight. You must come with me. I cannot trust you." Rebecca flushed hotly as she turned and walked beside him. Was more meant than met the ear? "There is not the least need you should," she said haughtily, and seemed disposed to say no more.

Bruce spoke first, in his abrupt peremptory fashion. He was absorbed and distrait. She tried not to feel disappointed at his words. "Lady Rebecca, is it true that you knew Edward MacAlister intimately for many years?" "Ever since I can remember. He was almost like a brother to us."

"Do you know if he ever had an enemy?" Rebecca looked up quickly into his pale face. "Why do you ask?" "That is my affair. I do not ask without a reason. Think before you answer—if you can." "Edward was always such a favourite," she began but was interrupted by a quick, impatient gesture from Bruce. "Don't chatter," he said, almost rudely, "think!" Oddly enough this brusque reminder did not offend her. She saw that Bruce's nerves were all on edge, that they were strung to a painful pitch of tension. She began to catch some of his earnestness and determination.

Rebecca was taken out of herself, and from that moment her manner changed for the better. She thought the matter over in silence. "I have heard that Sir David MacRae bore an old grudge against him, Ah!" breathed Bruce softly. "But I fancied, perhaps, that Catherine's influence had made them friends. Edward knew some disreputable story connected with Sir David MacRae's past life MacMurray knows more about it than I do-and he always hated him for it." "Ah!" said Bruce again. "Why do you ask?" questioned Rebecca again; but he gave her no answer. He was wrapped in deep thought. She looked at him once or twice, but said no more. He was the first to speak, and the question was a little significant.

"You were down on the shore with Catherine and MacAlister that night, were you not?" "Yes." "Was MacRae there too?" She looked at him with startled eyes. "No; certainly not." "Can you be sure of that? Was there moon enough to show plainly everything that went on?" Rebecca put up her hand to her head. "No." she answered. "I ought not have spoken so positively. It was too dark to see anything. There might have been dozens of people there whom I should never have seen. I was much too anxious and excited to keep a sharp look-out-why should I? And there was not a gleam of moonlight till many minutes after the boat got back, and the confusion was very great all the time. Why do you talk so? Why do you ask such a question?" She spoke with subdued excitement and insistence. "Somebody was in that boat unknown to the crew," he answered significantly. "Was there?"

"Somebody steered the boat to shore. You do not share, I presume, in the popular belief of the phantom coxswain?" Rebecca stopped short, trembling and scared. "You think——?" but she could only get out those two words; she knew not how to frame the question. He bent his head. "I do." But she put out her hand with a quick, passionate gesture, as if fighting with some hideous phantom. ""Ah! no! no! It could not be. It would be too unspeakably awful-too horrible! How do you know? How can you say such things? What has put such a hideous thought into your mind?" "I come from standing by MacRae's bed, listening to his words of wandering his delirious outbursts. It is plain enough what phantoms are haunting him now-what pictures he is seeing, as he lies in the stupor of drink and opium. He is trying to drown thought and remorse, but he has not succeeded yet."

Rebecca shuddered strongly, and faltered a little in her walk. Bruce took her hand and placed it within his arm. "You are tired, Rebecca?" "No; but it is so awful. Bruce"——calling him so as unconsciously as he had called her Rebecca "must Catherine know this? Oh! It was cruel enough before-but-this—— "She shall never know," said Bruce quickly. "To what end should we add this burden to what she carries now? No one could prove it——it may be nothing more than some sick fancy, engendered by the thought of what might have been. Mind you, I have no moral doubts myself; but the man is practically mad, and no confession or evidence given by him would be accepted. He has fulfilled his vow he has murdered-practically murdered his foe; but Catherine must be spared the knowledge: She must never know."

"No, never! never!" cried Rebecca; and her voice expressed so much feeling, that Bruce turned and looked at her in the fading light. "Have you a heart after all, Rebecca?" he asked. She made no answer; her heart beat wildly, answering in its own fashion the question asked, but not in a way that he could hear. "Rebecca," rather fiercely," why did you not marry the marquis?" "Because I loathed him." "You did not always loathe him?" "I did, I did, always." "You flirted with him disgracefully, then." She looked up with something of pleading in her dark eyes. "I was but eighteen." "Do you never flirt now?"

She looked up again, her eyes flashing strangely. "What right have you to ask such a question?" "The right of the man who loves you," he answered, in the same half-fierce, half-bitter way——"who loves you with every fibre of his being; and although he has proved you vain and unbecoming and heartless once and again, cannot tear your image from his heart. Do not think I am complaining. I suppose you have a right to please yourself; but sometimes I feel as if no man had ever been treated so abominably as I have been by you."

"You by me!" she answered, panting in her excitement," when it was you who left me in a fury, without one word of farewell." "I thought I had had my leave pretty distinctly." "You had had nothing of the kind-nothing but a few wild confused words from a mere child, frightened and bewildered by happiness and nervousness into the silliest of speeches a silly girl could make at such a moment. But you cannot understand-you never will-you are made of stone, I think." He turned upon her quickly. "I wish I were sometimes," he said; "I wish it when I am near you. You make love you—I am powerless in your hands, and you-you—" "I love you with all my heart. I have never loved anybody else, and you have behaved cruelly, disgracefully to me always." The words came all at once in one vehement burst of passion.

He stopped short, wheeled round, and stood facing her. He could only see her face as they stood thus in the gathering dusk. "Rebecca," he said slowly, "what did you say just now? Say it again." Defiance shone out of her eyes. "I will not!" She said, her cheeks flaming. He took both her hands in his and held them hard. "Yes, you will," he answered. "Say it again." She was panting with a strange mixture of feeling; the earth and sky seemed to spin round together. "Say it again, Rebecca." "I said—I love you; but I don't—I will never, never say it again—" She got not farther, for he held her so closely in his arms that all speech was impossible for the moment. "That will do," he answered. "I don't want you to say it again. Once is enough."

"Catherine", said Rebecca in the softest of whispers as she came into the quiet room where her brother lay asleep upon the sofa, and Catherine sat dreaming beside the fire. "Ah, Catherine, Catherine!" and then she stopped short, kneeling down, and turning her quivering face and swimming eyes towards the face bent tenderly over her. Somehow it was never needful to say much to Catherine. Always understood without many words. She bent her head now, and kissed Rebecca. "Is it so, then, dear?" she asked. "Did you know?" "I knew what you told me yourself, and I could see for myself that he had not forgotten any more than you."

"I did not see it." "Possibly not-neither did he; but sometimes loves is very blind-and very willful too." Was there a touch of tender reproach in the tone? Rebecca looked at her earnestly. "I know what you mean," she said. "We both want to be master; but I think––I am afraid––he will have the upper hand now." But the smile that quivered over the upturned face was full of such sweetness and brightness that Catherine kiss her again. "You will not find him such a tyrant as he professes to be. Bruce is very generous and unselfish, despite his affectation of cynicism. I am so glad you have made him happy at last. I am so glad that our paths in life will not lie very widely apart." Rebecca took Catherine's hand and kissed it. "I am so happy," she said simply. "And I owe it all to you."

Catherine caressed the dark head laid against her knee, as Rebecca subsided into her favourite lowly position at Catherine's feet. Presently she became aware that the girl's tears were falling fast. "Crying, dearest?" she questioned gently. A stifled sob was the answer" what is the matter, my child?" "Edward!" was all that Rebecca could get out. Somehow the desolation of Catherine's life had never come home to her with quite the same sense of realisation as now, in the hour of her deepest happiness. "He would be glad," answered Catherine, steadily and sweetly. "He loved you dearly, Rebecca; and he and Bruce were always such friends. It was his hope that all would come right. If he can see us now, as I often think he can, he will be rejoicing in your happiness now. You must shed no tears tonight, dearest, unless they are tears of happiness." Rebecca suddenly half rose, and flung her arms round Catherine.

"How can you bear it? How can you bear it? Catherine, I think you are an angel. No one in this wide world was ever like you. And to think––" she shuddered strongly and stopped short. "You are excited and over-wrought," said Catherine gently. "You must not let yourself be knocked up, or Bruce will scold me when he comes back. See, MacMurray is waking up. He had such a bad headache, poor boy; I hope he has slept it off. You must tell him the news––it will please him, I am sure." "You tell him," whispered Rebecca, and slipped away to relieve her over-burdened heart by a burst of tears; for one strange revelation following upon another had tried her more than she knew at the time.

MacMurray was quietly pleased at the news. He liked Bruce; he had fancied that he and Rebecca were not altogether indifferent to each other, so this conclusion did not take him altogether by surprise. He was sorry to think of losing Rebecca, but not as perplexed as he would have been some months before. Life looked different to him now––more serious and earnest. He began to have aspirations of his own. He no longer regarded existence as a sort of pleasant easy game of play.

Certainly it seemed as if the course of true love as regarded Rebecca and Bruce, after passing its early shoals and quicksand, were to run quietly and smoothly enough now. He came back from St. Maws in time for dinner, and when dessert was put on the table, he announced his plans with the hardihood characteristic of man. "Aunt Jennifer is delighted, Rebecca and so is Johnathon," he said. "I have told them that we will be married almost at once, within three months, at least-oh, you needn't look like that I think I've waited long enough-pretty well as long as Brian——" "Did for Melissa-and didn't like her in the end don't make that your precedent."

"Well, don't interrupt," proceed Bruce imperturbably. "We've got it all beautifully arranged. I'm going to take part of the practice, as Johnathon has always been bothering me to do ever since it increased so much, and we're to have half the house for our establishment, and he and Aunt Jennifer the other. It was originally two houses, and lends itself excellently to that arrangement, though I dare say practically we shall be all one household, as you and our aunt have managed to hit it off so well. Catherine, can't Rebecca be married from MacAlister when MacMurray is well enough to give her away? It would save a lot of bother. I hate flummery, and I'm sure she does too. Come now, Rebecca, don't laugh. Don't you think that would be an excellent arrangement? Here we all are; what is the good of getting all split up again? You'll be losing your heart to another marquis if I let you out of my sight."

Her eyes were dancing with mischievous merriment. She was more than ready to enter the lists. "Just listen to the tyrant-trying to keep me a prisoner already! Trying to take everything into his own hands——and not content without adding insult to injury!" His eyes too were alight; but his mouth was grim. "I have not forgotten how you served me last time, my Lady." "At Oxford?" "At Oxford." "Catherine, listen. I will tell you how I served him. I had eyes for no one but him, silly girl that I was; I was with him morning, noon and night. Child as I was at the time, careless and inexperienced, even I was absolutely ashamed at the open preference I showed him; I blush even now to think of the undisguised way in which I flung myself at a particularly hard head. And yet he pretends he did not understand! If that is so, then for real, down right, hopeless, stupidity, and obtuseness, command me to an Oxford double-first-class-man!"

Rebecca might get the best of it in an encounter of tongues, but Bruce had his own way in the settlement of their affairs, possibly because her resistance. What indeed, they had to wait for, when they had been waiting so many long years for one another?" Nothing clouded the horizon of their happiness. Even the hideous shadow which had been in a sense the means of bringing them together seemed to have vanished with the sudden disappearance of David MacRae from the neighbourhood. Upon the very day following Bruce's visit to him, he left his house, ill and weak as he was, to join by his sister at Mentone. His servant accompanied him. The desolate house was shut up once more, and Bruce Pendrill sincerely hoped the haunting baleful influence of that, wild and wicked nature had passed from their lives for ever.

So Rebecca after all was married at MacAlister, in the cliff church that seen the hands of Edward and Catherine joined in wedlock she resisted a good while, feeling afraid that it would be painful to Catherine––a second wedding, and that within a few months of her own widowhood. But Catherine took part with Bruce, and the bride elect gave way, only too delighted at heart to be with Catherine to the last. It was a very quiet wedding-as quiet as Catherine's own-even the people gathered together in the little church had hardly changed. Only one short year had passed since Catherine in her snowy robes stood before that little altar, with the marriage vow upon lip-only a year a year ago, now?

Yet Catherine's face was very calm and sweet. She shed no tears she seemed to have no sad thoughts for herself, however others might feel. One pair of grey eyes seldom wandered from her face as the simple ceremonies of the day proceeded. One heart was far more occupied with thoughts of the pale-face widow than of the blooming bride. MacMurray quitted MacAlister almost immediately after his sister. The words of thanks he tried to speak faltered on his tongue, and would not come. Catherine understood, and answered by one of her sweetest smiles. "You were Edward's friend; you are my friend now. You must not try to thank me. I am so very glad to think of the link that binds us together. I shall not lose sight of you whilst Rebecca is so near. You will come again some day?" "Yes, Lady MacAlister," he answered quietly, "I will come again;" and he raised the hand he held for one moment very reverently to his lips. As he drove away he looked back, Catherine still upon the terrace. "Yes", he said quietly to himself, "I will come back-some day."

Chapter 29

"As We Forgive"

A year had passed away since that fatal night when Edward had left his wife standing on the shore had gone away in the darkness and had returned no more: a year had passed, with its chequered lights and shades, but the anniversary of her husband's death found Catherine, as he had left her, at MacAlister alone.

Many things had happened during that year. Rebecca had married and settled happily in the picturesque red house at St. Maws as Bruce Pendrill's loving, brilliant wife. Catherine had been to Germany once again, to assure herself with her own eyes of the truth of the favourable reports sent to her. She had had the satisfaction of seeing how great an improvement had taken place in Matthew's condition; that although the cure was slow-would most likely need a second, possibly even a third year before it would be absolutely complete, yet it was practically certain, if he and those who held his fate in their hands would but have patience and perseverance. The boy was quite happy in the establishment of which he was a member. He had gone through the most trying part of the treatment, and was enthusiastic about the kindness and skill of his doctor. He had made many friends, and had quite lost the home-sickness that occasionally troubled him at first. He was delighted to see Catherine again. He was insistent that she should come to see him more often; but he did not even wish to return to MacAlister till he could do so whole and sound, as a man in good health and strength, instead of a helpless invalid.

Catherine was summoned from Germany by the news of the dangerous illness of Lady Louise, who died only a few days after the arrival of her niece. She had been talking of making a permanent home at MacAlister now that Catherine was so utterly alone, but her death stopped all such schemes; and so it came about that in absolute solitude the young widowed countess took up her abode for the winter in the great silent castle beside the sea.

The sea still exercised its old fascination over Catherine. Her happiest hours were spent wandering by its brink or riding along the breezy cliff. It was a friend indeed to her in those days, it frowned upon her no more. It had done its worst already––it had taken away the light of her life. Might it not be possible-was there not something of promise in its eternal music? Could it be that in some unexpected, mysterious way it would bring back some of the light that had been taken away-would be the means of uniting once again the hearts that had been so cruelly sundered? Strange thoughts and fancies flitted often through her brain, formless and indistinct, but comforting withal.

Returning to the castle at dusk one day, after one of these solitary rambles, she found an unusual bustle and excitement stirring there. Lorna hurried forward to explain the cause of the unwonted tumult.

"I hope I have not done wrong, my Lady. You were not here to give orders, and I could only act as I felt you would wish. A lad came running in with a scared face not half-an-hour back, saying there was a man lying at the foot of the cliffs, as if he had fallen over. I scarce think he can be alive if that be so; but I told the men that if he were-as there is no other decent house near––I thought you would wish––"

"That he should be brought here. Quite right, Lorna, is there a room ready? Has Mr Pendrill been sent for?" "The groom has been gone this twenty minutes. Living or dead, he must have a doctor to him. The maids are getting the east room ready, I doubt if he can be living after such a fall." "He may not have fallen over the cliff. He may have been scaling it, and have dropped from but a small height. See that everything to be needed is ready. He may be here almost immediately now." She went up to the bed-room herself, to see if it were ready should there be need.

It was probably only some poor tramp or fisherman who met with the accident-no matter, he should be tended at MacAlister, he should lie in its most comfortable guest chamber, he should have every care that wealth could supply. Catherine knew too well the dire results that might follow a slip down those hard treacherous cliffs not to feel peculiarly tender and solicitous over another victim.

The steady tramp of feet ascending the stairs, and approaching the room where she stood, roused Catherine to the knowledge that the injured man was not dead, and that they were bringing him up to be tended and nursed as she had directed. The door was pushed open; six men carried in their burden upon an improvised stretcher, and laid it just as it was upon the bed. Catherine stepped forward, and then started, growing a little pale; for she recognised in the death like, rigid face before her the well-know countenance of David MacRae.

She could not look without a shudder at that shattered frame, and Lorna shook her head gravely, marveling that he yet breathed. None save professional hands dared touch him, so distorted and dislocated was every limb; and yet by one of those strange coincidences, not altogether uncommon in cases of accident, the beautiful face was entirely untouched, not marred by a scratch or contusion. Death-like unconsciousness had set its seal upon those chiseled, marble features, and had wiped from them every trace of passion or of vice.

Bruce Pendrill was amongst them long before they looked for him. He met the messenger not far from MacAlister, and had come at once. He turned Catherine out of the room with a stern precipitancy that perplexed her somewhat, as did also the expression of his face, which she did not understand. He shut himself up with his patient, retaining the services of Lorna and one of the men.

It was two hours before she saw him again. Catherine wandered up and down the dark hall, revolving many things in her mind. What had brought David so suddenly back at this melancholy time of the year? She had believed him abroad with his sister, with whom he seemed to have spent his time since his disappearance early in the spring. What had brought him back now? And why did he so haunt the frowning, treacherous cliffs of MacAlister? Was he mad? But why did his madness always drive him to this spot? She asked many such questions of herself, but she could answer none of them. At last Bruce came down. His face looked as if carved in flint. She could not read the meaning of his glance.

"Is he dead?" she asked softly. "He cannot last long. If he has any relations near, they should be telegraphed for." "His sister is in Italy, I believe. There is no one else that I know of." "Then there is nothing to be done. He is sinking fast. He cannot live many hours. I doubt if he will last the night." Catherine's face was pale and grave. "Poor David!" she said, beneath her breath. Bruce started, and made a quick movement as if repulsion. "No one could wish him to live," he began, almost roughly;" he has hardly a whole bone in his body." "Is he conscious?" "No, nor likely to be. It is not at all probable he will ever open his eyes again. He will most likely sink quietly, without a sound or a sign. I have done all I can for him. Somebody must be with him to watch him, I suppose. It can only be a question of hours now." A dark cloud hung upon the doctor's brow. His mind was per-occupied. Presently he spoke again––a sort of mutter between his teeth. "He ought not to be allowed to die here––under this roof. It is monstrous-hateful to think of! Nothing can save him. Yet I suppose it would be murder to move him now." Catherine looked up quickly. "Move him! Bruce, what are you thinking of?" "I know it cannot done," was the answer, spoken in a stern, dogged tone. "Yet I repeat what I said before: he ought not to be under this roof." There was a gentle reproach in the look that Catherine bent upon him.

"My husband's roof and mine will always be always be a refuge for any whose need is as sore as his. Sometimes I think, Bruce, that you are the very hardest man I ever met. His life, I know, is terribly stained; yet it is not for us to judge him." It seemed as if Bruce were agitated. He gave no outward sign, but his face was pale, his manner curiously harsh and peremptory. "You do not know," he said. "Your husband––" She stopped him by a gesture. "My husband would be the first to bid me return good for evil. You know Edward very little if you do not know that. David is dying, and death wipes out much. He is about to answer for his life to a higher tribunal than ours. Ah! let us not condemn him harshly. Have we not all our sins upon our heads? When my turn comes to answer for mine, let me not have this one added-that I hardened my heart against the dying, and denied the help and succour mutely asked at the last hour." "Catherine," said Bruce, with one of those swift changes that marked his manner when he was deeply moved, "were I worthy, I would kiss the hem of your garment. As it is, I can only say farewell. God be with you!"

He was gone before she could open her lips again. She stood in a sort of dream, feeling as if some strange thing were about to happen to her. Night fell upon the castle and its inhabitants, but Catherine could not sleep. If ever she closed her eyes in momentary slumber, the same vivid dream recurred again and again, till she was oppressed and exhausted by the effort to escape from it. It was David, always David, begging, praying, beseeching her to come. Sometimes it seemed as if his shadowy form stood beside her, wildly praying the same thing-to come to him-to come before it was too late. At last she could stand it no longer. She rose and dressed. The clock in the tower struck five. She knew she could sleep no more that night. Why should she not take the watch beside the unconscious dying man, and let the faithful Lorna get some rest?

She stole noiselessly to the sick room. There had been no change in the patient's state. He lived, but could hardly live much longer. Lorna would fain have stayed, but Catherine dismissed her quietly and firmly, preferring to keep her watch alone. Profound silence reigned in the great house-silence only broken from time to time by the reverberating strokes of the clock in the tower, or by the sudden sinking of the coal in the grate and the quiet fall of the cinders. The place, and the place, and the office thus undertaken by Catherine.

David lay dying-David, once her friend and playmate, then her bitterest, cruelest foe, now?--ah yes, what now?--she asked that question many times of herself. What strange, mysterious power is that death! How it blots out all hatred, anger, bitterness, and distrust, and leaves in its place a tender, mournful compassion. Who can look upon the face of the dead, and cherish hard thoughts of him that is gone?

Not Catherine, at least. David had been to her as the evil genius of one crisis of her life-of more had she but known it. She had said in her heart that she could never forgive him, that she would never voluntarily look upon his face again, and yet here he lay dying beneath her roof, and she was with him. She could not, when it came to the point, leave him to die alone, with only a stranger beside him. He might never know, his eyes would probably never open to the light of this world again; but she would know and in years to come, when time should, ever more than now, have softened all things to her, she knew that she would be glad to think she had shown mercy and compassion towards one in death, who had shown himself in life her bitterest foe

Very solemn thoughts filled her mind as she sat in that quiet room, in which a strong young life was quickly fading away. Would the sin-stained soul pass into the shadowy land of the hereafter in silence and darkness, without one moment for preparation perhaps for repentance? Would some slight gleam of consciousness be granted? Would it be vouchsafed to him to wake once more in this world, to give some sign to the earnest, silent watcher whether he had tried his peace with God before he was called to his last account? The lamp burned low-flickered in its socket. That strange blue film, the first forerunner of the coming day, stole solemnly into that quiet room. Suddenly Catherine became aware that David's eyes were open, and fixed intently upon her face. She rose and stood beside him.

"You are here?" he said, in a strange low voice. "I felt that you would hear me call-and would come. I knew I could not-die-till I had told you all." She did not know how far he was conscious. His words were strange, but his eye was calm and quiet. He took the stimulant she held to his lips. It gave him an access of strength. "Where am I?" he asked. "At MacAlister." A strange look flitted over his face. "Ah! I remember now––I fell. And I have been brought to MacAlister-to die-and you, Catherine, are with me. It is well." She hardly knew what to say, or how to answer the awed look in those dying eyes. He bent a keen glance upon her. "Will it be soon?" he asked; and she knew that the "it" meant death. She could not deceive him. She bent head in assent, as she said "Very soon I think."

His eyes never left her face. His own moved not a muscle, but its expression changed moment by moment in a way she could not understand. "There is not much time left, Catherine. Sit down by me where I can see you. I must make a confession to you before I die." "Not to me, David," said Catherine gently. "Confess your sins to our Father in Heaven. He alone can grant forgiveness; and his mercies are very great." "Forgiveness! The word was spoken with an intensity of bitterness that startled Catherine. The horror was deepening each moment in his eyes. She began to feel that it was reflected in her own. What did it all mean?

"God is very merciful," she said gently, commanding herself so that he should not see her agitation. "You do not know," he interrupted almost fierily. "Wait till I have told you all." "Why should you tell me, David? I know much of your past life. I know that you have sinned. Ask God's forgiveness before it is too late. It is against, Him, not me, you have sinned,"

"Against Him and you," he answered with a grave intensity of manner that plainly showed him master of his faculties. "Listen to me, Catherine- you shall listen! I cannot carry the guilty secret to the grave. Death looks me in the face––he holds me by the hand, but he will not let me leave this world till I have told all." A nameless horror fell upon Catherine. She neither spoke nor moved. "Catherine, turn your face this way. I want to see it. I must see it. You remember the night, a year ago, when-your husband-went away?" She bent her head in silence. "Did you know that I was there––in the boat with him?" She raised her head, and looked at him speechlessly.

"I was there," he said, "but nobody knew, nobody suspected. I was on the shore before you. I saw you cling to him. I heard every word that passed. I think a demon entered into my soul as you kissed each other that night. Kiss her!' I said, 'kiss her but you shall never see her again!' Catherine, I think sometimes I am mad––I was mad, possessed, that night. I had no will, no power to resist the evil spirit within me. He went down to the boat. I followed. In the black darkness nobody saw me swing myself in. You know the story the men told when they came back––it was all true enough. The crew of the sinking vessel had been rescued. Your husband left the boat to help the little lad. I followed him, unknown to all. He had already handed the boy into the boat when I came stealthily up to him; the boat had swung round, and for a moment was lost in darkness before it could be brought up again. This was my chance. It was pitchy dark, and he did not see me though I was close beside him. I had the great boat-hook in my hand; we were both sinking with the sinking vessel. I steadied myself, and brought the metal end of the weapon with all my strength upon his head. He sank without a cry. I saw his head, covered with blood, and his glassy eyes above the water for a moment––the sight has haunted me ever since––then I sprang into the boat. 'All right!' I shouted, and the men pulled off with a will, without a suspicion or a doubt. Almost before the boat reached the shore I sprang out, and vanished in the darkness before any one had seen me. My vow of vengeance was fulfilled. I murdered your husband, Catherine-do you understand?––I murdered him in cold blood!

184

What have you to say to me?" She sat still as a marble statue, her hands closely locked together. She spoke no word.

"I thought revenge would be sweet; but it has been bitter-bitter-bitter! I have known no peace night or day. I have been ceaselessly haunted by the sight of that ghastly face-ah, I see it now! Every time I lie down to sleep I am doomed to do that hideous deed again. I have fled time after time from the scene of my crime, only to be dragged back by a power I cannot resist. I knew that a terrible retribution would come; yet I could not keep away. And now-yes, it has come-more terrible than ever I pictured. I am dying-- in this house-and you-his wife-are watching over me. Ah, it is frightful! Is there forgiveness with God for sin like mine? You say his mercies are great. Can they cover this hideous deed? Catherine, can you forgive?"

He spoke with the wild, passionate appeal of despair. The anguish and remorse in his face were terrible to see; but Catherine did not speak. She sat rigid and still, pale as death, her eyes glowing like living fire in the wild conflict of her feeling. This was terrible-too terrible to be borne.

"Catherine, I am dying-dying! The shadows are closing round me. Ah, do not turn away! It is all so dark; if you desert me I am lost indeed! If you were dying you would understand. Catherine, you say God is good-merciful. Have asked his pardon again and again for this black sin, and even as I pray it seems as if you-your pale, still face-rises ever between me and the forgiveness I crave. I read by this token that to you I must confess this blackest sin; of you I must ask pardon too. I have repented. I do repent. I would give my life to call him back. Catherine, forgive-forgive! Have mercy upon a dying man. As you will one day ask pardon at God's hands, even for your blameless life, give me your pardon ere I die!" Who shall estimate the struggle that raged in Catherine's soul during the brief moments that followed this appeal-moments that to her were like hours, years, for the concentrated tumult of feeling that surged through them? She felt as if she had grown sensibly older, ere, white and shaken by the conflict, she won the victory over herself.

She rose and stood beside him. "David, I forgive you. My God forgive you as I do." A sudden light flashed into his eyes. The awful unspeakable horror passed slowly away. The deep darkness lifted a little--a very little-and Catherine saw that it was so. "I think-you have-saved me," he whispered whilst the death damp gathered on his brow. "Catherine, you will have your reward for this——I know it——I feel it. Ah! Is this death? Catherine——it is coming-teach me to pray——I cannot——I have forgotten—— help me!" "I will help you, David. Say it after me. 'Our Father which art in Heaven, Hallowed be Thy name; Thy kingdom come, Thy will be done in earth as is Heaven; Give us this day our daily bread; And forgive us our trespasses; as we forgive'——" "As we forgive'——" David broke off suddenly; a strange look of gladness, of relief, of comprehension, flashing over the face that had been so full of terror and anguish. "'As we forgive'-and you have forgiven——then it may be that He will forgive too. I could not believe it before-now I can-God be merciful to me, a sinner!"

Those were his last words. Already his eyes were glazing. The hush as of the shadow of death was filling that dim room. Catherine knelt beside the bed, a sense of deep awe upon her, praying with all the strength of her pure soul for the guilty, erring man her husband's murderer-dying beneath his roof. And as she thus knelt and prayed, a sudden sense of her husband's presence filled all her soul with an inexpressible, indescribable thrill of mingled rapture and awe. She trembled, and her heart beat thick and fast; whether she were in the spirit or out of the spirit she knew not. And then——in deep immeasurable distance, far, far away, and yet distinctly, sweetly clear-unmistakable——the sound of a voice Edward's voice-thrilling through infinity of space: Catherine! Catherine! My wife!"

She started to her feet, quivering in every limb. David's eyes were fixed upon her with an inexplicable look of joy. Had he heard it too? What did it mean-that strange cry from the spirit world in this hour of death and dawn? She leant over the dying man. "David," she said, in a voice that was full of an emotion too deep for any but the simplest of words, "I forgive you-so does Edward; and I think God has forgiven you too." The clear radiance of another day was shining upon the earth, as the troubled, erring spirit was set free, and passed away into the great hereafter, whose secrets shall be read in God's time, when all but His Word shall have passed away.

Let us not judge him——for is there not joy with the angels in heaven over one sinner that repenteth? Yes, all was over now: all the weary warfare of sin and strife; and with a calm majesty in death, that the beautiful face had never worn in life, David MacRae lay dead in MacAlister Castle.

Chapter 30

Lord MacMurray

"And you forgave him, Catherine, you forgave him? The man who killed your husband?" It was Rebecca who spoke, and she spoke with a passion of horror in her tone. Bruce stood a little apart in the recess of the window, a heavy cloud upon his brow. Lord MacMurray was leaning with averted face upon the high caved mantel-shelf.

They had all come over early to MacAlister, to hear the fate of the hapless man who had died in the night. Rebecca felt an unquenchable longing to know if he had spoken before he died——if by chance the terrible secret had escaped in delirium from his lips; and she had insisted on coming with her husband. Her brother, who had arrived unexpectedly the previous evening, had made one of the party. He was hungering for another sight of Catherine, and MacAlister seemed to draw him like a magnet. Catherine's face had told a tale of its own when she first appeared; and the whispered question on Rebecca's lips "Did he speak, Catherine? Did he say anything?" elicited a reply that led to explanations on both sides, rendering further reserve needless; then Catherine told her tale with the quiet calmness of one who has too lately passed through some great mental conflict to be easily disturbed again.

But Rebecca, fiery, impetuous Rebecca, could not understand this calm. She was shaken by a tempest of excitement and wrath. "You forgave

187

him, Catherine? Ah! How could you? Edward's murderer!" "Yes, I forgave him." "You should not! You should not! It was not it could not be right! Catherine, I cannot understand you. I think you are made of stone!" She said nothing; she smiled. That smile was only seen by MacMurray. It thrilled him to his heart's core. "Why were you with him at all?" said Bruce, almost sternly. "It was not your duty to be there. It was no fit place for you." "I think my place is where there is sorrow and need and loneliness," answered Catherine, very gently. He needed me-and I came to him." "He sent for you?" "But you said——" Catherine lifted her head; she rose to her feet, passing her hand across her brow. "You would not understand, dear. There are some things Rebecca, that you are very slow to learn. You know something of the mysteries of life, but you do not understand anything of those deeper mysteries of death. I have forgiven a dying man, who prayed forgiveness with his last breath——and you look at me with horror. "Rebecca gazed at Catherine, but yet would not yield her point. "Mercy can be carried too far——" but she could not say more, for the look upon Catherine's face brought a sudden sense of choking that would have made her voice falter had she attempted to proceed. Her brother's murmured words, therefore, were now distinctly heard.

"Not in God's sight, perhaps." Catherine turned to him with a swift gesture inexpressibly sweet. "Ah! You understand." she said simply. "I am glad you have come just now, MacMurray. I shall want help. Will you give it to me?" "I will do anything for you, and esteem it an honour." She looked at him steadily. "Even if it is for one who-for the one who lies upstairs now-dead?" MacMurray bent his head. "Even for him-at your bidding." "Thank you" she said. "I will take you home now, Rebecca," said Bruce, curtly. "We are not wanted here." Catherine looked questioningly at him, as she gave him her hand, to see what this abruptness might signify. He returned her gaze with equal intensity. "I believe you are an angel, Catherine," he said, lifting her hand for a moment to his lips; "but there are times when fallen mortals like ourselves feel the angelic presence a little overpowering."

Catherine, as she had said, wanted the help of some man of business, as there was a good deal to be done in connection with David's sudden death: a good many trying formalities to be gone through, as well as much correspondence, and in Lord MacMurray she found a able and willing assistant. He saw much of Catherine in those days. He was often at MacAlister-hardly a day passed without his riding or driving across on some errand-and she was often at St. Maws herself, for Rebecca's momentary flash of anger had been rapidly quenched in deep contrition and humility; and both she and her husband treated Catherine with the reverential tenderness that seemed to meet her now on all hands.

Lord MacMurray watched her day by day, wondering if ever he should dare to breathe a word of the hopes that filled his heart, reading in her calm face and in the sisterly gentleness and fondness with which she treated him, how little conscious she was of the purpose the possessed his soul. Sometimes he paused and shrank from troubling the still waters of their sweet, calm friendship, but then again the thought of leaving her in her loneliness and isolation seemed too sad and mournful, if by any devotion and love he could lighten the burden of her sorrow, and bring back something of the lost happiness into her life. MacMurray was very humble, very self-distrustful; he did not expect to accomplish much, but he felt that he would gladly lay down his life, if by that act he could do anything to comfort her. To die for her would, however, be purposeless: the next thing was to try and live for her.

And so one day, as they walked the lonely shore together, on a chilly cloudy winter's afternoon, he put his fate to the touch. She had noticed his silence-his abstraction: he had not been quite himself all day. Presently they reached a sheltered nook amongst some rocks not far from the water's edge, and she sat down, motioning him to do the same. She looked at him with gentle, friendly concern.

"Is anything the matter?" she asked. "Have you something on your mind?" He turned his head, looked into her eyes, and answered—"Yes." "Can I help you?" she continued, in the same sweet way. "You help me so often, that it is my turn to help you now if I can." He looked at her with a glance she could not altogether understand. "Catherine," he said, "may I speak to you?—may I tell you something? I have tried to do so before, and have failed; but I ought not to go on longer without speaking. Have I your permission to tell you what is on my mind?" He did not often call her by her Christian name: only in moments of excitement, when his soul was stirred within him. The unconscious way in which it dropped now from his lips told that he was deeply moved. A faint vague uneasiness stirred within her, but she looked into his troubled, resolute face, and

Graham Lomas

answered——"Tell me if you wish it, MacMurray"——although she shrank, without knowing why, from the confession she was to hear.

Catherine," he said, not looking at her, but out over the sea, and speaking with a manly resolution and fluency unusual with him, the outcome of a very earnest purpose," I am going to speak to you at last, and I must ask you beforehand to pardon my presumption, of which I am as well aware as you can ever be. Catherine I think that no woman in the wide world is like you. I have thought so ever since I saw you first, in your bridal robes, standing beside Edward in that little church over yonder. When I saw you then-no, pardon me if I pain you; I should not have recalled the memory, and yet I cannot help it——I said within myself that you were one to be worshipped with the truest devotion of a man's heart; and the more I saw of you later, the deeper did that feeling sink into my soul. He, your husband, had been as a brother to me, and to feel that I was thus brought near to you, admitted to friendship and to confidence, was a source of keen pleasure such as I can ill describe. You did not know your power I think I would at any time have laid down my life either for him or for you. I know I would that fatal night-but I must not pain more. When I awoke, Catherine, from that long fever, to find you watching beside me, to hear that he, my friend, was dead, and you left all alone in your desolation Catherine, Catherine, how can I hope to express to you what I felt? It is not treachery to his memory believe me, it is not. If I could call him back, ah! How gladly would I do it!——at the cost of my life if need like-but that can never, never be! I know I can never fill his place. I know I am utterly unworthy of the boon I ask; but if a life-long devotion, if a love that will never change nor falter, If the ceaseless care of one, who is yours wholly and entirely, can ever help to fill the blank, in ever so small a degree make up to you for that one irretrievable loss, believe me, it will be the greatest happiness I can ever know.

Catherine, need I say more? Have I said too much? I only ask leave to watch over you, to comfort you, to love you; I ask nothing for myself only the right to do this. Can you not give it to me? God helping me, you shall never repent it if you do. "A long pause followed this confession-this appeal. Catherine's face had expressed many fluctuating feelings as he proceeded with his speech. Now it was full of an almost divine compassion and tenderness: a look sometimes seen in a pictured saint or Madonna drawn by a master hand. "You are so good," she said, very low; "so very, very good; and it grieves me so sadly to give you pain."

He turned his head and looked at her. His eyes darkened with sudden sorrow. "I have spoken too soon," he said, in the same gentle, self-contained way. "I have tried to be patient, but seeing you lonely and sad makes it so hard. I should have waited longer––it is only a year now since. Catherine, do not think me hard or callous to say it, but time is a great softener––a great healer. I do not mean that you will ever forget; but years will go by, and you are still quite young, very young to live your life always alone. Think of the years that lie before you. Must they all be spent alone? Catherine, do not answer me yet; but if in time to come––if you want a friend, a helper-let me-can you think of me? Ah! How can I say it? Can I ever be more to you than I am now? You understand: you have only to call me, to command me––I will come." He spoke with some agitation now, but it was quickly subdued. It seemed as if he would have left her, but she laid her hand upon his arm and detained him.

"MacMurray," she said softly, "I am lonely and I do want a friend. You have been a friend to me always; I trust and love you as a brother. May I not do so always? Can you not be content with that? Must it end with us, that love and trust? I should miss it sorely if it were withdrawn. "Her sweet, pleading face was turned towards him. There was a brief struggle in the young man's mind: then he answered quietly "It shall be so, if you say it," he said. "My chiefest wish is for your happiness. But––" She checked him by a look.

"MacMurray, I am Edward's wife!" His eyes gave the reply his tongue would never have uttered. She answered as if he had spoken. "Yes, he is dead. Did you think that made any difference? Ah, you do not understand. When I gave myself to Edward, I gave myself for ever-not for a time only, but for always. He is my husband. I am his wife. Nothing can change that." "Not even death?" The words were a mere whisper; yet she heard them. It seemed as if a sudden ray of light shone upon the face she turned towards him. He was awed; he watched her in mute silence.

"Ah! no," she said very softly," not death-death least of all. Death can only divide us, it cannot touch our love. Ah! You do not know, you do not understand. How can I make it clear to you? Love is like nothing else in the world––it is us, our very selves. Somewhere––"Catherine clasped her hands together and stretched them out before her towards the eternal ocean, with a gesture more eloquent than any words, whilst the light upon her face deepened in intensity every moment as her eyes fixed themselves upon the far horizon." Somewhere he is waiting for me to come to him––he, my husband, my love; and though he may not come back to me, I shall go to him in God's good time, and when I join him in the great, eternal home, I must go to him as he left me-with nothing between us and our love; and there will be no parting there, no more death, and no more sea."

Her words died away in silence; but her parted lips, her shining eyes, the light upon her face, spoke an eloquent language of their own. Her companion sat and looked at her in mute, breathless silence, not unmixed with awe. He knew his cause was lost. He knew she could never, never be his; yet strange to say, he was not saddened or cast down, for by this revelation of her innermost heart he felt himself uplifted and ennobled. His idol was not shattered. Catherine was as ever, enshrined in his heart––the one ideal woman to be worshipped, reverenced, adored. Even in this supreme hour of his life, when the airy fabric of his dreams was crumbling into dust about his, he had a perception that perhaps even thus it was best. He never could be worthy of her, and now he might still call himself her friend; had she not said so herself? There was a long, long silence between them. Then he moved, kneeling on one knee before her, and taking her hand in his.

"Catherine," he said, "I understand now. I shall never trouble you again. You have judged well, very well; it is like you, and that is enough. But before I go may I crave one boon?" "And that is––?" "That you forget all I have said, all the wild, foolish words that I have spoken; and let me keep my old place-as your brother and friend." She looked at him with her own gentle smile. "I wish for nothing better," she answered. "I cannot afford to lose my friend." He pressed her hand for one moment to his lips, and was gone without another word. Tears slowly welled up in Catherine's eye as she rose at last, and stood looking out over the vast waste of heaving grey sea-sad, colourless, troubled.

"Like my life," she said softly to herself. And yet she had just put away a love that might at least have cast a glow upon it, and gilded its dim edges. She stretched out her hand with a passionate gesture of entreaty. "Ah! Edward, husband, come back to me! I am so lonely, so desolate!"

Even as she spoke, the setting sun, it touched the horizon, broke through the bank of cloud which had veiled it all the day, and flooded the sea as with liquid gold-that cold grey sea that she had just been likening to her own future life. She could not help an involuntary start. "Is it an omen?" she asked; and despite the heavy load at her heart, she went home somewhat comforted.

~~ੴ~~

Chapter 31

~~ੴ~~

Christmas Eve

It was Christmas Eve; the light was just beginning to wane, and Catherine's work was done at last. She was free now until the arrival of her guest–– the Pendrill's and Lord MacMurray-should give her new occupation in hospitable care for them. Catherine had been too busy for thoughts of self to intrude often upon her during these past days. She wished to be busy; she tried to occupy herself from morning to night, for she found that the aching hunger of her heart was more eased by loving deeds of mercy and kindness that in any other way-self more fully lost in ceaseless care for others. But when all was done, every single thing disposed of, nothing more left to think of or to accomplish; then the inevitable reaction set in, and with a heart aching to pain, almost to despair, Catherine entered the music room, and sat down to her piano.

She played with a sad, passionate appeal that was infinitely pathetic, had any one been there to hear; she threw all the yearning sadness of her soul into her piano, and it seemed to answer back with a promise of strong sympathy and consolation. Insensibly she was soothed by the sweet sounds she evoked. She fell into a dreamy mood, playing softly in a minor key, so softly that through the door which stood ajar, she became aware of a slight subdued tumult in the hall without, to which she gave but a dreamy attention at first.

194

The bell had pealed sharply, steps had crossed the hall, the door had been opened, and then had followed the tumultuous sounds expressive of astonishment that roused Catherine from her dreamy reverie. She supposed the party from St Maws had arrived some what before the expected time, rose and had a few steps forward when she suddenly stopped short and stood motionless-spell-bound-what was it she had heard?––only the sound of a voice-man's voice.

"Where is Lady MacAlister?" The words were uttered in a clear, deep, ringing tone, that seemed to her to waken every echo in the Castle into wild surging life. The very air throbbed and palpitated around her––her temples seemed as if they would burst. What was the meaning of that sound-that wild tumult of voices? Why did she stand as if carved in stone, growing white to the very lips, whilst thrill upon thrill ran through her frame, and her heart beat to suffocation? What did it all mean? Whose was the voice she had just heard that voice from the dead? Who was it that stood in the hall without The door was flung open. A tall, dark figure stood in the dim light. "Catherine neither spoke nor moved. The cry of awe and of rapture that rose from her heart could not find voice in which to utter itself-but what matter? She was in her husband's arms. Her head lay upon his chest. His lips were pressed to her cold face in the kisses she had never thought to feel again. Edward had come back. She could not speak. She had no will to try and frame a single word. He held her in his arms; he strained her ever closer and closer. She felt the tumultuous beating of heart as she lay in his arms, powerless to move or think. She heard his murmured words, broken and hoarse with the passionate feeling of that supreme moment.

"My wife! Catherine! My wife!" And then for a time she knew no more. Sight and hearing alike failed her; seemed as if a slumber from heaven itself sealed her eyes and stole away her senses. When she came to herself she was on a sofa in her own room, and Edward was kneeling beside her. She did not start to see him there. For a moment it seemed as if he had never left her. She smiled her own sweet smile.

"Edward! Have I been asleep-dreaming?" He took her hands in his, and bent to kiss her lips. "It has been a long dream, my Catherine, and a dark one; but it is over at last. My darling, my darling! God grant I may not be dreaming now!" She smiled like a tired child. She had a perception that something overpoweringly strange and sudden had happened, but she did not want to rouse herself just yet to think what it must all mean.

Two hours later, in the great drawing-room ablaze with light, Catherine and Edward stood together to welcome their guests. She had laid aside her mournful widow's garb, and was arrayed in her shimmering bridal robes. Ah, how lovely she was in her husband's eyes as she stood beside him now! Perhaps never in all her life had she looked more exquisitely fair. Happiness had lighted her beautiful eyes, and had brought the rose back to her pale cheeks: she was glorified-transfigured——a vision of radiant beauty.

He had changed but slightly during his mysterious year of absence. There were a few lines upon his face that had not been there of old: he looked like a man who had been through some ordeal, whether mental or physical it would be less easy to tell; but the same joy and rapture that emanated, as it were, from Catherine was reflected in his face likewise, and only a keen eye could read tonight the traces of pain or sorrow in that strong, proud, manly countenance.

Catherine looked at him suddenly, the flush deepening in her cheeks. "Hush! They are coming!" she said, and waited breathlessly. The door opened, admitting Mrs. Pendrill, Rebecca, and Bruce. There was a pause——a brief, intense silence, during which the fall a pin might have been heard, and then, with one long, low cry, half-sobbing, half-laughing, Rebecca rushed across the room, and flung herself upon Edward. Catherine went straight up to Mrs. Pendrill, and put her arms about her neck. "Aunt Jennifer, he has come home," she said, in a voice that shook a little with the tumult of her happiness. "He has just come home-this very day Edward-my husband. Help me to believe it. You must help me bear this-as you helped me to bear the other." Bruce had by this time grasped Edward by the hand; but nether trusted his own voice. They were glad that Rebecca covered their silence by her incoherent exclamations of rapture, and by the flow of questions no one attempted to answer. It was all too like a dream for any one to recollect very clearly what happened. Johnathon and MacMurray came in almost at once, new greetings had to be gone through. How the dinner passed off that night no one afterwards remembered. There was a deep sense of thankfulness and joy in every heart; yet of words there were few. But when gathered round the fire later on in the evening, when they had grown used to the presence amongst them of one whom they had mourned as dead for more than a year, Edward was called upon to tell his tale, which was listened to in breathless silence.

"I will tell you all I can about it; but there are points yet where my memory fails me, where I have but little idea what happened. I have a dim recollection of the night of the wreck, and of leaving the boat; but I must have received a heavy blow on the head, the doctors tell me, and I suppose I sank, and the men could not find me. But I was entangled, it seem, in the rigging of a floating spar, and must have been carried thus many miles; for I was picked up by an ocean steamer bound for Australia, which had been driven somewhat out of its course by the gale. It was not supposed that I could live after so many hours exposure. I was quite unconscious, and remained so for a very long time. There was nothing upon me by which I could be identified, and of course I could give no account of myself. On board the boat were a kind-hearted wealthy Australian couple, who had lately lost an only son, to whom they fancied I bore some slight resemblance. Perhaps for this cause, perhaps from true kindness of heart, they at once took me under their special care and protection. There was plenty of space on board the vessel, and they looked after me as if I had indeed been their son. They would not hear of my being left behind in hospital on the way out. They took me under their protection until I should be able to give an account of myself.

"Of course I knew nothing about all this. I was lying dangerously ill if brain fever all the while, not knowing where I was, or what was happening. When we reached Sydney at last, and I was conveyed to their luxurious house on the outskirts of town, I was still in the same state, relapse following relapse, every time till I gained a little ground still for months my life was despaired of. I was either raving in delirium, or lying in a sort of unconscious stupor, and without all the skill and care lavished upon me, I suppose I must have died. But I did not die. Gradually, very gradually, the fever abated, and I began to come to myself: that is to say, I began to know the faces around me and to recognise my surroundings; but for myself, I knew no more who I was, nor whence I had come, than the infant just born into the world. My memory had gone, had been wiped clean away; I had no idea of my own identity, no recollection of the past. The very effort to remember brought on such pain and distress that I was imperatively commanded to relinquish the attempt. Gradually some things came back to my mind: I could read, write, understand the foreign tongues I had mastered, and the sciences I had studied in past days. As my health slowly improved this kind of knowledge came back spontaneously and without effort; but my personal history was as a blank wall, against which I flung myself in vain. It would yield to no efforts of mine. Distressed and confused, I was obliged to give up, and wait what with what patience I might for the realisation of the hope held out cheerfully by the clever doctor who attended me. He maintained that if I would but have patience, some strong association of ideas would some day bring all back in a flash, and meantime all I had to do was to get strong and well, so as to be ready for action when that time should come. I was restless sometimes, but less so than one would fancy, for the blank was too complete to be distressing. My new friends and protectors were unspeakably kind and good, and did everything in their power to ensure my mental and physical well-being; I recovered my health rapidly, soon my memory was to come back too."

Edward passed his hand across his eyes. No one spoke, every eye was fixed upon his face. "It did so very strangely: it was one hot afternoon in November-our summer, you know"––he named the date and the hour, and Catherine heard it with a sudden thrill. Allowing for the discrepancy of time, it was during the moments that she watched by David MacRae's dying bed that her husband's memory was given back to him.

"I was looking over some old English newspapers, idly, purposelessly, when I came upon a detailed account of the wreck, and my own supposed death. As I read––I cannot describe what it was like-my memory came back to me in a great flood, like over whelming waves. It seemed, Catherine, as if my spirit were carried on wings to MacAlister, as I were hovering over you in some mysterious way impossible to describe. I called your name aloud. I knew that I was close to you at MacAlister––it is useless to attempt to describe. What I felt. When I came to myself they told me I had fainted; but that was not so. I had been on a journey, that is all, and had returned. My memory was restored from that hour, clearly and distinctly; the doctor thought there might be lapses, that I might never be the same man again as I had been once; but I have felt no ill effects since. Little more remains to be told. My first instinct was to telegraph; but not knowing what had happened in my absence, knowing

I must long have been given up for lost, I was afraid to do so, lest hopeless confusion should result. Instead, I took the first home bound steamer, and reached London late last night. I found out at the house there where Catherine was, and came on here by the first train. I have come back to MacAlister to spend my Christmas with you."

Chapter 32

Home For Christmas

"Catherine, I could not tell you last night—it was all so sudden, so wonderful-but I think you know, without any words of mine, how glad, how thankful I am." It was MacMurray who spoke, spoke with a glad, frank, joyous sincerity, that beamed in his eye and sounded in every tone of his voice. Catherine gave him both her hands, looking up into his face with her sweetest smile.

"I know, MacMurray; I know. I am sure of it. Is he not almost a brother to you?——and are you not the best of brothers to me?" "At least I will try to be," he answered gladly. "I cannot tell you how happy this has made me." She was glad too: glad to see him so happy, so heart-whole. He had loved her with the loyal love of a devoted chivalrous knight, had loved her for her sorrow and her loneliness; but she was comforted now, and he was able to rejoice with her. It was all very good-just as she would have it. Ah! What a day of joy and thanksgiving it was! How Catherine's heart beat as she knelt by her husband's side that glad Christmas morning in the little cliff church, when in the pause just before the General Thanksgiving, the grey-headed clergyman, with a little quiver in his voice, announced that Edward MacAlister desired to return thanks to Almighty God for preservation from great perils and for restoration to his home.

His voice faltered too in the familiar words, and many suppressed sobs were heard in the building, but they were sobs of joy and gratitude; and tears of healing and happiness stole down Catherine's cheeks. It was like some beautiful dream, yet too sweet not to be true. In the afternoon Catherine and Edward went out alone together; first into the whispering pine woods, and then out upon the breezy cliff, hard beneath their feet with the winter's frost.

He let her lead him whither she would. He had no thought to spare for aught beside herself. They were together once again. What more could they need? But Catherine had an object in view; and as they walked, engrossed in each other, in sweet communion of soul and interchange of thought, or the almost sweeter silence of perfect peace and tranquility, she led him once more towards the little cliff church; though only when she was unlatching the gate to enter the quiet graveyard did he arouse to the sense of their surroundings, "Why Catherine," he said, "why have you brought me here? We are too late for service." "I know." she answered; "but come. I have something to show you. "Her face wore an expression he did not understand. He followed her in silence to a secluded corner, where, beneath a dark yew tree, stood a green mound, at the head of which a wooden cross had been temporarily erected. Edward read the letters it bore——"CF;" followed by a date, and beneath, the simple familiar words——rest in peace."

Strange, perhaps, that Catherine should have care for this lonely grave, in which was laid to rest one who had, as she believed, robbed her life of all its brightness and joy. Strange that she, in the absence of friend or kinsman, should have charged herself with keeping it, and of erecting there some monument to mark who lay below. Strange-yet so it was. Her husband looked at her questioningly. "David's gave-yes," she answered quietly. "Edward, look at the date." He did so, and stared a little. "He died at dawn that day, Edward. You know what was happening then at the other side of the world? There was a strange look of awe upon her face as she spoke, which was reflected in his also. She came and stood close beside him. "Edward, do you know that he was there-that night?——that he tried to kill you?" He had taken off his hat as he stood beside the grave, with the instinctive reverence for the dead even though it be a foa-characteristic of a noble mind. Now he passed his hand across his brow and through his thick dark hair. "I thought that was a delusion of fever——a sort of hideous vision founded on no reality. Catherine, was it so?" "It was." "How do you know?" "I heard it from his own lips." He gazed at her without speaking; something in her face awed and silenced him.

"Edward, listen," she said. "I must tell you all. Six weeks ago, the evening before that day, he was brought, shattered and dying, to MacAlister; he had fallen from the cliffs, no skill could serve to prolong his life. I knew nothing then—he was profoundly unconscious, yet as the night wore away some strange intuition came upon me that he wanted me, that was beseeching me to come to him. I went—he was still unconscious. I sent Lorna way and watched by him myself. Edward, at dawn he awoke to consciousness—he told me all his awful tale he said he had murdered you—I believed it was true. He was dying-dying in darkness and in dread, and he prayed for my forgiveness as if his salvation hung upon it. Edward, Edward, how can I tell you?—I cannot-no one could understand," for a moment she pressed her hand upon her eyes, looking up again in a few seconds with a calm glance that was like a smile. "He was dying, Edward, and I forgave him—I forgave him freely and fully-and he died in peace. Stop, that is not all. Edward, as I knelt beside his bed, praying for the sin-stained spirit then taking its flight, I felt that you were with me; I had never before felt the strange overshadowing presence that I did then-you there, your own self. I heard your voice far away, yet absolutely clear, like a call from some distant, snow-clad mountain-top, infinitely far—'Catherine! Catherine! My wife!' I think David heard it too, for he died with a smile on his lips. Edward, I am sure that you were with me in that strange, awful hour. I knew it then—I know it better now. Edward, I think that love is stronger than all else-time, space, death itself. Nothing touched our love. I think it is like eternity."

A look of deep awe had stamped itself upon Edward's face. He put his arm round Catherine, and for a very long while they stood thus, neither attempting to speak or to move. At last he woke from his reverie, and looked down at her with a strange light shining in his eyes. "And you forgave him, Catherine?" She looked up and met his gaze unfalteringly. "I forgave him, Edward; was I wrong?" He stooped and kissed her. "My wife, I thank God that you did forgive him. His life was full of sin and sorrow-but at least its end was peace. May God pardon him as you did as I do." There was a strange sweet smile in her eyes as she lifted them to his. "Ah, Edward!" she said softly, "I knew you would understand. Oh, my husband, my husband!" with a sweet, tender smile. Then her eyes wandered dreamily out over the wide sea beneath them. "There is nothing sad there now, Edward. It will never separate us again."

He looked down at her with a world of love in his eyes; yet as they turned away his glance rested for one moment upon the lonely grave he had been brought to see, and lifting his hat once more, he murmured beneath his breath——"Requiescat in pace." Then drawing his wife's hand within his arm, he led her homewards to MacAlister, whilst the sun set in a blaze of golden glory over the boundless, shining sea.

The End

Printed in the United States
By Bookmasters